THE INVESTIGATION
OFFICER'S FILE

INSPIRED BY ACTUAL EVENTS

DALLAS CLARK

Black Rose Writing | Texas

ISBN: 978-1-68433-688-3
PUBLISHED BY BLACK ROSE WRITING
www.blackrosewriting.com

Printed in the United States of America
Suggested Retail Price (SRP) $18.95

The Investigation Officer's File is printed in Palatino

*As a planet-friendly publisher, Black Rose Writing does its best to eliminate unnecessary waste to reduce paper usage and energy costs, while never compromising the reading experience. As a result, the final word count vs. page count may not meet common expectations.

My special thanks to Black Rose Writing for taking this chance on me.

I dedicate this novel to each of my Beta readers, whose contribution made all the difference in this novel.

And to Jessica for her technical support which was invaluable to this writing.

Finally, with all my heart, I dedicate this novel to my daughter Katie and her husband Keith, and their children Andrew, Thomas and Jake; and to my daughter Joanna and her husband Jeff, and their children, Frances and Dallas, and to my daughter Hannah Camille and her mother Melanie, whose support of me has been helpful beyond measure.

THE INVESTIGATION OFFICER'S FILE

1315 Hours, Mon, 30 Sep 68
Officer Candidate School
United States Marine Corps Base
Quantico, Virginia
Candidate White

"Maggot, in the one hundred ninety-three-year history of my Marine Corps, that is the worst pushup ever. You ain't got the chance of a snowball in hell of being a second lieutenant in my Corps. I'll see to that. Get your fat ass up and haul it over to the candidate reporting station right over there, if you can find it, and tell them you won't be here long, and you tell them that Sergeant Gonzalez said you ain't got what it takes to lead Marines to the chow hall, much less on a mission to kill the Cong. Now get outta here."

As Woody White struggled to his feet, exhausted by the pushups he had attempted, and scared as he had never been before from the tirade of Sergeant Gonzalez, he was thinking he made a big mistake when he enlisted in the Marines during his second year of law school at Wake Forest University.

He had parked his car in the "Candidates Park Here" lot and was heading to the "Candidates Report Here" building when he first met Sergeant Andros Gonzalez. The meeting started pleasantly enough.

"Good morning," Sergeant Gonzalez asked." Do you have the time, please?" He was dressed in utilities, with the three stripes of an E-5 sergeant pinned on the collars and his barracks cap, and the name "Gonzalez" printed over the right breast pocket of his utility shirt.

Woody put his suitcase down and looked at the Hamilton watch he had inherited from his father. "Yes, sir, it is one-thirty-five."

Sergeant Gonzalez rushed to Woody, standing so close to him that his nose almost touched Woody's, and he was yelling so loudly that Woody thought he could be heard in Washington, DC, 25 miles to the north." Why did you call me 'Sir'? I'm not an officer, 'cause I WORK for a living. And what do you mean one-thirty-five? Do you know you are on a military base?

"Yes, yes sir, I know…"

"What did I tell you five seconds ago, you maggot. I am not an officer. I'm giving you a direct order, don't call me 'Sir' again, or I'll have your ass. Understood?"

"Yes, sergeant."

"That's not right either, you worm. You address me 'Sergeant yes Sergeant' or 'Sergeant no Sergeant' Understood? What is your name, candidate?"

"Woody White, sergeant. I mean Sergeant, Woody White, Sergeant."

"Did you cut your engine off when you parked your car, Candidate White?" Sergeant Gonzalez continued to have his face in Woody's. His eyes bulged, and he looked as mad as anyone Woody had ever seen.

"Sergeant, yes Sergeant."

"Why did you do that, White?"

"Sergeant, because I am reporting to Officer Candidate School, Sergeant, to become a Marine Corps second lieutenant, Sergeant."

"Well, White, you shoulda left the motor running, 'cause I can already tell you ain't gonna be in MY Marine Corps. You don't even know how to tell time. I'll bet you tell time by seeing where Mickey's hands are at, don't you? Well, let me tell you, as long as you are trying to become a Marine in MY Marine Corps, your clock is a twenty-four-hour clock, so what you know up to now was one pm, is now and forever after thirteen-hundred hours, understood?"

"Sergeant, yes Sergeant."

"How much do you weigh, White?"

"Sergeant, about one-hundred ninety-six pounds, Sergeant."

"White, do you know what an order is?"

"Yes, sir, an order is…"

Sergeant Gonzalez's voice decibel somehow reached a new high, and he was so close to Woody's face that his spittle hit Woody's nose.

"Numb-nuts! I gave you a DIRECT ORDER to address me as 'Sergeant' when addressing me. And you violated my order, didn't you, maggot?"

"Sergeant, yes Sergeant."

"And I asked you what an order was, and that only requires a 'yes' or 'no', correct?"

"Sergeant, yes Sergeant."

And then Sergeant Gonzalez's voice dropped almost to a whisper. "Well, Maggot, if I asked you if you knew what an order was, and your answer had to be either a 'yes' or 'no', then tell me why you started to tell me what an order was. I didn't ask you what an order was, now did I?"

Woody felt like his brain was turning to oatmeal. "Sergeant, no Sergeant."

"What are you going to do if you are leading my Marines in the jungle, and your company commander orders you to move your platoon 100 meters east, but you move west, and the F-4 Phantom jet drops napalm on you and your men, burning you and some of my Marines to a crisp, like bacon, 'cause you didn't follow orders. What are you going to do?"

Woody had taken about 2 seconds to try to think of an answer when the sergeant was again yelling at him. "Maggot, drop and give me 10."

As Woody finished the pushups and stumbled towards the reporting office, he knew one thing for sure: OCS was going to be ten weeks of pure hell, and he hoped he could make it through and be commissioned a second lieutenant in the United States Marine Corps.

What Woody did not know was that the United States Senate would pass a law within two weeks of Woody's reporting to OCS that would have a life or death impact on his Marine Corps career.

Woody also did not know that the murder of an officer in Vietnam, a Marine's following an order about that murder, and the handling of the investigation would result in his most important case as a Marine.

0935 Hours, Tue, 31 Dec 68
First Platoon, Alpha Company
First Battalion, Ninth Marine Regiment
Third Marine Division
Vandegrift Combat Base
I Corps
Republic of South Vietnam
"Listen Up"

"LISTEN UP!" Sergeant Maurice Smith didn't have to give orders a second time. The thirty-nine men of First Platoon, Alpha Company, First Battalion, Ninth Marine Regiment, Third Marine Division (Alpha 1/9), directed their attention to him because he was their platoon sergeant. He was a 6'3" Black man from Dothan, Alabama, strong as an ox, and fearless. He was midway through his second consecutive tour in South Vietnam, both with Alpha 1/9. He knew what to do in a firefight, and first platoon, Alpha 1/9 had been in a number of firefights. The men of the five squads of the first platoon not only respected Sergeant Smith; they feared him and looked to him to lead them in combat.

"Well, here we are at beautiful Vandegrift Combat Base, aka VCB, within spitting distance of the DMZ, in beautiful South Vietnam, on this beautiful New Year's Eve." The men chuckled, because there was nothing beautiful about VCB, previously named LZ Stud.

VCB sat in a valley which was, in parts, flat as an IHOP pancake. It had military value because it could serve as a landing place for the many choppers supporting the Marines fighting in I Corps, which was the northernmost of the four combat sectors of South Vietnam and the sector closest to North Vietnam. Men and supplies constantly came into and out of VCB either by chopper or a road named Route 9. Steel Marston Matting had been placed on the floor of the valley and offered some foundation for the choppers to land, take on or off-load supplies or Marines wounded or killed in action. There were more landings and take-offs than you could keep up with. One began to not even notice the choppers, except when the larger CH-53 Sea Stallion choppers lifted heavily with a swinging load of bodies of KIA Marines in body bags, bundled in a large tarp swinging slowly below the chopper on the way to the Division morgue, wherever it was.

Sergeant Smith continued. "The word has come from on high! Since we ain't got a lieutenant platoon leader until Lt. Williams' replacement gets here, and that should be in a day or two, I was ordered to join the lieutenants of the other platoons of Alpha to meet with the company CO. That was when he told me our new platoon leader would be checking in soon. But the main reason for meeting was to tell us that our mission, it be challenging. The CG of the Third Division, Davis — you remembering hearing about him, he was on the Canal in WW2, won The Medal in Korea, he don't think we's doing what Marines are supposed to do by just holding the line, if that's what we're doin'. He wants us to kick ass and take names. The NVA been moving supplies down the Ho Chi Minh trail, scooting into Laos where they've been safe 'cause our tactical area of operations don't go into Laos. It's called Operation Dewey Canyon, if that matters. The brass comes up with these names but for us, we just go out and do the grunt work. Don't know when this starts, but it will be soon.

"Now, about our new lieutenant. Name's Speight. He ain't gonna be able to hold Lieutenant Williams' jock strap. Lieutenant Williams was a Naval Academy grad who opted for the Corps, and the Corps don't take every Academy grad who wants into the Corps. We take only the best. The next lieutenant is gonna come straight from The Basic School, so we'll have to take it slow with him until he gets his sea legs. Be on the lookout on ways to help him through your squad leaders to me."

One other point — important point. Somewhere, it may have been south of I Corps, don't know, an Army unit was on patrol. One of the guys had to take a dump, so they held up while he went behind some bushes. Next thing they heard was the roar of probably a tiger, and one scream from the soldier. All they found was his rifle and helmet. They looked for him, no luck. The lesson is to take a dump before you go on patrol, and if you have to pee or take a dump while on patrol, the whole platoon stops, forms a perimeter around the guy taking care of bidness, until he's done. That is one hellava way to go. Okay, dismissed."

For the first time since arriving in South Vietnam 110 days ago, Lance Corporal Ricardo Jackson felt he would not make it back home alive. He had basically been forced to join the Corps. He and five of his Philadelphia buddies had broken into a home in their neighborhood when that family was on vacation. He was the only one caught. After the judge heard the evidence from the arresting cop — that he heard noise from the home, saw a broken window, went to the front door and knocked, and chased after the five kids who ran out the back door and caught only Jackson, the judge gave Ricardo a choice, right there in the courtroom: Take a year in county jail, or join the Marines.

Ricardo, who was only 18 years old, had only the vaguest idea that there was a war in South Vietnam, or that Marines, and other US servicemen and women, were getting killed in Vietnam. Since he didn't want to spend a year in jail, he agreed to enlist. When he brought a copy of the enlistment papers to the courtroom clerk two weeks later, the charges were dismissed.

Two weeks after the case was dismissed, Jackson was on a Greyhound bus, heading from Philadelphia to Parris Island, South Carolina, boot camp for the Corps on the East coast.

Ricardo actually thrived in boot camp. He was the top recruit in his platoon. He was small but athletic, strong, aggressive, and kept his mouth shut and his eyes and ears open. He had been approached in the ninth week of the ten-week boot camp and asked if he wanted to be sent to Officer Candidate School, in Quantico, Virginia. He was told there was no guarantee he could pass OCS and be commissioned, but if he did, it would add a year to his two-year enlistment. He declined, and after boot camp, was sent to advanced infantry training at Camp

Lejeune, in Jacksonville, North Carolina. His next stop was First Platoon, Alpha, 1/9, Third Mar Div at VCB.

He had taken an instant liking to Lieutenant Williams, his platoon leader, who seemed to have a sixth sense of what was going to happen in combat. Their platoon had some troops wounded and killed in action while Williams was the platoon leader but not because the lieutenant made stupid decisions. Ricardo had followed Lt. Williams' orders to the letter, and was rewarded with more responsibility, and more rank, when we was promoted to lance corporal and made assistant squad leader.

But Lieutenant Williams had rotated back home, and he was going to be replaced by a lieutenant who was fresh out of The Basic School. Ricardo had heard that Basic School was a five- or sixth- month school, with both classroom and tactical exercises. He knew there was just no way a second lieutenant could learn all he needed to know about leading men in combat by shooting blanks and running around Marine Corps Base, Quantico, Virginia. Now with this new directive by the CG of the Third MarDiv, to seek and destroy the enemy in Operation Dewey Canyon, the war took on a different feel for Lance Corporal Ricardo Jackson.

He had the feeling there was a body bag with his name on it.

It never crossed his mind that he could leave Vietnam as a prisoner in handcuffs and leg irons, convicted of first-degree murder.

1100 Hours, Thurs, 2 Jan 69
Da Nang Airbase
Republic of South Vietnam
Lieutenant Speight

Second Lieutenant Alvin Speight, USMC (Reserves), Service number 0108920, was scared shitless. He hoped no one could tell, because Marine officers in combat zones were not supposed to be scared shitless.

Three days before arriving at Da Nang Air Base in Vietnam, he had boarded a commercial jet at Norton Air Force Base in southern California for a flight to Okinawa, where he was given shots, including a shot that felt like a one-pronged pitch fork shooting maple syrup into his ass, and other shots to ward off diseases endemic to South Vietnam. He wished they had a shot to ward off any bullets with his name on them. He was well aware of the old saying — You can't do anything about the bullet or rocket with your name on it, but you worry about bullets and rockets addressed 'To whom it may concern.'

His body clock was all screwed up too because he had flown through the International Date Line and so many time zones, he couldn't count them. The commercial flights, both the one from Norton to Okinawa and from Okinawa to Da Nang, had stewardesses, who served meals and flirted with the enlisted men. It was surreal as hell and only added to his confusion.

He had put his orders — *'Report to the company commander of Alpha Company, First Battalion, Ninth Marine Regiment, Third Marine Division, Vandergrift Combat Base, I Corps, Republic of South Vietnam, for assignment as an infantry officer'* — in the left pocket of his utility jacket. As he moved through the busy terminal at Da Nang, it was easy to distinguish those who were starting their tour — all wearing stateside utilities, from those lucky bastards going home, all of whom were wearing jungle utilities and jungle boots. There were a few catcalls from those preparing to board the commercial jets to go home to the "Land of the big PX" but for the most part, those coming into country and those leaving were respectful of each other.

As he waited in the terminal for someone to tell him where to go next, Alvin felt out of place. He was not only was scared he also didn't even look like a Marine. He was 5'7" tall and weighed only 150 pounds. He had sandy hair and a fair complexion, and he wasn't very well coordinated or strong and had problems with the obstacle course at OCS.

He had been in the seating area of the airport for about forty-five minutes when sergeant came out and announced: "All enlisted and officers with orders to report to any unit in the Third Marine Division follow me." Alvin joined forty or so other Marines and followed the sergeant to another waiting area. As an officer, he moved to the front of the line to give a sergeant his orders. After reviewing the orders, the sergeant took the top copy and placed it in a pile of other orders and told Lt. Speight to go through a passageway to the left, which led to the tarmac.

When Alvin stepped onto the tarmac, he felt like he had entered a blast furnace in one of the steel mills in his native Pittsburg. It was hot, even though it was only the middle of the morning. He and the other Marines who were going to Quang Tri, followed a corporal to an aircraft which, to Alvin, appeared to be from the World War Two era.

There was no talking as the men got on the aircraft. The seats on the aircraft faced the rear, something Alvin had never seen. He was seated near the cockpit, which was then unoccupied. His sea bag — issued by the Corps as the only permitted luggage — was propped next to him. There were no overhead storage areas. There were no stewardesses.

His concern about this flight was exacerbated when the pilots came on board. They looked like two guys just barely old enough to ask cheerleaders for a date. Alvin was thinking he didn't have to worry about dying in combat — the plane crash would take care of that. Alvin heard the pilots go through their checklist, after which they started the engine and taxied away from the hanger. Alvin looked out the window and saw a F-4 Phantom jet taking off. He wondered if any of them would ever fly in support of a combat mission he would be on. The plane taxied and then stopped for about five minutes. Then it turned, the pilots gunned the engines, the aircraft started down the runway and was shortly airborne.

As the aircraft climbed, Alvin could see how huge Da Nang Air Base was. The plane banked to the left and continued to climb. Alvin had no way to know the cruising altitude, but he could see a hilly green countryside, with red clay splotched here and there. As the plane continued its flight, Alvin saw they were over water, which he correctly guessed was the Gulf of Tonkin, but they never got out of sight of land.

Alvin had no idea how long they had been airborne but could tell the pilots were beginning their landing pattern. Alvin could see what appeared to be a village here and there, and what he guessed were rice paddies because the water reflected the sun. He became concerned as the descending plane veered left and right, and wondered if they were under fire, or if the plane was just lining up on the runway for its landing. But then they made the smoothest landing Alvin had ever experienced, so while these flyboys may have been young, they were good.

After the aircraft came to a stop, Alvin took his sea bag and stepped from the plane. The building which served as the terminal for the Quang Tri airfield had signs for the units in I Corps, and Alvin headed for the sign which read "1/9." He was met by a gunnery sergeant, commonly referred to as a 'gunny', which meant two things: He was an E-7, and since the highest enlisted rank was E-9, he'd been around the block a few times; and it also meant that he knew how to get things done. Since Alvin and the gunny met inside the building, the gunny didn't salute as neither of them was wearing their cover — Marine for 'hat'.

The gunny stood on a bench and spoke: "Everyone going to 1/9 needs to wait here for a few, until the six-by's get here. There's not enough choppers available to get everyone there, so we're getting to VCB by vehicles. Just so you know, we go north on Route 1, and then hang a louie onto Route 9, going west, to VCB. Don't know how long it will take. I know you have not been issued firearms, but all the personnel who are driving the six-by's are armed, and each vehicle has an Marine with a M-60. There ain't been a lot of attacks on traffic on these roads in some time, so we should be good to go. Once you get to VCB, find the company HQ for your unit and report in. They'll take over then. If you're smart, you'll take a dump or pee before you get on the trucks, 'cause this is a non-stop trip."

Alvin hated six-by's. These large trunks were frequently used to transport Marines at OCS and TBS to various duty stations, such as the rifle range, or to the area where they were taught how to toss grenades. They had benches to sit on, and if they had shock absorbers they didn't work worth a damn. But the thing Alvin hated most about the six-by he was getting on was that it was taking him to a duty station which was close to the DMZ between North and South Vietnam, an area full of the North Vietnamese Army and Viet Cong, and in which he would lead men in warfare. He was not full of confidence.

Alvin lost track of time when the six-by's pulled out. There was no talking during the trip, not because there was a rule against it, there just was no point. The vehicles were so loud no one could hear any being said. Alvin could tell when the vehicle turned left off Route I and headed west, to VCB.

The vehicles finally stopped, and the Marines jumped out of the six-by's and someone in the truck threw down their sea bags. Alvin looked around at this sprawling combat base. The buildings had sandbags — what appeared to be two deep — stacked up to the window areas, around all four sides. Alvin guessed the buildings, with tin roofs, couldn't withstand a direct hit of a rocket or mortar, but the sandbags could perhaps protect Marines on the inside when shrapnel from rockets or mortars landed close to the buildings.

Alvin got directions to HQ for Alpha 1/9 and hiked about two hundred yards to report for duty. He knocked on the screen door and was told to 'enter'. He came in with his sea bag and stood before a desk being manned by a PFC. "I'm Lieutenant Alvin Speight and I'm reporting for duty. Can you tell me where the company CO is?"

Two officers came to the PFC's desk. "I'm right here, Lieutenant. I'm Captain Jason Aldridge. This is Lieutenant Rip Bernhardt, my XO. Welcome to Alpha 1/9." Both officers extended their hands. Captain Aldridge continued. "Here's what needs to happen. I'll get the sergeant to get you to a bunk, and he'll take you to supply, where you will get your jungle utilities and boots. He will take you to the armory to get your M-16 and some rounds. We have perimeter security which is damn good and lately there's been no effort by the bad guys to probe the line, but you need to be prepared.

"I've arranged for Sergeant Maurice Smith to be your platoon sergeant. He's very good — this is his second tour, both with Alpha 1/9. He can help you get your bearings out in the bush. It would be smart to listen to what he says and do what he suggests when things get hot. Any questions so far?"

Alvin shook his head 'no' and Captain Aldridge continued. "We've recently received orders to conduct an operation named Dewey Canyon. We'll have a conference about it at 0900 hours tomorrow. You'll need to be there. Sit tight and I'll get the company sergeant to take you to supply and to show you our lovely base."

After dropping off his sea bag in his hooch — his living quarters — Alvin and the sergeant went to supply, where Alvin got three sets of jungle utilities. He also tried on three pair of jungle boots until he got a pair that fit him. The sergeant advised him to always pack at least two extra pairs of socks for switching out when the feet got wet in the bush. Alvin asked the supply sergeant for some skivvies. "Sir, we don't issue many skivvies over here, 'cause they ride up, you can get the red-ass real quick with all the humping you do, so it's a bad idea."

Alvin responded, "Give me three sets of skivvies, sergeant. I wear underwear."

"Whatever you say, lieutenant. Here you are. And here's your 782 gear too." The sergeant handed Alvin his canteen, web belt, ammo pouch, poncho liner and the rest. The supply sergeant handed Alvin a form with the number '782' and a pen. Alvin wondered if 782 gear got its name from the form you had to sign to have it issued.

Alvin asked for a Marine Corps watch, which had a dark green band and a luminous dial. The supply sergeant said, "Here you go, lieutenant. You'll need to get some tape — something like adhesive, to cover the face. Those dials show up at night in the bush. Excellent target for a sniper."

Alvin and the company sergeant each had a load of gear when the returned to Alvin 's hooch, all of which they dumped on his rack — Marine for 'bed'. Alvin met the other three platoon leaders for Alpha 1/9, and the platoon CO, for putrid iced tea. Alvin was wiped out, so he hit the rack and did best to get a good night's sleep his first night in a combat zone.

The next day, Alvin's first Friday in 'Nam, all platoon leaders for Alpha 1/9 and their platoon sergeants met with Captain Aldridge and Lieutenant Bernhardt in the CO's office. Captain Aldridge had some maps of the area south of VCB.

Aldridge addressed the group. "Most of you know about the change in our mission, but Lieutenant Speight is the rookie on this, so we're going over it again for him, and 'cause it won't hurt for all of us to review what's going to happen. The Division CG, General Davis, believes we should go looking for the PAVN, not sit on a hilltop and wait for them to come to us. This change in approach to the mission of the Corps in I Corps is consistent with Marines, who kick ass and take names."

Lieutenant Speight raised his hand. "What's PAVN?"

Aldridge replied. "That's the People's Army of Vietnam, the bad guys. We tangle with both PAVN and Cong up here. What's happening is that while the outposts we have set up are supposed to stop the bad guys, the so-called McNamara Line, it ain't working, and it ain't consistent with our mission, to seek and destroy. So, the CG has ordered us to leave our combat bases and engage and kill the enemy where we find them. What these bad boys are doing is hitting our firebases and patrols, and then scooting into Laos, and our area of operation won't allow us to go after them. Or, they're coming down the Ho Chi Minh trail with supplies and men and then crossing into 'Nam, hitting us and then going back across the border into Laos. What I hear is that we're gonna change that and go after them and to hell with the border, so they won't have a place to hide."

As they were leaving the meeting, Alvin's platoon sergeant, Maurice Smith, said, "Lieutenant, you haven't asked about the men in the platoon, who can do what, who has a hard time doing things, and it's a good idea for you to know about the men you're gonna lead." When Sergeant Smith finished his run-down of the members of the first platoon, Lieutenant Speight had no questions, and Sergeant Smith had misgivings about the lieutenant which he kept to himself.

0835 Hours, Wed, 22 Jan 69
Alpha, 1/9
I Corps, South Vietnam
Operation Dewey Canyon

Alvin could not believe how fast time passed between 3 January and 22 January, when the unit started Operation Dewey Canyon. The four rifle platoons and the weapons platoon loaded onto nine CH-46 choppers for the trip to Firebase Jasper. Alvin had ridden in a 46 during a training exercise at TBS but didn't pay much attention to the chopper then. He did now. It had gunners on the port and starboard sides, right behind the cockpit area, and one at the rear of the chopper, each manning a 60-caliber machine gun. Each M-60 had a bandolier of rounds that snaked to the floor. They looked like they were loaded for bear. The choppers weren't too vulnerable flying to Jasper, but when they went into their landing patterns, there was always cause for concern, since they came in slowly and hovered so the men could disembark.

There was no such thing as a smooth chopper ride. A big chopper, like the 46, just moved around a lot, even when it was loaded with Marines. Alvin felt like he would get sick on his stomach, not so much because of the ride but because of the situation. He was able to keep his composure, because he didn't want his men to know just how nervous he was.

When the choppers landed, Alvin had his first look at a combat base. The top of the hill had been leveled. There were firing pits, a mortar pit, barbed wire topped with concertina barbed wire wound around the perimeter, some holes dug around in which sandbags were positioned, a 106 mm recoilless rifle, lots of empty ammo boxes, and aiming stakes. The Marines of Alpha 1/9 hustled off the choppers and went to their previously assigned sectors on the perimeter, where they got a 'sit rep', a situation report, from the men of Charley 1/9 they were replacing. Then they hunkered down. The weapons platoon took its position, and Captain Aldridge met with the CO of Charley to discuss what to expect. The men of Charley 1/9 then got on the choppers, which had never cut its engines off, and the choppers lifted and headed back to VCB.

Captain Aldridge yelled out an order. "Platoon leaders. Check the wire and the claymores in your sector. We need to be sure the wire is tight as a tick, and that the claymores are positioned to fire toward the bad guys, not us. The bad guys may sneak up and turn them around so when they are detonated, it hits us, not them." Alvin crouched and quickly ran around first platoon's sector, checking the claymores.

As the company got in place, Lieutenant Speight found a big foxhole, surrounded by sandbags, and placed his gear in it. He dragged an ammo box into the foxhole to use to sleep on. This would be his living area as long as the company was on Jasper. His bunking area at VCB looked like the penthouse at The Plaza next to 'Hotel Jasper'.

When night fell, the company went on full alert. The PAVN could not have missed the choppers coming and going, and it was their practice to probe the lines of a firebase when one company replaced another. And they did, starting with mortar fire. Everyone got in their firing positions. The aiming stakes gave the company maximum opportunity to cover every foot of the perimeter with some overlap without shooting each other. The PAVN came up the eastern side of the firebase, which Alvin's platoon was responsible for. The men of First Platoon fired into the advancing PAVN. As they neared the wire, Captain Aldridge yelled out the order to weapons platoon: "Willie Peter, Willie Peter." The order was followed by the unmistakable sound of a mortar round being fired from the mortar tubes — a hollow thump-like sound, and in a few seconds, the night sky was brilliant when the white phosphorus in the mortar rounds ignited. The men of Alpha 1/9 could see the PAVN were in the wire, and with the light provided from the willie peter rounds, they were able to kill a number of the enemy.

But the PAVN kept coming. Sergeant White, who was next to Alvin, said, "Lieutenant, they in the wire. We need to fire the claymores." The claymores were positioned between the fighting positions and the wire. Alvin didn't react, so the sergeant gave the order to detonate the claymores. When detonated, the ball bearings in the claymores have a kill-zone distance of at least fifty yards. But two of the claymores in Alvin's sector were facing his own men, not the wire, and when they were detonated, the ball bearings hit the sandbags of some of the Marine's firing pits and some of the Marines of First Platoon. Sergeant Smith hollered the order, "Cease firing the claymores." The men of First Platoon kept firing their M-16s, the M-60 machine gunner kept firing and the PAVN finally retreated.

Once the attack ended, Captain Aldridge and the company corpsman came over to Alvin's sector. "What the hell happened, were the claymores positioned to hit us?" Aldridge was livid. Alvin answered, "Captain, I checked when we got here, they must have snuck up and reversed them."

Captain Aldridge ordered Alvin to follow him to the center of the firebase, which the CO thought was out of the hearing of the company, but one man could hear him. "Lieutenant, you screwed up. I'm telling you this privately, so the men won't hear me, but it is your job to make sure you and your men protect your sector. You dropped the ball. Don't let that happen again. Lucky no one was hurt too bad. Get your head and ass wired together, got it?"

"Yes, sir."

But Alvin did NOT get it.

Pvt. Grant, in the First Squad, heard the conversation and was thinking that Lieutenant Speight couldn't hack it, and that worried him.

The next day, at 1300 hours, Captain Aldridge led First and Second platoons on a patrol, moving down a path on the east side of the perimeter of Firebase Jasper. The XO, Lieutenant Bernhardt, the third and fourth platoons, and the weapons platoon, stayed at the firebase. The patrol was no more than two klicks (a little over one mile) from the perimeter when the point man on the patrol held up his right hand, the signal to stop in position. He had seen something. Sergeant Smith was next to Alvin, and said, "Lieutenant, you needs to go up to the front of the platoon to see what he's got." After waiting a few seconds, Alvin moved from his crouch and ran to the front of the platoons.

The point man pointed to the east, and Alvin saw several bunkers, a smoldering fire, and several boxes. Alvin called up Sergeant Smith, and Captain Aldridge came forward also. "What do we do with this stuff?", Alvin asked.

Captain Aldridge answered. "Lieutenant, we need to record what's here, get that info to S-2, battalion intelligence, destroy it, and move on. See that box over there, Lieutenant, the one with 'CCCP' on it, you know what that means?"

Alvin shook his head. Aldridge answered, "Well, Lieutenant, that means the gear in that box, whatever it was, came from the Russians. We're fighting them, too." The order was given to set up a perimeter around the site and the inventory and destruction began. The site contained bags of rice, some rounds for the AK-47 rifle — the Russian-made rifle of choice for the PAVN and Vietcong, some fuel drums full of diesel fuel, and a box with vehicle parts.

Sergeant Smith walked around the site and came back to Lieutenant Speight and Captain Aldridge. "Sir, they some vehicle tracks over that way, leading to the west toward Laos. This may be a place where the bad guys stop to work on vehicles, eat up, rest and plan their next attack. They be back, so what you think about us setting up an ambush in that tree line over there?" Captain Aldridge agreed and gave the order to set up the ambush.

The first platoon set up at a trail head to the left of the little roadway, and the second platoon set up on the right. Aldridge made sure the men had firing lines which kept them from firing on each other and gave a final order to his platoon leaders. "It's getting to be dusk. The best time for those guys to move is at night. We're staying here for the night. I'm radioing the XO to tell him what's going on. But — and listen up — we don't want to start firing until the main body of men and vehicles is in our kill zone so we can kill as many as possible. There's enough moonlight for us to tell when that is. Don't fire until I give the order, everyone understand?" Each platoon leader said they understood the order. The squads moved into their positions, hiding behind whatever they could find, and waited.

At 2300 hours, the Marines heard vehicles heading in their direction. Everyone took their safeties off and kept their eyes on the kill zone. One vehicle, which was surrounded by five men, came into the kill zone. The driver cut off the engine. The platoon heard more engines coming down the road. Lieutenant Speight began firing and then all the platoons joined in. When the firing stopped, it was so quiet Sergeant Smith could hear the engines from the other vehicles going away from the ambush site. Captain Aldridge ran up to Speight. This time he didn't bother to speak privately to Speight. "Lieutenant, you screwed up. We got a few bad guys and their vehicle, but we weren't supposed to start firing until I started firing and I wasn't doing that until we had as many vehicles and enemy in the kill zone as we could. You didn't follow my order, and we missed a great opportunity."

This time, the conversation between Aldridge and Speight could be heard by all members of the First and Second platoons. Including Private Grant, who was six-feet-six inches tall, and the strongest and meanest man in the first platoon. He had been in the Corps long enough to have obtained the rank of corporal but had been demoted twice for fighting and insubordination. Grant didn't care about rank, he just wanted to get back to the US in one piece. All of the men of Alpha 1/9 were afraid of Grant, because of his quick temper and reputation as a gang member from Chicago, a reputation he fostered. He was one scary dude.

Grant realized that his odds of making it back home in one piece were dropping as long as Lieutenant Speight kept making mistakes. He had to do something about that but didn't know yet what to do or when to do it.

The platoons returned to Jasper at first light the next day. Alvin and Platoon Sergeant Smith were near the front of first platoon when it came to the same path they came down when they began the patrol. Alvin gave the order for the point man in the group, PFC Scully, to start up the path. Sergeant Smith spoke. "Lieutenant, we ain't supposed to go back the same way we left, 'cause they can lay some mines on the path. Shouldn't we go 'round and come up the west side."

Speight responded. "I got the red ass from wearing these skives and need to get back to Jasper the easiest way. Go up this way. It's the quickest and easiest way to get back. Get going." PFC Scully had taken about ten steps up the path when he stepped on a land mine placed in the pathway. The mine's detonation, and Scully's scream, occurred simultaneously. Lance Corporal Jackson was right behind Scully and the force of the explosion knocked him down. When he looked up and opened his eyes, he saw Scully's severed leg, from the knee down to the boot, bleeding like nothing Jackson had ever seen. The corpsman came forward, wrapped a tourniquet around Scully's right thigh, and Captain Aldridge called HQ for a medevac chopper to come get Scully.

Grant was right behind Lance Corporal Jackson and had a clear view of what had happened to Scully. His hatred of Speight, and his fear Speight would make a mistake again, intensified. He knew Speight had to go.

When the patrol made in back to Jasper, Sergeant Smith spoke to the company commander. "Sir, Lieutenant Speight ain't cutting it. He made three big time mistakes and he ain't been here a day. The men are grumbling about him. Have you thought about sending him back to HQ? If he stays out here, he may get a M-16 round in his back. That's happened before."

Aldridge replied. "Sarge, I agree. I just got word that Lieutenant Colonel Brinson is coming out here to check on us. When he gets here, I'll ask him if the battalion has some place for Speight off the lines and if he has a replacement for Speight."

Within the hour, a Huey gunship was spotted in the skies north of Jasper. Captain Aldridge got on the horn to talk to the pilot." We're popping our smoke grenade now. What smoke do you see?

The chopper pilot answered, "Green."

"Roger green Flyboy. It's windy down here as you can see from the smoke. You may want to come in from the west to get a headwind."

"Will do. See you in five."

The Huey made a perfect landing, and Lieutenant Colonel Brinson hopped out to meet Aldridge, who gave the battalion CO the written inventory and location of enemy gear and supplies they found, and the body count of killed PAVN from the attack on the base camp and from the ambush. He also summed up the actions of Lieutenant Speight, and told the colonel he hoped there was a spot somewhere — anywhere — off the line so Speight wouldn't get men killed, and so Speight wouldn't be in danger from his own men. Both Aldridge and the battalion CO knew there had been cases in the Corps, and the Army, of officers being fragged, being killed when a live grenade tossed by one of their own men exploded near them. Colonel Brinson spoke. "Well, two intelligence officers just rotated out of S-2 and we need replacements. I'll take Speight back to VCB with me and tell the S-2 that he is being assigned to his unit. A lieutenant just reported for his second tour, so I'll get him out here today so your company will have everyone in place."

In five minutes, the Huey gunship, and Speight, were on the way to VCB. No one explained why Speight was on the chopper.

Grant didn't need or want an explanation. He was glad Lt. Speight was leaving the company and that he did not have to kill him.

Grant was wrong.

S-2, the intelligence section of a unit, is tasked with taking information from units, such as the size and location of enemy units, caches of enemy supplies, times of contact with the enemy unit movement, body count of killed enemy, and the like, to try to make sense out of where the enemy had come from, and where it was going. On many occasions, that data was sent up the chain of command and led to B-52 strikes, artillery bombardment, and other tactical maneuvers.

Lt. Speight fit in well with 1/9's S-2 unit. He was an organized learner and processer of information, which was needed in S-2. Gathering information sent from units in the fields, and trying to make sense of it so as to increase the fighting efficiency of Marines in the field, was a job which took time, attention to detail, and an organized mind and approach. Alvin possessed those traits and was given added responsibility shortly after he arrived from Firebase Jasper. He had found a good niche for himself in the Corps. He hoped he would finish his thirteen-month tour with S-2 instead of being in the bush, fighting the NVA.

BUT he wouldn't.

1830 Hours, Sat, 22 Feb 69
Blackie's House of Beef
1217 M Street, Washington, DC
Chow Time!

Woody was commissioned a second lieutenant on 8 November '68, three days after Richard Nixon won the 1968 presidential race. Woody had no illusions that, in spite of Nixon's promises, the newly-elected President would not bring the war to an end during Woody's tour in the Marines. Immediately after the commissioning ceremony, he reported to The Basic School at Quantico to begin six months of training as a Marine combat officer, learning how to lead Marines fighting the North Vietnamese Army and the Vietcong. The training was rigorous and challenging, so he and three of his fellow second lieutenants had taken a night off from TBS to dine at Blackie's House of Beef, one of Washington, DC's most famous restaurants.

Woody could tell by the way the maître d' looked at him, Ernie, Paul and George that they really weren't welcome at this fine restaurant. He guessed, correctly it turned out, that they would be seated in the back, in a corner, near the kitchen, as out of sight as possible.

As soon as they were seated, their waiter, in a tuxedo — all the waiters wore a tux — came to the table and asked what each wanted to drink. Ernie, Paul and George each ordered Pabst Blue Ribbon beer. The waiter — somewhat snootily Woody thought — said they didn't serve Blue Ribbons. They changed their orders to gin and tonics, and Woody ordered Old Grouse scotch on the rocks. A server brought bread and whipped cinnamon butter and filled their water glasses.

Ernie said, "Damn, Woody, how did you know about this place?" The walls were paneled, the carpet was deep, the room had a muted sound, and the wait staff moved with a quiet purpose. In a word, it was elegant.

"Well, when I was thirteen, that would have been 1956. My dad flew our family up here. First airplane flight. We stayed at the Willard Hotel, which is near the White House, and Dad and I went to the major league baseball All Star Game, at Griffith Stadium. Saw Mantle, Mays, Ted Williams — second time I saw him 'cause Dad, I, and some other dads and sons, saw the Red Sox play the Senators one weekend. The players I remember the most were Ted Kluszewski of the Cincinnati Reds — his shirt sleeves were cut off at the shoulders so he could show off his huge biceps, and Nellie Fox of the White Sox, who looked like the smallest player out there. He went up to Ted and kinda messed with those huge biceps. Everyone got a laugh. Don't remember who won the game, but after the game, Dad brought all of us here for dinner. It was the fanciest place I'd ever eaten — no place close to it back home, and I've never forgotten it. Thought we'd enjoy it. The food is better than the chow hall, to be sure."

The waiter returned with their drinks and asked for their orders. They asked the waiter what he would suggest, and he recommended the prime rib, which was a favorite at Blackie's. Each man gave his preference for rare, medium or well-done, and the waiter left. The server brought some more bread and whipped cinnamon butter.

Ernie, who was from Hershey Pennsylvania and a graduate of Temple, spoke up. "You know what happens next week? We get to give the Corps our three preferences for duty stations when we graduate TBS. I've looked around, and I'm gonna ask for Kolona Bay, in Hawaii. Girls dancing in grass skirts, sandy beaches, what a dream. How about you guys?"

Woody replied. "Ernie, the Corps' base on Hawaii is called Kaneoha Bay, not whatever you called it. Second, tell me how many Cong and NVA are attacking that base, and if the answer is 'none', then you're probably wasting your time asking for that duty station. Besides, the very idea of the Corps wanting to know what WE want just ain't happening. They haven't cared about our feelings — and shouldn't — since we reported for OCS. They care as much about our preference as I do in reading *The Illiad and the Oddessy* in the original Greek, and I can't read or speak Greek."

Ernie replied, "OK smart-ass, what are you going to write as your three preferences?"

"Well, I'm putting 'Republic of South Vietnam' all three times."

George asked, "Woody, why in hell would you do that?"

"Well, I think, no, I know, all of us are going to 'Nam. They're teaching us how to fight, not push papers. Remember that captain who spoke to us about going into armor, he said the military was in the business of war, and business was good. So, we're going, sooner or later. There are three bad things which can happen to me when I come back from 'Nam. First, I can get killed, in which case it doesn't matter when I come back; second, I can come back maimed for life, and it won't matter much then; third, if I come back healthy but at the end of my three years, and get released from active duty in California or someplace other than North Carolina, with no job, and no time to really look for one, I'm up the creek. I want to get it over with, and if I'm real lucky and come back alive without being seriously injured, I'm hoping to get assigned for the remainder of my time to Camp Lejeune or Cherry Point, in North Carolina. I've passed the NC Bar exam, and don't EVER want to take another bar exam, so depending when I leave for 'Nam and then rotate back home, I may have up to a year to find a job. Makes sense to me for my situation. But don't get fooled into thinking we're not going to 'Nam. It ain't *if*, it's *when*."

All four men were lost in their own thoughts, about their futures, drinking and eating the delicious bread and butter. Then Paul spoke up. "I wonder if we'd have gotten a better table — one away from the kitchen, if we'd worn our uniforms?"

George said, "Well, our buzz haircuts tell everyone who sees us that we are in the military. They may not know the branch but could guess we're Marines. But don't you remember what our company commander warned us about? There was a guy in TBS last year who went into either DC or Georgetown in his dress whites after their mess night, went to an all-night diner, got in an argument with someone about the war, and the other guy shot the Marine, right in the heart —

killed him. They told us to keep a low profile when we went into the 'civilian world'. There are a lot of folks who are against the war, who don't think much of us who have signed up. We need to be careful."

Woody said, "I remember that warning. I am avoiding conflicts folks may try to start just because I look like I'm in the military. But look, our dinners are here. Boys, dig in, this prime rib will change your life. It's chow time!"

1300 Hours, Fri, 2 May 69
I-95 North
Northern Virginia
Report to Naval Justice School

Woody never appreciated President Eisenhower as much as he did on Friday, 2 May 1969, when he took the overpass over I-95, turned left onto the on-ramp for I-95 North, put Quantico and The Basic School in his rear view mirror, and headed north to his next duty station at the Naval Justice School in Newport, Rhode Island. The NJS was established after World War II to teach military law to Marines, Navy and Coast Guard lawyers and legal personnel.

Woody appreciated Ike because he started the Interstate Highway System after seeing the autobahns in Germany as the Allies pushed the Germans to defeat. The President realized our country needed a way to get around faster. Woody was hoping he would not hit a red light or stop sign before he got to Newport.

Woody's first memory of an American president was Dwight David Eisenhower. When Woody was in the fourth grade, in January 1953, his class walked to the home of the one student in his class whose family had a television set and watched the Presidential Inauguration of the hero. The television commentators discussed Ike and World War II, and that evening, after school, Woody asked his dad about the war. His dad told him it was bad, it lasted a long time, it was cold, and he didn't want to talk about it. Woody Senior didn't tell Woody that his World War II experience had probably shortened his life expectancy.

The Basic School had been quite the experience. Woody now knew how to fire and clean a rifle and a.45 pistol — an officer's standard issue firearm. He knew how to call in artillery fire on a target. He knew how to read a topographical map, at least one of the woods around Quantico, Virginia, and he hoped that would be enough for him to read a map in the middle of a rice paddy or under a jungle canopy so he could lead his men or call in artillery to blast away the bad guys but not him and his men. Most importantly, Woody learned how to lead men. He thought every officer and enlisted Marine who instructed him at OCS and TBS had served in Vietnam. Just as every professor he had at Wake Forest had a PhD, the instructors at TBS had 'advanced degrees in warfare'.

As he headed North to Newport, Woody also realized that the next time he started on a long road trip, he would be heading west, to the Marine Corps Base at Camp Pendleton, California, for duty as the executive officer of a training battalion, after which he would report for duty to Headquarters Company, Third Marine Division, in Quang Tri, South Vietnam, which was right below the DMZ that delineated the northern border of South Vietnam and the southern border of North Vietnam. He didn't know what he'd be doing with the Third Mar Div, but after OCS and TBS, he felt as prepared as one could be for the uncertainty of war. At NJS, he was going to be instructed how to be a military lawyer. He hoped that when he reported to the Third Division, he would have the opportunity to use his soon-to-be-acquired legal skills, rather than go into battle.

Woody arrived in Newport at 1300 hours on Sunday, 4 May. He had a wonderful lunch of the best fried shrimp he had ever eaten, but the coleslaw couldn't touch the coleslaw served with barbeque at Respass Brothers BBQ in Greenville. The two Bloody Mary's were perfect. When he came into the restaurant, he bought a copy of The Boston Globe. He had been a Red Sox fan since his Dad took him to see Ted Williams and the Sox play the Washington Senators. The American League had split into two divisions for the 1969 season, so Woody checked the sports page for the schedule of the Sox at Fenway Park and the fabled Green Monster left field wall.

He reported to the Naval Justice School the next day. There were twenty-two other officers in Woody's NJS class, sixteen Marine second lieutenants, and six US Navy lieutenants, which was the equivalent of captain in the Marines. Woody didn't know any of his classmates.

When a Marine captain entered the room, each Marine stood at attention. The Navy Officers did not initially stand, but after they saw the Marines stand, they stood but were not at attention.

The captain addressed the group. "I'm Captain Gray Hite. I'm a Captain in the Marine Corps. You may take your seats. I will be your ONLY instructor for your six weeks at NJS. How many of you Navy guys are graduates of an Ivy League school, either undergrad or law?" Three of the six Navy lieutenants raised their hands. Captain Hite asked the other three where they went to law school and was told UCLA, Illinois, and Wisconsin.

"Did any of you Marines go to an Ivy League school?" No hands were raised. "I didn't think so. This is my second year at NJS. I served in Vietnam from '67 to '68. I tried cases, AND I led men in combat. Do any of you Marines think you will go to Vietnam?" All hands shot up. "Well, you're right. And how many of you think you will lead men in combat during your tour?" Again, all hands were raised.

"Well, you may be wrong. I'll explain later. But first, a little exercise. Get out a sheet of paper, write your name and whether you are Marine or Navy on the top, and look up when finished". When all were looking up, Captain Hite addressed the lawyers. "In this exercise you are the trial judge. The defendant, a Marine private first class, has just been convicted by the military panel of barracks larceny by stealing the wallet and watch of a fellow Marine who left them on his bunk while he was in the head, which is the bathroom for you Navy lieutenants. For the purposes of this exercise, your sentencing options are (1) fine and reduction in rank, or (2) bad conduct discharge. That's all you know. You've got 15 seconds to write down your sentence and pass the sheets to the front".

When Captain Hite had all the papers, he looked at each and put them in two piles on the desk he stood behind. "Well, I have the results. Every Navy lieutenant gave the defendant a fine and reduction in rank, and every Marine gave a BCD." He looked at the clipboard he brought to class. "Navy Lieutenant Peabody — what do you think about all the Marines giving the defendant a BCD, and don't hold back."

When Peabody stood up, Woody thought his name fit his appearance. He was tall, thin, had a pointed nose which Woody thought would look perfect with a *prez nez*, and he talked in a high-pitched voice. He sounded and looked rich, both of which he probably was. Even his voice sounded like he was talking down to the listener. "Sir, I think the bad conduct discharge was a barbaric sentence".

"Well, Marines, I guess Lt. Peabody thinks you Marines are prehistoric. Not sure if that is a compliment or an insult. Whichever, I'll call on — let's see, Marine Lieutenant Kitchen, for a rebuttal. Kitchen, stand and defend the Marines from this vicious attack by the Navy."

Lieutenant Kitchen was 5'9" and weighed about a buck sixty. "Well, my guess is that the lieutenant — was it Peabody? — is not stupid, he is just uninformed in the ways of barracks life and military life. In the Corps, you are trained to be trusted by, and to trust, your fellow Marines. Your life may depend on it. This defendant violated that trust. He has to go. That's the way I see it."

"Exactly." Captain Hite went to the front of his desk, sat on it and faced his class. "Here's the point. And, by the way, I do this same exercise at the beginning of every class, and the sentencing results are the same every time. Although, this is the first time Marines have been referred to in pre-historic terms. You Navy guys — you've been in the military what — two weeks?" They all nodded 'yes'. "And that consisted of what I call 'salute school', where you learn how and who to salute — who is a higher rank than you, how to wear the uniform of our Country properly, and some other military protocol. But even though you are not experienced in military matters, you are expected to know something about the military lives of the men you will be representing, prosecuting or advising. Therefore, you're giving advice and counsel to someone when you don't even know or understand his environment. Every Marine in this class has earned his second lieutenant's commission through OCS or PLC, and then they all went

TBS, where they not only learned how to lead men in combat they also learned about things military."

"So, at this school, in this class, I am going to give you Navy guys as much of a taste of military life as I can in the time we have, so when you go on active duty you will not only 'book smart', but you will also have some idea about things military. You all WILL know military law if you pass my test and become certified as a military lawyer. If you Navy guys pay attention, you will also learn a little bit — better than nothing — about how the military operates and how sailors live their everyday lives. You can't give good advice, or prosecute or defend a case, if you don't have some idea about the environment in which sailors live. The law is more than what is in the books, it involves the practical experiences people have and how the law impacts their lives."

"Now, remember when I said that I had been to 'Nam, tried cases there, and led combat patrols? Remember I asked if any of you Marines thought you'd be lawyering and in combat in 'Nam and you said 'yes'? And remember when I said that you may be wrong? Well, now you're going to find out what I meant by all of that. I call on Lieutenant Woodrow White."

Woody came to attention. "Men, when called upon, you do need to stand, but not at attention, Lieutenant White, why do you think you will be in combat in Nam even though you have passed the bar?"

"Sir, you come out of Marine OCS and either go air wing, or grunt. I can't fly, so I'm a grunt. That is what I was trained to do. The way this war is going, they will need a lot of lieutenants to be in combat positions. So — I'd be pleasantly surprised if all I did was try cases in Vietnam."

"Well, Lieutenant, let's discuss that thought. Have you heard the name 'Clarence Gideon'?"

"Yes, sir, I have."

"Now, all of you pay attention to what just happened. I asked him one question, and I got one answer. He didn't tell me WHO Gideon was, he just answered my question 'yes' because it called for a 'yes' or 'no' answer. We will be conducting mock trials in this class. You will be prosecutor, also called trial counsel, defense counsel, military judge, and military court panel members in these mock trials. The number one rule of preparing your own witness is to train him to answer only the question asked by either you, opposing counsel, or the judge. Now, Lieutenant White, tell us what you know about Clarence Gideon."

"Sir, he had been convicted of several crimes before he was charged, I believe, with the felony which gave rise to the Gideon matter. He asked for a lawyer to be appointed to represent him because he was indigent and faced prison, but his request for counsel was denied. He was convicted and sentenced to prison, and he hand-wrote a <u>certiorari</u> petition requesting the court reverse his conviction on the grounds that the Constitution entitled him to have a lawyer appointed to represent him if he couldn't afford one since he faced a prison sentence. The Supreme Court allowed his petition for <u>cert</u>, heard the case, and decided that Gideon was entitled to appointment of counsel because he was indigent, faced a prison sentence, and couldn't afford an attorney. I believe the decision was handed down in 1963. Anthony Lewis wrote an excellent book about the case called <u>Gideon's Trumpet</u>."

Captain Hite responded. "That's exactly right. And what difference does it make to the military lawyer that the Supreme Court handed down <u>Gideon V Wainwright</u>? Anybody? Well, I wouldn't expect you to know this, but to you Marines, it is the most significant legislation you could imagine. Lt. White, what were you doing on 10 October 1968?"

Woody answered, "Sir, I was at OCS at Quantico".

Captain Hite continued. "Lieutenant White, is that a Southern accent."

"Yes, sir."

"Well, do you know who Sam Ervin Jr. is."

"Yes Sir."

"Who is he?"

"He is one of the Senators from North Carolina."

Captain Hite continued. "That is right. The Honorable Senator has enjoyed the well-earned reputation of being a fair-minded man, and he has a law degree, from Harvard I believe. He thought it was right and fair for a civilian like Gideon to have an attorney represent him if he faced a prison sentence and was indigent, but — and here's the point — he did NOT think it was fair for military defendants to not have a licensed attorney represent them if they faced a discharge or a prison sentence. The old rule was that an officer, not necessarily an attorney, would represent a defendant. The good Senator felt that had to change, and there were other things Senator Ervin didn't like about the laws for men, and women, in the military. So, it took him several years, but he got Congress to pass a bill which, in effect, provides that military defendants have the right to have a REAL lawyer — a lawyer who had passed the bar of a state — to represent them when they were a defendant in a court martial that could result in their being discharged or receiving a prison sentence. That law is called The Military Justice Act of 1968, and the House passed it on 3 October 1968, and the Senate on 10 October. So, when you Jarheads get to Nam, there is a good chance you will not be in the bush, you'll be in a courtroom, defending some Marine in a special or general court martial facing a BCD or a dishonorable discharge, or a prison sentence. Maybe you can now breathe more easily.

"Now, the Uniform Code of Military Justice, the UCMJ, is the bible of military law. It came into existence in 1950 and has been changed over the years. I am NOT going to teach you the military law by having you sit down and memorize the elements of the crime, the rules of evidence and all that stuff. You are going learn it by living it, practicing it. You are my third class. We will learn through mock trials. If you are the trial counsel, you'll draft the specs of the crime and 'try' the case; if you are the defense counsel, you'll prepare the defense; if you're a court member — a juror — you will decide guilt or innocence. After each exercise, we'll critique the work of each of you, and learn that way. Let's get started."

And so it was that on his first day at Naval Justice School, Woody found out he would probably be in a courtroom, and not in the jungles, of South Vietnam. He had six weeks to learn how to be a military lawyer, and after thirty-days leave, he had to drive to California, to catch that Big Bird to South Vietnam.

0600 Hours, Sun, 2 Jun 69
Alpha, 1/9, A Shau Valley,
I Corps, South Vietnam
Operation Apache Snow

"Lieutenant, just how long have we been in this god-forsaken valley?"

Jordan Crawford, First Lieutenant, USMC (R), had previously been with Second Battalion, Ninth Marine Regiment, but had taken command of Alpha Company about seven days before Apache Snow, his first op with Alpha. He answered Second Lieutenant Overton, "Now Lieutenant Overton, you know the Corps wouldn't send us to a god-forsaken place. This is a wonderful, tropical paradise. It has elephant grass eight feet high which is so pleasant to walk through, even when it cuts your jungle utilities. It has triple canopy trees which provide wonderful shade from the tropical sun and also provide excellent hiding spaces for the PAVN and which do a great job of keeping the humid weather from being reached by any wind. In fact, when — make that if — this so-called 'war' ends, I'm thinking about building a golf course here. It has great elevation changes — which are probably easier to hump with a golf bag than humping with the military gear, weapons and ammo we are carrying. It could well be a destination place. But to answer your question, the choppers dropped us off on 10 May, so — about three weeks. I'm assuming the Army and ARVN were airlifted at the same time, but who knows."

Lieutenant Overton replied. "Well, thanks for the tourist info, Skipper. I beg to differ with you about the triple canopy trees, 'cause some of them don't even have leaves after the folks in charge of this war sprayed that orange crap on them. You know, if that orange stuff will eat through leaves and kill them, what the hell are they doing to our lungs or eyes? No telling. Beside, who comes up with the names for these ops? Who ever heard that Apaches had snow?"

"Lieutenant, I can't believe you are so cynical about our beloved..."

Crawford heard the rifle shot at the same time Lieutenant Overton's head exploded, filling the air with the mist of Overton's blood and brain matter. He immediately knew nothing could be done for Lieutenant Overton. Instinctively, he ducked behind a tree and yelled "SNIPER", grabbed his M-16 and looked up at the trees. He saw a puff of smoke from a tree above their position, about thirty-feet high. He fired his entire clip and was reaching for a second clip when he looked up. The rounds from his M-16 had shredded the branches and leaves between him and the puff of smoke. He could now see the sniper, with blood coming from the limp body, but Crawford fired more shots at him, not so much to make sure he was dead — he knew the shooter was dead, but out of frustration for having lost a man under his command. He could see the shooter was tied to a tree limb. Crawford thought there was no way this war could be won by the US and South Vietnam when the enemy was willing to go to such extremes as this shooter did by, essentially, committing suicide.

His platoon sergeant came to his side, and Crawford gave orders. "Sergeant, the lieutenant is dead. No need to call the corpsman. Have the RTO get up here and get 1/9's CO on the horn."

In a minute, the Company's radio transmission operator, PFC Ronald Lassiter, whom everyone called Sparky, came to Crawford's position. The long aerial for the PRC-25 radio was wrapped around the radio so it would not present a target. Sparky contacted regiment's frequency.

Crawford talked to the regimental commander of 1/9. "Colonel, we're down to one platoon CO and myself. Lieutenant Overton was just KIA. Yesterday a platoon commander was WIA and airlifted to battalion aid station. I know we're here as a blocking force when the NVA are pushed toward us heading for Laos, but we need at least one more platoon leader. Could really use two. And we can use some M-16 rounds, some .50 cal rounds and some M-60 rounds."

"Lieutenant, has a dust-off chopper come to get the KIA's body?"

"No sir. I called you first, and no call has been put in for the dust-off."

The battalion commander responded, "Lieutenant Crawford, I'm in touch with the Hundred First Airborne. They are driving some NVA your way. You need to set up an ambush for the NVA. I'll give you the radio frequency for that CO so you can contact him to make this happen. I'll personally order the chopper to you, and I'll make sure there is a lieutenant on that bird. I'll make it happen. And the chopper will resupply ammo and C Rats. We have some Cobra gunships on call. Go through me if you need them. What is your position?"

After giving the colonel the company's coordinates, Crawford called the platoon leader and platoon sergeants of Alpha 1/9 to meet with him for a sit rep. He ordered the company to get into a defensive position as they awaited the chopper.

It soon started raining, hard, so it took the Huey some time to get to the position of Alpha 1/9. A platoon sergeant popped a red smoke grenade to mark their position. When the chopper landed, a Marine jumped to the ground. When Sergeant Smith saw him, he said, "This be bad news."

Crawford asked the sergeant what he meant.

"Well, Lieutenant, it means that if that Marine is the replacement for Lieutenant Overton, we's got a problem. Can't remember his name — Smith maybe, but he was with us on Dewey Canyon and screwed up so bad, our platoon leader asked the brass to get him out of the bush and to some desk job, where he won't get men killed because he's stupid. Sorry, Lieutenant, shouldn't speak that way about an officer, but this ain't some place to be nice."

"No problem Sergeant. Rather know what I'm dealing with. No need to detail his screw-ups. I'm going to put him with you, tell him why and have you to keep him from screwing up."

Sergeant Smith replied, "Yes sir. I keep a sharp eye on him."

Crawford signaled Speight to come to him as members of his company were off-loading boxes of ammo and C-rats and placing Lieutenant Overton's body bag in the chopper. He gave Speight a run-down of the company's mission and position, told him he would be platoon leader of first platoon, again, and that Sergeant Maurice Smith would again be his platoon sergeant. "Now, Speight, you listen to what Sergeant Smith says and follow his advice. He's very experienced, as you know. You can't go wrong listening to him, got it?"

"Yes sir, got it."

Woody was wrong.

Private Roosevelt Grant was shocked to see Lieutenant Speight back in the field. He remembered that Speight had triggered the ambush on Dewey Canyon too early and that platoon leader had blown him out about it. Grant also remembered that Speight's decision to return to base camp by the same route they left on caused Scully to lose his leg to a land mine. Grant was hoping Speight would get WIA or KIA, and then he wouldn't have to worry about Speight messing up again. Grant knew that one way or another, Speight had to go and he knew he may have to make that happen.

Two hours after the chopper left with Lieutenant Overton's body, the men of Alpha 1/9 heard sporadic gunfire from the east. Lieutenant Crawford called Sparky to his side and pulled a piece of paper from the left pocket of his utility jacket. "Sparky, this is the Hundred First's frequency, don't know which unit. I was given this so we can coordinate with them if it turned out they were driving the NVA towards us, which is what it sounds like is happening. Get them on the hook for me."

Sparky unhooked the radio aerial, so it was at full length, adjusted his frequency button to the frequency of the Hundred First, pushed the transmit button and said, "This is Alpha 1/9, USMC, calling CO of Hundred First, over."

Within ten seconds, a voice came over the radio. "This is Captain Witherspoon of the 101, over."

Crawford responded, "Lieutenant Crawford, Alpha/1/9, Marines here. Sounds like you've got them on the run, just as was planned. Over."

"Roger that Lieutenant. There's about two companies of NVA, no heavy weapons like RPGs that we know of. They're doing the 'fire and maneuver thing' so that about half of them fire, the other half moves toward you and then vice versa. What are your coordinates?"

After hearing the coordinates for Alpha 1/9's position, Witherspoon keyed his transmission button and spoke. "If we keep them going the way they've been going, they'll be at your place in an hour or so. What can we do to help you get the welcome mat out?"

"Captain Witherspoon, if you can, pinch them in on their north and south ends and drive them this way, kinda like herding cattle into the pen, We can have sort of a horseshoe ambush to deal with them, over."

"Crawford, no guarantees but we'll try. We don't want to be in your line of fire, so when you're ready to unload on them, let us know and we'll stop our pursuit and leave them for you, over."

Crawford replied, "Sounds like a plan. Thanks. By the way, you know you airborne guys are a bit nuts, jumping out of perfectly safe airplanes, don't you?"

"No, just another way to show you that the Army has bigger studs than you pansy Marines. Good hunting, over."

After completing the transmission, Crawford ordered all platoon leaders to his position. He gave them a run-down of Witherspoon's report. Then he brushed some leaves out of the way, and, using a stick, drew his ambush plan in the dirt. Moving the stick from left to right, Crawford said, "We're going to set what I'm calling a modified horseshoe ambush. Speight and Sergeant Smith, First Platoon will be on the left end, the north end. Then Second Platoon. Then weapons platoon — by having you in the middle you can support the entire company and I'll be with Weapons, then Third Platoon and Fourth — you'll hold down the south end, the right end, of the ambush. The 101 says they think these bad guys have only small arms — no RPGs, but we don't know that, so be ready. The 101 is going to try to drive them to us and pinch them in on each end, so when they get to us, they're like cattle being herded into a pen.

"The woods are so thick we won't be able to see them until they are about on us, but they'll have to slow up when they're crossing that stream and that's when we'll unload. Whatever happens, we cannot let any of them get outside either the First or Fourth platoon positions. Then they'd be behind us. Can't let that happen. Have your men at least ten feet apart — don't want one grenade taking out two men, and, set up your firing lines so the First and Fourth Platoons don't fire at each other. First and Fourth, pick a point at each end and make sure your men don't shoot behind that point, 'cause if they do, they'd be shooting our men. Give that point to the other platoons. If we can pinch them into our middle, like herding cattle to the pen, we'll be okay. This valley is too narrow for us to call in arty or napalm–don't want to get roasted or hit ourselves. So, we're on our own, and the NVA ain't got a chance. Questions?" There were none. "Okay, set up, lock and load, and we'll open fire on my command. Got that Lieutenant Speight?"

"Yes sir."

"Oh, I forgot one important thing. Everyone needs to have some tracer rounds in their ammo clips to make sure they aren't shooting each other. Okay, let's get ready."

Crawford moved to his position with the weapons platoon, which put him in the middle of the spread-out ambush. Sparky and his radio were with Crawford so he could contact the Hundred First when the time was right.

Sergeant Smith, Lieutenant Speight, and the platoon leader and platoon sergeant of Fourth Platoon went to the northern end — the left side of the ambush site, and discussed their respective lines of fire. The platoon leader of Fourth Platoon spoke first. "It looks to me that if First Platoon sets up right here, and doesn't fire to the right of that big tree at the right end of the ambush, the one with bark missing (he pointed to the tree), and if Fourth Platoon doesn't fire at anything to the left of this tree we're under, and if that info is given to Second, Third and weapons platoons, we won't be shooting at each other. Sound ok?" They all agreed and went to their respective fighting positions and gave the orders to the rest of the men of Alpha not to fire in the restricted areas.

Roosevelt Grant had been in ambushes before and knew what he was doing. Sergeant Smith was to his immediate right, and Lieutenant Speight was to the sergeant's right. Grant was glad he had his eyes on Speight and wondered if he'd screw up again.

And then the men of Alpha 1/9 waited.

As the small arms fire between the 101 and the NVA got closer, Lieutenant Crawford began to see NVA soldiers moving toward the ambush, hiding behind trees. He thought — they ain't dummies and probably smell our ambush. He had Sparky raise Witherspoon of the 101 on the radio. "This is Crawford of Alpha 1/9. Can you read me?"

"101 here. Affirmative. Can read you."

Crawford continued, "We're beginning to see the NVA. You need to back off, we're going to open up in a couple of minutes."

"Roger that. We'll push them a little and then back off. Looks like we've got them herded like we talked. Good luck. Over and out."

The men of Alpha 1/9 had either scooped out fighting holes in the dirt of the A Shau Valley or positioned themselves behind a tree or rock. Each Marine was intensely looking across the stream, ready for the NVA to emerge from the thick woods on the east side of the stream. They took their weapons off safety and were as ready as they could be.

Lieutenant Crawford did not know the size of the enemy force, except for Witherspoon's estimate of one or two companies. It was going to be difficult to know when to spring the ambush. If sprung too soon, too many of the NVA could take cover in the thick trees on the east side of the stream and they would be hard to deal with. If sprung too late, the force of the NVA may be large enough to engage in close combat with Alpha 1/9. When Crawford estimated twenty NVA had crossed the stream, he yelled the order "OPEN FIRE!"

The firepower from the M-16s, the M-60 machine guns, the 50 cal, and the M-79 grenade launchers manned by Alpha 1/9 brought down most of the NVA who had crossed the stream. The remaining NVA took positions behind trees, rocks, and anything else they could find, on the east side of the stream and began moving from tree or rock, closing in on Alpha 1/9's position.

Grant knew from his tracer rounds that he was killing NVA. He emptied his first clip and was reaching for another when he heard Platoon Sergeant Maurice Smith cry out. "NO LIEUTENANT." Grant looked up and saw that the tracer rounds from Lieutenant Speight's M-16 were to the right of the tree with no bark, landing in Fourth Platoon's position. Speight was shooting at his fellow Marines! Smith grabbed Speight around the neck with his left arm and grabbed the stock of the M-16 with his right hand, pointing the barrel to the sky. "Dammit Lieutenant, you be firing into our own positions. See that tree with no bark, don't fire to the right of that tree."

The fire fight intensified as more NVA came across the stream. They knew they could not retreat — the Hundred First was waiting for them. They knew if they stayed in the kill zone — between the stream and Alpha's position, they would be killed. They could only move forward into the Marines of Alpha 1/9.

They never had a chance. The ambush was so well-conceived and implemented that the fire fight was over in about fifteen minutes, with only two friendly WIA, both from the Fourth Platoon, whose positions were near the tree with no bark.

When the NVA stopped firing, Lieutenant Crawford ordered Alpha to stop firing. He gathered his platoon leaders and platoon sergeants around him. "We're taking no prisoners. We aren't the Red Cross, and they'd slow us up. Each of you assign one man from your platoon to make sure each NVA is dead. If not dead, leave them. Also remember, those bastards may pull the pin on a grenade to explode if their body is moved, so be careful. Gather all their weapons, get the clips and the rounds and dump them in the stream. Lieutenant Speight, you and your platoon dig a pit big enough to dump all the weapons and we'll burn 'em. Have those four men get an accurate count of the number of NVA KIA. Battalion will want to know." Lieutenant Crawford was disgusted that the brass — the colonels and generals, and the folks in the administration in Washington DC, all of whom were supposedly running this war — often seemed to be more interested in the number of enemy killed than they were in the number of Americans WIA or KIA. He thought it was a stupid way to keep score in a war.

For the next few minutes, fifteen Marines from Alpha carried out Crawford's orders. Sometime a Marine fired a round into the head of an NVA because that was the quickest way to make sure he was dead. They reported to Crawford there were 103 enemy KIA. Crawford then got on the horn to battalion, reported the success of the ambush and requested enough choppers for the company to be airlifted to VCB.

Alpha 1/9 formed a defensive perimeter around what would become the LZ for the choppers and kept a sharp eye out for NVA or Cong. In a few minutes they heard the "whop-whop" of the choppers heading toward them. Sergeant Smith popped a smoke grenade, and the green smoke gave the chopper pilots the location of the LZ and the wind direction. There were several choppers, and since the LZ could handle only two choppers at a time, it took Alpha about thirty minutes to evacuate the area.

Grant was on the last chopper to leave the LZ. He had time to think about Lieutenant Speight. He knew he'd never know for sure if the two WIAs in Fourth Platoon were wounded by Speight, but given the direction of Speight's firing shown by the tracer rounds from his M-16, Grant was satisfied that Speight had messed up again. He knew he had to kill him. The question was when and how. Those questions were about to be answered.

1215 Hours, Fri, 13 Jun 69
Near the Paracel Islands
South China Sea
Latitude 16 Degrees, 29 minutes
Longitude 112 Degrees, 0 minutes
Typhoon

Typhoons can be formed in the Northwestern Pacific Basin. On 13 Jun 69, the surface temperature was sufficiently warm in the South China Sea, near the Paracel Islands, for the formation of a typhoon. There were other meteorological circumstances which contributed to the formation of the typhoon: atmospheric instability, a high humidity force to develop a low-pressure center, and a low level focus or disturbance which existed prior to the surface temperature becoming warm. A typhoon formed at high noon on 13 Jun 69.

After it formed, the typhoon gained strength and knot speed from the water and atmospheric circumstances as it moved west, toward South Vietnam.

When the typhoon's leading edge reached the shore of South Vietnam, in the Da Nang region, it covered a hundred miles in all directions out from the eye, and its winds were reaching one-hundred knots. It veered sharply in a northwesterly direction, toward Quang Tri Province and Vandegrift Combat Base. The leading edge reached Quang Tri at 1700 hours on Saturday, 14 June.

At the office of the Commanding General of the Third Division, the powers that be realized that the force of the typhoon would severely impact the abilities of Marines to wage war, primarily because air and vehicular support essential to the Corps waging war would not be available for use in this weather. The word was passed down the chain of command to 'stand down' until the 'all clear' was given after the typhoon had passed. The Third Division Marines were reminded that the enemy could use the weather to their advantage.

When Grant heard the 'stand down' order, he knew three things; First, the typhoon would give him his best — maybe his last — chance to murder Speight; second the M61 grenade he kept after Apache Snow was the perfect murder weapon; and third, he couldn't use his left hand because he had paid someone to slam the stock of an M-16 on his hand to break it so he could avoid combat, so Grant needed someone to open and hold the door while he pulled the grenade pin and safety before tossing the grenade under Speight's rack.

He needed someone weak.

He needed someone he could fool.

He needed Greenfield.

0300 Hours, Sun, 15 Jun 69
Alpha 1/9
VCB, I Corps
Fragging

Grant knew he could not discuss his plan to frag the lieutenant with Garland Greenfield before it was time to kill the lieutenant. He had to surprise Greenfield, giving him no time to think about it and less chance to back out. Grant hoped the cover of the typhoon would help them get away with it.

Grant went to Greenfield's rack and placed his right hand over Greenfield's mouth to keep him quiet as he shook Greenfield awake. Grant whispered to Greenfield, "Keep quiet and come with me." Greenfield got out of his rack and followed Grant out of the hooch. It was raining like hell, and each man was instantly soaked. "I'm gonna play a joke on Lieutenant Speight. I got me a smoke grenade from that last op and I'm gonna toss it into the lieutenant's hooch. It's got green smoke. But I've got this bad left hand and can't hold open the door and pull the pin on the smoke grenade with my good hand. I just need you to hold the door, I'll toss the smoke grenade, and then we'll run back to the hooch. Alright?"

Greenfield was intimidated by Grant and felt he had no choice but to agree, so he told Grant he'd help. The lieutenant's hooch was about one hundred yards from their hooch. They crouched as they ran to the hooch. The thunder, lightning, howling wind and sheets of rain gave them cover. Grant couldn't imagine anyone would be up and about in this weather.

He was wrong.

They reached the lieutenant's hooch. As Garfield opened the hooch door with his left hand, Grant turned his back to Garfield and bent at his waist. He then threw the grenade into the hooch. They both heard it roll on the wooden floor as they ran from the hooch. They were about ten yards from the lieutenant's hooch when the M61 fragmentation grenade exploded. Every Marine has thrown a M61 grenade and knows the sound of its explosion. Even with the thunder, lighting and rain, Greenfield heard the grenade explode and he knew Grant had not tossed a harmless smoke grenade. He had fragged the lieutenant.

When they got to their hooch, Greenfield stopped running and turned to Grant. "You fragged the lieutenant, and he's probably dead. I can't believe this!"

Grant grabbed Greenfield by his wet t-shirt. "You're damn right I killed him. He was a shitty officer. He deserved to die. You're just as guilty as I am. Better keep your mouth shut, or you'll go to jail as long as I do. We both keep quiet and no one will know who did it. We'll say we were up talking when we heard the grenade go off. Nobody liked the lieutenant. Keep quiet and we're ok."

Greenfield went back to his hooch, changed out of his wet utilities and climbed back onto his rack. He was more afraid than at any time in combat. He knew Grant would just as soon kill him as a bug, and realized his only hope was to keep his mouth shut. He knew he was in a hurt locker in the worst way and could see no way out.

0600 Hours, Sun, 15 Jun 69
Office of Commanding Officer
Alpha Company, 1/9
VCB
"Breckinridge, you're the Investigation Officer"

Jordan Crawford, First Lieutenant, USMC (Reserve) became CO of Alpha 1/9 a few days before Operation Apache Snow. At 6'2" and with the body of an NFL defensive back, he looked like a Marine, even in jungle utilities, which hung loosely so to be as cool as possible in the steamy, hot environment. Lieutenant Crawford was born ready.

His father was a lawyer in Rawlins, Wyoming, and knew John Joseph Hickey, who also practiced law in Rawlins. Mr. Hickey was appointed US Senator from Wyoming in 1961, Jordan's junior year in high school. When Jordan's dad sent a letter to his friend the Senator, requesting an appointment for his only son to the Naval Academy at Annapolis, Maryland, the appointment was speedily dispatched. By the end of January 1962, his senior year in high school, Jordan knew he was headed to Annapolis.

In his fourth year at the Academy, he opted to select his commission as a second lieutenant in the Marine Corps rather than the Navy. The Corps selection committee, after reviewing Jordan's record at the Academy, gladly welcomed Jordan as one of their own. He was proud, but in a quiet way, that he had graduated from the Academy class of 1966.

He graduated first in his TBS class and was then posted to Second Battalion, Ninth Marine Regiment as platoon leader of second platoon.

On Thursday, 30 January '68, he, another platoon commander, and two sergeants from 2/9, were ordered to drive from Quang Tri to Hue', the ancient imperial capital city of Vietnam, to reconnoiter the lay of the land and the streets and buildings. The battalion intelligence officers felt the NVA and the Vietcong may attack Hue'.

Their intelligence was accurate. At approximately 0230 hours on 31 January '68, the NVA and the Vietcong launched a full-scale attack on Hue', as well as numerous other sites in South Vietnam. Since he was somewhat familiar with the city of Hue', Lieutenant Crawford was given the assignment of planning and executing the effort to re-take Hue' from the enemy. The Marines engaged in a furious battle with the NVA, which included house-to-house fighting, even though the Marines had received little training in house-to-house warfare at OCS or TBS. Crawford's leadership during the battle for Hue' was exceptional. As a result, he was awarded the Bronze Star with 'V' device for valor and was promoted to First Lieutenant.

During the presentation of his after-action report, Crawford suggested to the battalion commander that the Corps start house-to-house combat training at The Basic School, an idea that was implemented almost immediately. First Lieutenant Crawford was highly regarded by 'the brass' — the ranking officers — of the Third Mar Div.

When he was assigned to Alpha 1/9, Lieutenant Jordan Crawford contemplated his short military career. He felt the Academy, as well as his in-country experience as platoon leader, had prepared him for anything which would come his way as he continued his tour of duty in South Vietnam.

He was wrong.

He was not prepared to deal with the murder of an officer under his command.

Jordon was winging it when he met with Lieutenant Donald Breckenridge, his new executive officer, and with S/Sgt Maurice Smith, from First Platoon, and the platoon leaders of Alpha, at 0600 on 15 Jun 69. There was no textbook which gave direction to a CO how to handle the murder of a Marine under his command. There was also the challenge of the vestiges of the typhoon, because even though the winds had abated, torrential rains continued.

Crawford started the meeting. "Here's where we are now. The body of Lieutenant Speight has been placed in a body bag and the bag has been placed in the reefer for cold storage until a chopper can get out here to remove it to the Division morgue, though with this weather there really is no idea when that will be. There is no point in endangering a chopper and its crew to get out here to take a body back to Division. It may be different if we had a seriously wounded Marine who needed immediate medical attention we couldn't give him. So the chopper will get here when it gets here.

"Except for Sergeant Smith, each of you was in the bunker Speight was in, so I need to know what you know."

Second Lieutenant Jerry Johnson spoke up. "Lieutenant, we've discussed this and knew you'd want a summary. We agreed I'd give it to you, but we don't know much. If I misstate something, forget something, or say something which doesn't match the memory of one of the other guys, they'll pipe up. None of us heard anything before the grenade detonated. Lieutenant Speight's rack was next to the door. The deck below the lieutenant's rack is blown all to hell. I guess the explosion would have been more widespread if the deck had been concrete, or something like that. The ply board deck just disintegrated. The racks in that hooch are only a couple of feet off the deck, so the blast probably killed him instantly. None of us heard the door open. Not sure we could have done anything had we heard anything. The thunder and lighting, and the rain on the metal roof, made it tough to hear yourself think. None of us was hit. We got to the lieutenant within seconds after the blast, but he was not breathing or moving. There was blood — "

Crawford interrupted Lieutenant Johnson. "I saw the body and the damage to his rack and deck. Don't need to discuss that. We've got to figure out who did this. None of us are trained in murder investigations, but with the uncertainly of communication with HQ, or with Naval Investigative Service, we're on our own until we can tell HQ what happened and until they can get an investigative team out here.

This is what we're going to do:

First, Jerry, get ahold of a good camera. If none of you have one, get the platoon sergeants to check with the men in their platoon. We need a nice Nikon or Minolta. We need to load it up with film, and take as many pictures as we can of the door, the rack, the deck, the hooch door, and go to the reefer and remove the body from the bag and take pictures of it. We can give the film to NIS or the trial counsel to get developed.

But second, the most important thing we can do is to start asking questions and get someone talking about who did this. I know Speight — I mean Lieutenant Speight — had some big problems in the bush, he had some KIAs and WIAs in First Platoon that may have occurred because of what he did or did not do. Members of his platoon may have had it in for him. Happened before. Sergeant Smith, you're his, or you were his, platoon sergeant. What are you hearing, or what have you heard, from the Marines about Speight's performance that would lead to this. We've got to find this killer ASAP, hopefully before NIS gets here."

Sergeant Smith answered, "Sir, Lieutenant Speight was not a good field commander. After Dewey Canyon, before you got here, on his first op, he was taken off the line…"

Crawford interrupted. "Well, we know he could not, or did not, hack it in the field. We can't do anything about any screw ups, so no need to discuss them unless his screw-ups help us ID the murderer, or murderers. Sergeant Smith, who do we start with to find out who did this? And, something else — do we think there was only one man, and is there a chance the killer or killers came from another unit?"

Sergeant Smith replied, "Lieutenant, maybe the best place to start is to round up the guys who hang out in that underground bunker. They get in there, shoot the shit, grab a few beers, probably smoke some pot. I'm not saying one of them did this, but they maybe got a feel for who is doing what in the platoon."

Lieutenant Crawford replied. "OK, so Sergeant, you'll need to find out if there were any Marines in that bunker last night or this morning, and if so, round them up. We need to set up the plan for asking those guys questions. Since the weather is keeping NIS from getting out here, we need to start the investigation, even if it probably won't be done the same way NIS would do it.

"XO, you're in charge of interviewing those people. One or more of them may be the guy or may know who the guy is or the guys are. So, question them one at a time.

"Sergeant Smith, you find anyone who was in the bunker last night and escort them here. Don't tell them what is going on — although they'll probably know what it is about. Stay with those waiting to be interviewed until the XO is ready for the next man, and make sure the one interviewed does NOT talk to those to be interviewed. Keep an eye on the situation.

"XO you'll need to make notes of what each of them says, even if there is no info about who may have done this. Just get details from each of them, kinda the 'who, what, when, where and how' of what they were doing, what they heard, and what they saw, last night, before and after the murder. Be sure to make a list of who you talk to for the SJA and NIS. If the 'stand down' order is lifted while you're doing your investigation, you're off the line, until we hand this off to the SJA's office and to the NIS. This is your job one. Got it?'

"Yes sir." The XO got it loud and clear: He was off the line for the foreseeable future and that was damn fine with him. The fact was that 1st Lieutenant Donald Breckinridge the Fourth, was ready to get out of Corps. He still had a couple of months left in 'Nam, then less than a half-year remained on his three-year commitment, and then he was out. His field commander skills weren't really up to snuff with what was needed from 1/9 in I Corps.

One reason Lieutenant Breckinridge was ready to get out of the Corps was that he just did not fit in. He was not 'one of the guys'. He didn't know why he wasn't accepted, but his fellow officers not only didn't like him — one of them suggested you took an instant dislike to him because it saved time. They also did not respect him. Donald always let it be known that he came from 'blue blood' of the deepest kind — the Main Line in Philadelphia. Even though both his granddad and dad had graduated from Penn and Wharton, their combined pull fell short when Donnie — as his mother called him — applied to Penn. He was lazy, and his Ivy League prep school grades reflected it. He graduated from Hampton-Sydney College, an all-male school located in southern Virginia. During his sophomore year, he enlisted in the Marine Corps, and attended The Platoon Leader's Course, the PLC, at Quantico during the summers of his sophomore and junior years, and upon graduation, he received his gold second lieutenant's bars. Since he had no post-graduate work, he began active duty training at The Basic School immediately following graduation.

Near the end of TBS training, the Corps conducts a peer-eval, the only question of which was to list, in order, the top five men in your TBS platoon you would want to lead you in combat. No one in Donald's forty-nine-member platoon listed him. His TBS platoon leader tried to counsel Donald about his attitude and demeanor, but Donald, who didn't think anyone was better than he, didn't listen or learn.

Even as XO at VCB, Donald demonstrated an ability to get people pissed off at him. On one occasion at VCB, he became angry with a Marine who was outdoors, filling sandbags, and who wearing his tee shirt and his cover (Marine for hat) but who did not salute the XO who came into the Marine's area. Not saluting an officer when outside, wearing your cover, at a State-side billet would, at a minimum, earn the offending Marine a rebuke from the officer. But at a combat base like VCB, the requirement of such military protocol was over the top. His fellow officers tried to talk Donald from writing up the Marine for such a minor offense, but Donald persisted, and the Marine faced what was commonly called 'Office Hours'. Donald had made a big deal about the alleged offense, so when the hearing officer found the Marine was not responsible for violating a rule or regulation in the combat zone, Donald was razzed unmercifully by his fellow officers, mainly for being stupid and unreasonable. If there was one thing Breckinridge couldn't handle, it was being made fun of.

The Marine was Lance Corporal Ricardo Jackson, and Breckinridge never forgot his name and silently vowed to get back at him.

As far as Smith could tell, he had rounded up the seven men who had been in the bunker. He and the men were outside the company office, waiting for the XO to begin the interviews. The XO called in

PFC Ratcliff, the first Marine in line. Smith and the other Marines could see, but could not hear, the XO and Ratcliff.

Breckinridge decided to file the interview notes in a folder, so he wrote on the outside of the folder, "Speight murder investigation. Gov't Witnesses — Prepared by 1ˢᵗ Lt. Donald Breckinridge IV." He then wrote Ratcliff's name, rank and service number on the inside of the folder and prepared to write notes of his questions and the Marine's answers on a legal pad. He asked Ratcliff to have a seat and began the questioning. He wanted to make the Marines he was interviewing be as comfortable as possible during the interview.

"Ratcliff, were you in the underground bunker last night, or this morning, during the storm, and before Lieutenant Speight was murdered?

"Yes, sir."

"Who else was in the bunker, from the time you got in it until you left it — I guess you left the bunker at some time, right?"

"Yes, sir, I left the bunker probably about midnight. It was still raining and thundering. There were guys in and out, can't remember who all. But when I left the bunker, Jonesy was there, Parker was there, Walters, Evans, Singletary was there, and Douglas. And, I forgot, Jackson was there for about a minute, but he left before the rest of us left. That was it. Singletary, he came in after Jackson left."

"Ratcliff, while you were in the bunker, did anyone discuss anything about Lieutenant Speight, good or bad."

"Oh, sir, I don't wanna…"

"It's ok to speak freely, Ratcliff, we're just trying to figure out who did this."

"Well, sir, he was a sorry platoon leader in the bush. At Dewey Canyon, after an op, he ordered us to came back up the hill back to the firebase the same way we left out, and one of the guys — it was Corporal Scully — tripped a mine and lost his leg. We were always taught to not come back the same way we left out 'cause the bad guys may mine or ambush the route you left on, which they did. The lieutenant just didn't know his stuff."

"No problem Ratcliff. Did hear anyone say anything about wanting to hurt or kill the lieutenant?"

"No sir, but we were afraid he didn't know his head from his ass — sorry, Sir. But no one really said anything about wanting to hurt him.

After a pause, Ratcliff said, "Wait, I just remember. Jackson was in the bunker for only a minute and then he left. He was real close to Corporal Scully, the guy who got his leg blown off with that mine on Dewey Canyon. That hit Jackson hard. We were talking about the lieutenant when Jackson left the bunker, and Jackson said that he wished the lieutenant was dead. He did say that."

"Do you know if anyone else heard him say that?"

"I guess everyone heard it. Even with the storm and rain, you could hear ok in the bunker. None of us talked about what he said, he just said it. I ain't heard nothing else about this."

Lieutenant Breckinridge asked, "So I have this clear, when you left the bunker, there were six Marines left, Jones, Parker, Walters, Evans, Singletary and Douglas, and Jackson had come and gone, right?

"Yes, sir."

Sergeant Smith could see the lieutenant interviewing Radcliff but could not hear what was going on. He saw that Lieutenant Breckinridge remained seated when he dismissed Ratcliff.

Breckenridge tore the page on which he made the interview notes and put it in the folder. He ordered Sergeant Smith to send in the next man, a Lance Corporal Jones. As Jones was sitting down, Breckinridge wrote Jones' name on the inside of the folder, below Ratcliff's name. He was trying to be meticulous.

Breckinridge wondered if Ratcliff and Jones had discussed what they each would say, because Jones' report of his time in the bunker was almost verbatim to Ratcliff's statement. Sergeant Smith saw that the lieutenant remained seated as he dismissed Jones. Breckinridge again placed the notes of the interview in the file folder.

Breckinridge followed the same procedures with Parker, Walters, and Evans. Their stories were so similar it was again difficult for Breckinridge to know whether they had previously discussed what they would say, or if they were all telling the same truth as they saw it. But Breckinridge didn't need to figure that out, all he had to do was to give the witness file to the NIS, whenever they got to VCB.

The sixth Marine interviewed by Breckinridge was Corporal Jason Singletary. After the XO wrote Singletary's name on the inside of the folder, he asked him to have a seat and began asking questions and writing Singletary's answers on the legal pad. Sergeant Smith remained outside the CO's office because there was one more Marine to be interviewed.

After a few minutes, Smith saw the XO stand, and he saw Singletary stand and come to attention. Breckinridge said something to Singletary, but Sergeant Smith couldn't hear the lieutenant. Smith then saw Singletary do an about face and leave the office. As Singletary left the CO's office, Sergeant Smith saw the XO turn his back to the sergeant and walk to the corner of the room and, with his back to Smith, bend over. Smith could not see what the XO was doing, and he wondered what that was all about.

The seventh and last Marine to be interviewed was PFC Douglas. After he was ordered to sit, the XO wrote Douglas' name on the inside of the folder, and the questions began. "Were you in the bunker last night, or this morning, before Lieutenant Speight was murdered?"

"Yes sir, I was."

"And was Jackson in the bunker along with Ratcliff, Jones, Parker, Walters, Evans and Singletary?"

"Yes, sir, he was, but Jackson left before the rest of us?"

"Did Jackson say anything about Lieutenant Speight?"

"Yes, sir, he said he wished the lieutenant was dead. Then he left. But, sir, I saw him later."

The XO looked up and paused. "Where?"

"Sir, after I got to my hooch, the thunder kept me up and I seen Jackson was running with Grant away from the lieutenant's hooch, right after I heard the grenade explode. They was running back towards their hooch."

"How did you know it was Grant?"

"Sir, 'cause Grant is so big, the biggest man in our platoon. It was Grant."

"Are you sure it was Jackson with Grant, PFC Douglas?"

"Yes, sir. It was dark, and the storm was really bad, but I knowed Grant and Jackson was close, spend a lot of downtime together, shoot the shit a lot of time. It had to be Jackson. I could see him when it lightened."

"Did you see them at Lieutenant Speight's hooch right before the grenade exploded?"

"No sir, I didn't, but when I see them, it was after the grenade exploded. They won't more than a few yards from the lieutenant's hooch, and they was hauling ass, like they'd done something."

The XO continued. "Now, Douglas, you're sure it was Jackson with Grant, right, I mean there's no doubt about that, is there?"

"Well, sir, it was dark and raining like hell and lighting but as best I could tell, it was Jackson. Grant is black and Jackson is white. It was Jackson, as best I could tell."

After Breckinridge dismissed PFC Douglas, he knew he was ready to report to the company CO, and he knew what he would say. He found the CO in the mess hall, nursing a cup of coffee.

The XO addressed Lieutenant Crawford. "I interviewed six men, and I've got the killers Grant and Jackson. PFC Douglas heard Jackson say — all of them heard Jackson say — that he wished the lieutenant was dead, and then after Douglas went to his hooch, he saw Grant and Jackson running from Speight's hooch after the grenade exploded. Grant was never in the underground bunker, but Jackson was. Looks like we've got this solved, in record time, I might add. What's the next step, arrest them, or what?"

Crawford answered. "Well, good job, but we're not arresting anyone. We're not the NIS. Even though the winds are too high for the choppers to get up, except for emergencies, the rain has stopped in Quang Tri, and probably between there and here. There are some NIS agents — don't know how many — in Quang Tri, and so we can contact them and get them to round up a convoy to drive up here. Could get here soon, unless there is road washout on the way. We're not going to do anything until NIS gets here, and then we'll confab with them and hand it off to them. The Naval Investigative Service knows what to do. We'll meet with NIS and tell them what was told to you. There will be an Article 32 Preliminary Hearing which Legal will handle, and then Legal will decide whether and who to charge with what. You and I are the only people who know what these six guys said, and I'm not telling anybody, so if it gets out, it's on you, and I'll be very unhappy if I hear the results of your interviews. So, keep it buttoned up, understand? That's a direct order."

The XO replied, "Yes, sir. I'll see NIS when they get here and shut up until then."

It is the responsibility of the Naval Investigative Service to investigate alleged criminal activity in the Navy, Marine Corps and Coast Guard. Its agents are civilian, not military, so they are not under the command of the officers and enlisted they investigate.

John Gates and Ben Harrelson had been NIS agents since they completed training in 1964, and they were very good. They worked in tandem so well that they were assigned the same duty stations. They knew how to solve crimes, and they were legendary. Throughout the Navy and Corps, wherever they were assigned, Gates was known as "Sherlock" and Ben was known as "Doctor Watson," after Sir Arthur Conan Doyles's characters.

Their convoy from Quang Tri to VCB encountered no road problems, and no interaction with the NVA or the Viet Cong. Gates and Harrelson arrived at VCB around 1300, and immediately went to Alpha 1/9 headquarters, where Crawford and Breckinridge were waiting for them.

After introductions, Crawford began his report of the situation. "Second Lieutenant Alvin Speight was the platoon leader for first platoon. We came off an op in Apache Snow. During the typhoon last night — I need to back up — when the typhoon hit us, we got the 'stand down' order, so everyone hunkered down. About 0300 hours this morning, someone fragged Lieutenant Speight — opened the hooch door and rolled or tossed a grenade under his rack. You can of course see the murder site and we have taken beaucoup pictures, but they are not developed. The person, or persons, who did this had to know where Speight slept. There were other officers bunking in that hooch, none of whom saw who did it. The explosion occurred right under Speight. When the other officers in that hooch — none of whom were wounded fortunately — got to him right after the explosion, he was not breathing or moving. He probably never heard or felt a thing.

I ordered my XO, along with Sergeant Smith — Speight's platoon sergeant — to start questioning members of Speight's platoon. Smith suggested they start with the Marines who regularly hang out in an underground bunker we have here. They didn't bunk there, but it was kinda hangout place for the enlisted in Alpha, and I guess other companies too. That turned out to a good idea, thanks to Sergeant Smith, 'cause Breckinridge, we think, may have hit the jackpot with one of the witnesses, a PFC Douglas, who ID'd two Marines as the murderers — or at least ID'd two Marines running from Speight's bunker right after the grenade exploded. The XO and I haven't told anyone what we know. He took notes when he interviewed the guys from bunker." Crawford nodded to Breckinridge.

Breckinridge pulled out papers from a folder. "I've got these notes from my interviews with the six Marines. One of them — "

John Gates interrupted. "Hold on a second, Lieutenant. First, ya'll did a perfect job of interviewing the Marines and we appreciate it. But Ben and I have a protocol in every case, and that is, even if someone else has interviewed witnesses, we want to start with a clean slate with each potential witness when we interview them, so we don't ever look at interviews someone else has done, until maybe after we've interviewed those potential witnesses. So, Lieutenant, I appreciate your good work but what you need to do with that interview file is to give it to whoever is assigned as trial counsel, you know, the prosecutor, and we can look at it later if we need to. I don't know who will be trial counsel in this case, probably Captain Mike McMurry or Navy Lieutenant Kevin Ross. They're the most senior trial counsel, and they absolutely know what they are doing, so it won't surprise me if one or both of them get the case since it is a big case. Just give that interview file to them. They'll probably show it to the defense counsel, but that's up to them."

Gates continued, "Our plan is to conduct our investigation, and then meet with the SJA and the assigned trial counsel who will prepare the charges if they think there is a case, and then we'll arrest the defendant or defendants."

Breckinridge interjected, "But I've got statements from…"

Ben Harrelson spoke quickly and harshly to the XO. "Lieutenant, you weren't listening when we told you our protocol. We don't ever look at what someone else has done. We do our own thing. Then we may look at your work. So please butt out."

Ben continued. "Lieutenant Crawford, is it possible for first platoon — well, first, I guess we have to know if there is a thought that someone from a platoon other than Lieutenant Speight's who may have done this. Doesn't seem likely, but should we look elsewhere?"

Crawford answered. "You should certainly be free to ask around, but we doubt anyone from any platoon other than First Platoon had any issue with Speight. He was not a very good field commander. In fact, after Dewey Canyon, at the first of the year, he messed up so badly his company commander asked regiment or battalion CO, — I don't know which — to give Speight an admin job, which happened. Unfortunately for Speight, we had to get him back in the bush during Apache Snow 'cause some of our lieutenants were WIA or KIA. Then, he messed up again. But I'd say his biggest detractors — the most likely suspects — are in First Platoon."

"Okay." Ben replied. "Is it possible for First Platoon to be off the line until we make our report to the SJA and to the trial counsel and until we make the charges and arrest anyone we think should be arrested?"

"Well, we've still got that 'stand down' order 'cause of the storm. I don't know when it will be lifted, but I can discuss your request with battalion to see what they say."

Gates spoke. "OK, please do that, and let's get started. Can you provide us a place to meet, and can we start with the — how many was it, seven?"

Lieutenant Breckinridge corrected him, "Six, there were six and I can get them for you to interview if you like."

Gates answered. "That would be good. Also, we'll need somewhere to bunk, 'cause I don't imagine we'll be done today. And although we know the cause of death, we'd like to see the lieutenant's hooch."

Lieutenant Crawford responded, "You can use this office. I'll take you to Lieutenant Speight's hooch. XO, you get the witnesses you interviewed back to this office. The agents will be back after we've looked at Speight's hooch."

Neither Sherlock or Watson felt they would learn anything to help their investigation by seeing where and how Lieutenant Speight had died, but as part of their investigation, they followed Crawford to the murder scene. They were familiar with the explosion radius of a M-61 grenade, which was the type issued to Marines and which was probably used to kill the lieutenant. They didn't believe there was evidence regarding the murderer's identity to be gleaned from the lieutenant's hooch. The lieutenant's rack was only eight feet from the door, and the door did not have a latch, so they pictured the killer opening the door, probably with his left hand, letting his body keep the door from closing, and then pulling the pin and safety clip and tossing the grenade right under the sleeping Lieutenant. That was probably the 'how'. They knew the 'when' was around 0300 hours earlier that day. The question was: Who?

Then they went back to Lieutenant Crawford's office. His 'desk' consisted of a piece of ply board placed on two sawhorses, with two green fans blowing towards his chair. Gates sat at the desk, and Harrelson pulled up a chair. Lieutenant Breckinridge said he had the six witnesses waiting. He was told to bring one of them in. Ratcliff came to the door, knocked and was told to come in.

Gates and Harrelson had a routine for interviewing witnesses which worked for them. One of them would ask questions and each would take notes. If the other had any follow-up questions he would ask them after the other had finished, but neither would interrupt the other during the other's interview. After each interview, they would compare notes to see if they had captured the same information. The other would be the primary interviewer of the next person, and so forth.

After they had interviewed Ratcliff, Jones, Parker, Walters, and Evans, they stopped for some chow and talked before they interviewed Douglas, the last witness.

Even though there was no one else in the mess hall, they sat in a corner. Gates spoke first. "Either they all heard the same thing, or they got together and agreed what they'd say. No way probably to know which it is, but so far none of them liked Speight, all of them wanted to have a different platoon leader, but only Jackson said anything specifically about the lieutenant."

"Agreed. So far, we got nothing of any use to charge anyone. I just don't think either Mike or Kevin would issue articles and specifications against this Jackson just based on what he said when he left the bunker. But we've got to talk to the last Marine Breckinridge talked to."

When they got back to Crawford's office, PFC Douglas was waiting for them. They went inside and after Ben asked Douglas a few preliminary questions, he began to focus on timelines.

"So was Jackson in the bunker when you left the bunker, and how long after you left the bunker did the fragging take place?"

Douglas answered. "No sir, Jackson left the bunker before I left. Don't have no watch — really no reason to worry about time, 'cept the day I rotate back home. The fragging happened maybe an hour or two, maybe more, after I left the bunker."

"Did Jackson say anything about Lieutenant Speight at any time while he and you were in the bunker?"

"Yes, sir, I heard him say he wished the lieutenant was dead."

"Did anyone else hear him say that?"

"Yes, sir, I think all of us heard him say that."

"So, when you left the bunker, where did you go?"

"Back to my hooch."

"Where is your hooch and the Lieutenant's hooch?"

"I'm on the same side as the lieutenant's and I'm two — no three — down from his."

"Did you see anything about the fragging while you were in your hooch?"

"Well, the thunder was so loud it woke me up. I got out of my rack and looked at the storm. It was lighting and I saw Grant and Jackson running from the direction of the lieutenant's hooch and then I heard the grenade explode."

"How far were you from them?"

"I don't know, maybe about twenty yards."

"Were you looking at them from their left or right."

"Right."

"How long did you see them, Douglas?"

"Sir, I don't know, just a few seconds."

Ben continued his questioning. "Well, could you see their faces with all the storm?"

"Yes, sir. Grant is the biggest guy in the platoon. About six feet and a half foot tall. He's black and you can't miss him. His best pal in the platoon is Jackson, who is white. I seen them together all the time. It was Jackson with Grant. I could see them when it lightened"

"Where is Jackson's hooch?"

Douglas answered, "It's across from mine and down about three hooches...next to the head."

Ben had more questions. "Where is Grant's hooch?"

"Sir, it's past Jackson's and on the same side of Jackson's."

"Did you see either Jackson or Grant go into their hooch?"

"No sir."

"Douglas, would you step out of the office for a minute, just wait outside the door?"

"Yes, sir", Douglas said as he went to the door.

When Douglas was out of earshot, Ben leaned close to John. "What do you think?"

John replied. "Well, it's eyewitness testimony of two men running, and his ability to see and ID isn't the strongest I've ever heard. I mean, making an ID on seeing someone running when it lightened is kinda weak. I don't know what Mike and Kevin will think of it, assuming they are appointed as trial counsel. I think we need some more info. I think we need to get Grant in here, see what he says, and then talk to Jackson. I think we should warn Grant and Jackson of their rights, though."

"Agreed," Ben said. He got up, walked to the door and told Douglas he was free to go. Then he waived to Sergeant Smith to come over. "Sergeant, we need you to bring Grant to us." Smith left the office area, and Ben went back in and sat at the desk.

Douglas was right about one thing: Grant was huge. He had to duck coming into Crawford's office. He was invited to sit but remained standing. He loomed over the NIS agents.

After introducing himself and Harrelson, John began his questioning of Grant. "We're here to investigate the fragging of Lieutenant Speight. You were in his platoon. We want to ask you some questions."

"I ain't saying nothin' to nobody."

John responded, "Well, all we're doing is interviewing you, we aren't charging you. We're just gathering facts through this investigation. We just want..."

"Don't care what you want. I ain't saying a damn thing."

John responded, "Well, you must have done something wrong if you won't talk to us, so what was it?"

Grant just folded his arms, glowered at John and Ben, and said nothing. They were certain they would get nothing from Grant. They called Sergeant Smith and asked him to have Grant report back to his unit. At least they didn't have to worry about Grant leaving the area — too many Cong and NVA. After Grant left, they asked Smith to bring Jackson to the office.

John's first thought about Jackson was that he didn't look like he could kill anyone, but he also knew that meant nothing. He'd seen killers come in all sizes and shapes. Jackson was scrawny, had acne and had the biggest nose John had ever seen. He asked Jackson to sit down, and he and Ben picked up their pads to take notes.

John began, "I'm NIS Special Agent John Gates, and this is NIS Special Agent Ben Harrelson. We're here investigating the death of Lieutenant Speight. We'd like to ask you some questions. Do you mind talking to us, or would you like to have a lawyer? You have the right to ..."

Jackson interrupted, "I don't need no lawyer. I'll answer what you ask. I ain't done nothin', got nothin' to hide."

John thought for a minute and decided to go straight to the jugular. "Did you say that you wished Lieutenant Speight was dead, last night in the bunker?"

"Yes, sir, I did."

"Why did you say that?"

"Well, I didn't mean it, but I was just sayin' that he was a shitty platoon leader and I wished he won't our platoon leader. He got us, and he kept us, in trouble. He ordered us to do something that caused one of my best buddies to get his leg blowed off."

"What did he do."

"Well, he screwed up a couple of times when he got here, when we were on Dewey Canyon. We was goin' back to the firebase after the patrol, and the lieutenant, he wanted to get back to our firebase using the same path we left out on. It won't as steep as the other paths, and he said he had the red ass and needed to get back to our position. My friend Scully told him he shouldn't go back the same way he left, 'cause the Cong may either set up an ambush or plant a mine. The lieutenant said go anyway. They planted a mine on the path and Scully stepped on it, lost his leg. Lieutenant Speight also screwed up on Apache Snow."

Gates interrupted Jackson. "Let's focus on what happened last night. Where did you go when you left that underground bunker and what time was it?"

"I don't know the time, ain't got no watch. But I went back to my hooch and tried to sleep which was hard with the storm goin'."

"Who else was in your hooch either when you got there, or after you got there?"

Jackson answered, "No one, sir."

John continued, "Did you later leave your hooch?"

Jackson answered, "Yes, sir, I did, don't know what time, but I left to take a leak."

"Where's the head in relation to your hooch?"

"Right next to it."

John said, "Well, we have a statement from someone that he saw you, and Grant, running from the lieutenant's hooch right after the grenade exploded."

Jackson stood up — all five feet six inches of him. "That's a damn lie. I ain't done nothin'. I didn't kill the lieutenant and I don't know who did. Who said that?"

John didn't answer Jackson and resumed the questioning. "Sit down, Lance Corporal. Can you prove where you were when the lieutenant was murdered? Did anyone see you in your hooch, or did anyone see you go into your hooch when you left the bunker?"

"I done said, no one else was in my hooch, and I didn't see no one."

"Do you know Grant?"

"Yeah, I know him. I know all the guys in the platoon, 'cept some of the new ones. Grant is a buddy of mine."

John took off the gloves. "He's such a good buddy you and he agreed to kill the lieutenant, didn't you?"

"I done tell you, I didn't kill the lieutenant. Besides, we got to turn in all unused ordinance to the armory here. I had two grenades on me when we came back from Apache Snow and I turned in both of them. I didn't have no grenade to toss at the lieutenant."

John pulled his chair back, stood up, and extended his hand to Jackson. "Well, Lance Corporal, thanks for your help. You can go back to your unit."

Jackson stood up. "What's gonna happen?"

John answered, "Well, we haven't completed our investigation, so we'll keep you posted. You can go now."

After Jackson left, Ben asked, "What is our plan of attack now? Think we should take this info to the SJA's office, meet with Mike and Kevin, and see what they think? We've done all we need for the preliminary investigation. No need at this point to interview every man in each platoon."

John responded, "Agreed, but first I think we should just take a stroll in the company area. If we need to, we can ask Sergeant Smith the locations of everybody's hooch, but I don't think we should really inspect the area carefully, don't want to show what we're interested in, yet. How does that sound?"

"That's a good plan. Maybe Sergeant Smith can help us get hop back to Quang Tri. This didn't take as long as I thought it would. Sergeant, can you come in here?"

Gates and Harrelson walked around the company area while Sergeant Smith arranged for them to get on a chopper back to Quang Tri. When they got to Quang Tri, they hitched a ride to the Office of the SJA of the Third Marine Division and were told to meet with the SJA, McMurry and Ross at 0900 hours the next day. They were assigned bunks for the night, and they finished their day at the O Club, where the beers were cold.

0900 Hours, Monday, 16 Jun 69
Office of the Staff Judge Advocate
Headquarters Company, Third Mar Div
Quang Tri
Trial Counsel

"Well, lookie here, it's Sherlock and Watson. Put your hands on your wallets, they aren't safe with these guys around!" Mike McMurry and Kevin Ross were happy to see Gates and Harrelson. The four of them had been involved in four major cases for the Third Mar Div in Quang Tri, all of which were successful, at least from their perspective. The defendants who were convicted, and in two cases dishonorably discharged, probably didn't care a bit for NIS or the two most senior trial counsel in I Corps. They met each other in the outer office of the SJA's office.

John and Ben were just as happy to see Mike and Kevin again. They knew how zealous and fair these experienced trial counsels were. They felt Mike and Kevin would be tested in what was shaping up as a he said-he said murder case, the type of case which was always problematic and unpredictable.

Mike grew up in a Catholic family, in Indiana, about one-hundred miles from Notre Dame. He was an altar boy at their church and became a devout Catholic. Even though no one in his family had attended Notre Dame, or any other college, everyone in the family was a rabid Irish fan. His dad was a county clerk and a small claims judge, a position for which a law degree was not necessary. Mike spent much time in his father's 'courtroom' and was quite impressed with the lawyers who appeared before his Dad. Even though his Dad was not a lawyer, he was highly respected by all the lawyers in the county.

One year, Mike's Christmas gift came in November, when his Dad took him to see the Fighting Irish play Michigan in South Bend. It was his first trip to Notre Dame. They had seats on the first row, fifty-yard line, right behind the Irish bench. And at that game, Mike decided he wanted to be a US Marine after he saw the Marine in the color guard wearing his dress blues. He had never seen a Marine in dress blues, but he knew he wanted to wear that uniform one day.

He was accepted to Notre Dame. His fraternity nickname was Lep, short for leprechaun, because he was short, he had a perpetual grin, and his eyes seemed to literally twinkle. He had a great sense of humor which endeared him to those who got to know him. His course of study — his major — was political science, and his favorite professor advised him, during his junior year, that there were more than enough political science professors, and law school was a better plan for him. So, when he graduated from Notre Dame, he had a degree in political science, and a seat in the Notre Dame Law School, from which he graduated. He enlisted in the Corps during his undergraduate freshman year and attended the PLC program at Quantico during the summers of his sophomore and junior years. His gold bars were pinned on him by his proud mother when he graduated from the undergraduate school, and his active duty report date was deferred so he could attend law school.

Kevin was born and reared in Charlestown, in the Boston area. His Mom worked at a dry-cleaners, and his Dad worked for the sanitation department. They were a prototypical 'paycheck-to-paycheck' family. Kevin's first paying job, when he was twelve, was at the grocery store owned by their next- door neighbor. He was paid a small wage and got tips for bagging groceries and taking them to the cars of the ladies who frequented the store. He gave all his money, including tips, to his mom to help with family expenses.

Kevin had a brother, Paul, who was six years older. Paul was a troublemaker and ran with the wrong crowd. Late one Saturday night, Paul and some of his friends had been drinking at one of the many Irish pubs in 'The Town', as Charlestown was called, and got in a fight with some punks from a different part of Boston. One of the punks had a concealed pistol, with which he shot Paul, who was taken to the hospital When Kevin, and his mom and dad, got to the hospital, Paul was in *extremis* and only opened his eyes for a minute. He signaled for Kevin to come close. His last words, before his eyes closed the last time, were, "Do good."

There was an arrest and trial of the punk who shot Paul, but even at age thirteen, Kevin was able to understand that the district attorney dropped the ball on a technicality, and the punk walked. It was then that Kevin knew he wanted to be a lawyer so he could prosecute criminals.

Neither of Kevin's parents had a college education. His Dad had dropped out of high school in his sophomore year to work. But both of Kevin's parents valued education, and they made every effort to instill in Kevin an appreciation of the benefits of education. It turned out that Kevin was an exceptional student, garnering top grades in his public high school graduating class. Kevin was also an aggressive, quick and intelligent hockey player. He received and accepted an offer to attend Boston College on an athletic scholarship. Kevin later received an academic scholarship from Boston College and after law school at Boston College, he completed OCS, having committed to the Corps after his first year in law school.

Kevin and Mike were in the same Naval Justice School class, and since neither was married, they spent a lot of time together, going to Boston to see the Red Sox play, and shooting the bull. The subject of religion often came up, since Mike had attended a Catholic School, and Kevin a Jesuit-Catholic school.

They were pleased when each of them received orders for Headquarters Company, Third Marine Division, Quang Tri. They felt it was fortunate that each was assigned to a legal billet, specifically in the trial counsel shop. They tried a number of cases together, particularly the more complicated ones.

After the greetings and good-natured ribbing, Mike asked John Gates to give the NIS version of the crime and investigation. When John finished, he told the two attorneys, "That's the Reader's Digest version. What's next?"

Kevin answered. "Well, let's see what the colonel has to say about this. He'll probably hand this off to the ASJA, but John, why don't you give the colonel the summary you gave us?"

Kevin knocked on the SJA's door and was ordered to enter. The SJA, Lieutenant Colonel Raoul Suarez, did not move from behind his desk or look up when the four men entered. He asked Kevin, "What's up?"

Lieutenant Colonel Suarez was scheduled to rotate back home, to New Mexico, near the end of August. He was spending as little time running the SJA's office as he could, and as much time as he could planning his campaign to run for county judge back home. He often deferred his command decisions to the Assistant Staff Judge Advocate, Major Bert Forrest, who was a career Marine.

Mike introduced John and Ben to the colonel, said they had investigated the fragging, and had a synopsis for the colonel. He was interrupted by Lieutenant Colonel Suarez. "Captain, I'm involved in some important work now, and think the best thing to do is for you to run your thoughts by Major Forrest, and follow his lead. Thank you."

After they left the SJA's office, Ben spoke up. "Not exactly an 'in the weeds' kind of guy, is he?"

"No, and it's a good thing, frankly", Kevin answered, "I guess it's like being in a firm, with a senior partner who is senior in name only, and who will let you do your own thing. Let's go to the courtroom and discuss in detail just what we will recommend to the ASJA, who is very much an 'in the weeds guy'."

The Third Mar Div courtroom was in a Quonset hut, a building which looked like a huge piece of metal underground pipe that had been cut in half and placed on top of a concreate slab. It had doors at each end, one small window on each side, a spectator seating area for no more than thirty people, a judge's bench which was flanked by the American and Marine Corps flags, a witness chair to the left of the bench, and to its left, against the wall, the military panel, or jury, box, which had three chairs, the normal complement for a special court martial. A table and chair in front of the judge's bench accommodated the court reporter. The trial counsels and NIS agents knew a general court martial would require more chairs.

Kevin spoke first. "Major Forrest is a 'process' guy. Wants to know how we're gonna attack the problem. So, what's our plan of action now that we have a general idea what happened?"

Mike responded. "Well, there are several things to do, maybe not in this order. First, Kevin, don't we need to check out the murder site, and the Alpha 1/9 area, and get this guy Douglas to show us where he was, and where Grant and Jackson — or whoever it was, were when he saw them running? Eyewitness cases are hard as hell when there is no other evidence. We may want to draw a schematic map of the area as an exhibit for the military panel. You know, with the storm and all, this ain't a cakewalk.

Kevin answered. "Good ideas. Then with John and Ben present, we need to interview all of the witnesses they interviewed, to see if their stories have changed. Hope they haven't. We need to think about interviewing other members of the platoon — and maybe even the company — to see what they may know. That may slow down the case, so we need to have someone above us — the ASJA — tell us whether to interview more than the six guys already interviewed, so we have a little CYA if the big brass starts hollering about why this is taking a lot of time. We need to discuss the charges, too. Mike, what do you say about who we should charge and what we should charge? And one other thing, I know the XO of Alpha acted as an informal investigator when NIS couldn't get there because of the storm. Do we want to look at his interviews? And we need to have the Article 32 hearing."

John interrupted, "I leave the charges to you lawyers, but regarding the XO's investigation — his name was Breckinridge, he tried to push his interview notes on us. I told him that we don't ever look at the interviews done by anyone else until after we've completed our interviews and then we might not review his interview notes, but he should offer his notes to you guys. We started from scratch, so I don't know if those six guys told him the same thing they told us. I suggest you get him to give you his interview file and then if you want to, you can compare his notes with our notes, and with your own interviews of those who are going to testify."

Mike said, "We'll get his interview file and may give it a quick review, but we probably won't mess with it assuming that it jives with what those six guys tell us and told you.

"On the Article 32 Hearing, the hearing officer will have to be equal to or above the rank of the defendant's counsel, whoever that is. And there's the question of whether we charge a defendant or the defendants before or after the 32. Probably before is my thought. Based on what we now know, it sounds like the charges should be murder, accessory after the fact and conspiracy. If my memory is right, the elements of accessory are that the accused knew, comforted, assisted, and so forth, the offender — in this case the murderer — to keep him from being caught, and that the man accused with accessory knew that the crime — murder here — had been committed. So going to the lieutenant's hooch with the man who tossed the grenade and maybe helping him toss the grenade, and then not pointing him out, would probably qualify at least as accessory after the fact.

"Unless our investigation takes us elsewhere, maybe both men — Grant and Jackson or whoever it was — should be charged with all three crimes, since we don't know who the 'trigger man' was, and maybe we can squeeze the 'non-trigger man' to testify against the 'trigger man'. I'm more interested in a murder conviction than an accessory or conspiracy conviction. By the way, what do Grant's and Jackson's SRBs show?"

Every Marine, from the Commandant to the lowest private, has a Service Record Book, which lists everything of importance about the subject Marine — where he has been stationed, the schools he has attended, his marksmanship records, his fitness reports, and information about their intelligence if the Marine engages in sensitive matters.

"Grant is still a private, same rank as when he finished boot camp two years ago. Every time he gets a promotion, he gets busted for everything from insubordination to some minor stuff. He's a troublemaker. On the other hand, Jackson is pretty squared away. At Parris Island, he did so well he was offered to try OCS but he turned it down, probably 'cause it would have added a year or so to his enlistment. He's got high marks all around. Got a Purple Heart and

Bronze Star for Valor four weeks after he came in country. So if we go on SRBs, Grant was the more likely 'trigger man'."

Kevin stood up. "So, we'll see if Major Forrest can see us, and lay this out for him, particularly the part about whether he wants to us to interview everyone in the company. We'll need to discuss the Article 32 also. Is everyone ok with this?" Everyone nodded. Kevin continued, asking the NIS agents if either of them had met Major Forrest. They both shook their heads 'no'. "Well, I doubt he's ever laughed at anything. Knows the law and he is the judge in special courts martial for the division. No close buddies, but a straight shooter."

They left the courtroom and walked to the office of the Assistant Staff Judge Advocate, which was located in the same building as the SJA's office. Major Forrest was in the outer office, the admin area, and Mike asked if they could see him. They all went into the major's office. Mike began the conversation by introducing the NIS agents to Major Forrest. The major didn't extend his hand to either agent, so Mike proceeded to outline the case status and the plan and concerns for moving ahead, after which the major finally spoke. "Well, sounds like a good plan to me. What questions do you have?"

Mike said, "Sir, you will have to appoint an Article 32 investigation officer, and since the highest-ranking defense counsel will probably be a captain, the IO will have to be a captain or higher. And Major, another thing is, we don't know whether we should take the time to interview everyone in the platoon, or anyone else. We don't think it is likely — though possible — that someone in another platoon did this, because the lieutenant who was killed, by all accounts, unfortunately was not a good field commander, and the guys that impacted most would be in First Platoon."

The major replied, "I think the more thorough approach is for everyone in the company to be interviewed. These 'he said-he said' cases are the toughest if there is no other evidence, like this case, so you need to be particularly thorough. If that's all, you are dismissed."

The major stopped them. "Wait a minute. Just thought of something. When you interview each man in the entire company, don't use the company roster to start that that process. Instead, make a list of everyone you interview, and then compare it to the roster.

With guys rotating in and out, or going to sick call, that's the best way to get it done. I don't imagine anyone rotated between the murder and now but check that out too. And I'd have each platoon leader bring his platoon to the interview site and confirm those are all his men, no one is missing or whatever.

"I can handle any pushback you get if this takes longer, 'cause it is the thorough way to do it. But all I'd do is ask each Marine his name, rank, service number, and unit, and did he hear or see anything relating to the fragging. There is no need to cross-examine each of them. This is probably going to be more for show than a real deep dive. Then, when you get back from VCB, report to me on how it went. Now you are dismissed."

The four men went to the airstrip at Quang Tri. They were the only passengers on a CH-46 chopper, which was carrying supplies, including C-rats, so Marines would have chow, such as it was, when they were in the bush.

When they landed at VCB, the NIS agents led the way to the Alpha Company area, because although Mike and Kevin had been to VCB when preparing other cases, they did not know Alpha's location. They were met by Lieutenant Crawford, who was asked to order each platoon leader have all Marines in his platoon come to the area of the company office and to also bring the latest platoon roster so it could be compared to the men then interviewed. Crawford then showed Mike and Kevin the locations of Speight's and Douglas' hooches, as well as the underground bunker.

After the inspection of the area, the two NIS agents and the two trial counsel were seated in the CO's office. Lieutenant Breckinridge came in and addressed them. "I'm the XO, and I interviewed six Marines and have their interview sheets. Do you want them? Do you want me to help you interview the Marines?"

Ben answered him. "Lieutenant, for the second time, no, for the third time, we don't need your help. You can leave. And leave that interview file with Captain Ross." Breckinridge gave Kevin his interview notes and folder and left. Kevin put the file in his briefcase and planned to look at it later.

The men of Alpha 1/9 were in formation. As a Marine came into the office, Kevin asked his name, rank, service number and unit, and

John wrote that information and checked that name off the company roster provided by Lieutenant Crawford. Two of the men interviewed were not on the roster since they just joined the company.

Kevin began asking each Marine these questions: "Were you here at VCB the night Lieutenant Speight was murdered; did you see anyone at or near the lieutenant's hooch at any time during the night of the murder; did you see anyone up and about the company area after midnight and before daylight on the night the lieutenant was murdered; what have you heard anyone say about who may have committed the murder and who said it?"

There were 123 Marines in Alpha, including Grant, all of whom were asked these questions. Except for Grant, who said nothing, and Douglas, who repeated his statement about seeing Grant and Jackson running, each of the remaining one-hundred twenty-one Marines gave the same answers: "They were at VCB; they saw no one at or near the lieutenant's hooch; they saw no one up and about the company area after midnight and before daylight on the night of the murder; and they heard no one say who may have committed the murder."

Two of those Marines were lying.

After completing the interviews, the lawyers and NIS agents caught a chopper back to Quang Tri and went to the empty O Club to discuss the plan. Mike began, "I don't know what else we can do to vet Douglas' story. His ability to ID whoever it was running from the lieutenant's hooch is suspect, because of the distance he was from them and the weather."

Kevin responded. "I agree, his testimony will be weak, but we've got no other cards to play. It isn't enough if all we have is that Jackson said he wished the lieutenant was dead. I don't think an Article 32 investigation officer would recommend charges based just on that evidence. I wouldn't. But we should have the guys who heard what Jackson said, which includes Douglas, testify at the 32 hearing."

"Agree," said Mike. "As to the possible charges, since we don't know who tossed the grenade and since they were both seen running from Speight's hooch after the grenade detonated — or from Douglas' testimony they were both running, let's recommend charging each of them with murder, accessory after the fact, and conspiracy. I'm not sure who we should try first, or if we should try them at the same time.

I know this isn't in your NIS wheelhouse, John, but what's your gut reaction regarding the charges?"

John thought a minute before answering. "Well, Grant was more likely the 'trigger man', the one who tossed the grenade, and it is more important to convict the defendant who threw it on the murder charge, than the person who was with him, 'cause whoever threw it probably came up with the idea. Maybe by charging both with all three crimes, and trying Jackson first, you can get him to flip on Grant. Facing a murder charge and the death penalty could give him incentive to testify against Grant if he was the one with Grant."

"Damn, John, that's downright scary, 'cause you're thinking like a lawyer. So, let's report to Major Forrest — no point in taking the time to go to the SJA — and see if he agrees and ask him to get an Article 32 hearing officer designated. Agreed?" All nodded, so they headed to the ASJA's office.

Major Forrest had a habit of walking back and forth in his small office when discussing serious matters, and the murder of Lieutenant Speight was such a matter. Kevin and Mike had presented the plan they, and the NIS agents, had formulated.

The major stopped pacing. "Well, the process is that I have already appointed Major Womack as the Article 32 Hearing officer. We will have to designate an attorney for both Grant and Jackson. Captain Peterson can handle Jackson's case, and Lieutenant Allen will be Grant's counsel. Are you going to serve charges on them before the Article 32?"

Kevin Ross responded, "Yes, sir. We'll prepare the charges, go to VCB, serve them with the charges, arrest them, get them in the brig here, keep them separate, and have the hearing. That way, we're moving as fast as we can."

Major Forest commented. "I approve. Let me see the charges before you serve them and arrest Grant and Jackson."

1330 Hours, Tues, 17 Jun 69
Third Mar Div
Quang Tri Province
Jackson Is Charged

In that Lance Corporal Ricardo Jackson, US Marine Corps (Reserve) did, on or about 15 Jun 1969, at Vandegrift Combat Base, I Corps, Republic of South Vietnam, with premeditation, murder Second Lieutenant Alvin Speight, US Marine Corps (Reserve), by causing a live grenade to be thrown under the bed of Lieutenant Speight, causing the death of Lieutenant Speight, a violation Article 118 of the Uniform Code of Military Justice.

In that Lance Corporal Ricardo Jackson, US Marine Corps (Reserve) did, on or about 15 Jun 1969,at Vandegrift Combat Base, I Corps, Republic of South Vietnam, knowing that the offense of the murder of Second Lieutenant Alvin Speight had been committed, assist the offender who murdered Lieutenant Speight, by hindering or preventing the apprehension, trial or punishment of the murderer, a violation of Article 78 of the Uniform Code of Military Justice.

In that Lance Corporal Ricardo Jackson, US Marine Corps (Reserve), did, on or about 15 Jun 1969, at Vandegrift Combat Base, I Corps, Republic of South Vietnam, conspire with another person to commit the crime of murder, a violation of Article 118 of the Uniform Code of Military Justice when one or more of the conspirators did an act to effect the object of the conspiracy, to wit, the murder of Second Lieutenant Alvin Speight, US Marine Corps (Reserve).

Jackson had read the charges against him at least ten times on the ride from VCB to the brig at Quang Tri, and still didn't believe this was happening to him. All he could remember was that he was in his hooch when the two NIS agents — the same two he talked to when he denied killing the lieutenant — came into the hooch with two sergeants and told him he was being charged with murder, conspiracy to commit murder and accessory after the fact to murder. Jackson had no idea what conspiracy and accessory after the fact even meant, but he sure knew what 'murder' meant.

After he was handcuffed, the NIS agents and one of the sergeants left Jackson's hooch while the other sergeant guarded Jackson. The next thing he saw was Grant, who was handcuffed, walking in front of the NIS agents and the other sergeant. He and his guard joined them, got into separate jeeps, and left VCB. His guard told Jackson he would be placed in the division brig at Quang Tri. The road ran thorough unsecured territory, so Jackson was relieved to see two Huey gunships overhead, providing security.

Jackson and Grant were each put in solitary confinement in separate parts of the brig and were unable to communicate with each other. Jackson had never felt so alone, so hopeless, in his life. He was half-a-world away from his family, in the brig, facing three charges, one of which carried the death penalty. He knew he was innocent and did not know why he was picked out from all the other Marines in first platoon to be charged.

Jackson did have one thing going for him, even though he didn't know it. His lawyer was the best lawyer — defense or prosecution — in the Third Marine Division.

First Lieutenant David Peterson received his undergraduate degree, with honors, in philosophy from Williams College, a small, elite liberal arts college located in bucolic Williamstown, Massachusetts. He was accepted to Harvard Law School and finished in the top tier of his class. During law school, he enlisted in the Corps, obligating himself to attend the ten-week OCS class at Quantico which began in January 1968, after his graduation. He was at OCS when the Tet Offensive began on 31 January 1968. After completing OCS and, TBS, David was sent to the Naval Justice School in Newport, Rhode

Island to take classes for certification as military trial counsel. In August 1968, he was assigned to a platoon leader's billet in Charlie Company, 1/9 of the Third Marine Division, in I Corps.

Peterson distinguished himself in the field, earning the Bronze Star with the V combat device. Due to the passage of the Military Justice Act, in October 1968, Peterson was made a defense counsel with Headquarters Company, Third Mar Div in November 1968.

Many, if not all, of the defendants represented by Peterson were not only guilty, but the government could prove it. But Peterson made the government work hard to win convictions. He filed novel motions and was a skilled trial counsel. He frequently engaged in legal battle with either Mike McMurry or Kevin Ross, or both of them. Sometimes these legal battles were followed with the sharing of beers at the O Club. These three professionals felt it was possible to be civil with their adversaries. They were friendly, worthy, lawyers who shared a love for the law and for the professional practice of law.

Major Forrest called Peterson to his office, told him of his new assignment, gave him a copy of the charges, and suggested he meet with Kevin and Mike about the case.

Kevin and Mike were upfront with David, giving him copies of the NIS interviews of the six men in the underground bunker, as well as the interview folder from the XO, Lieutenant Breckinridge. David glanced at the NIS interviews as Kevin and Mike filled him in on the case. He put the Breckinridge interview folder in his file. He could sense that Jackson was in for a tough legal ride.

Jackson was at the brig in Quang Tri for no more than four hours before Peterson came for his first attorney/client conference. He saw Jackson to be a very frightened, small man with the largest nose Peterson had ever seen. Jackson told Peterson his mind was still 'messed up', as he described it.

David began the interview. "Lance Corporal, anything you tell me is confidential, and that means I can't tell anyone what you and I talk about. But if you tell me something, you can't say something different in the courtroom. Understand?" Jackson nodded he understood.

"So, Jackson, did you say you wished the lieutenant was dead?"

"Yes, sir, but I didn't mean it, I just meant he won't a good platoon leader and we could do better if he won't our platoon leader. He messed up in Dewey Canyon, they took him off the line, and he came back to the platoon in Apache Snow, and he messed up in there. My best buddy lost his leg because of the lieutenant on Dewey Canyon."

David replied, "So, you had a motive, a reason, to kill the lieutenant. That's what the prosecutor is going to say."

"But I didn't. I was in my hooch when the grenade exploded!"

"OK, tell me about that night, after you left the bunker."

Jackson continued. "Well, I left the bunker, and went to my hooch. There was no one there, and no one came to the hooch before the grenade exploded. I don't think no one came until daybreak. I guess they were holed up somewhere else, and it didn't matter 'cause we were on stand down. I was in my rack when I heard the grenade, but with all the thunder and lightning, and rain, I didn't go see what was going on. Oh yeah, I remember getting up and going to the head to take a wizz before the grenade exploded, but I didn't see nobody."

Peterson asked, "How did you and PFC Douglas get along, any problems?"

"No, sir, never got cross-legged with him. No problems."

"Douglas told NIS that he saw you, and Grant, running from the direction of Lieutenant Speight's hooch right after the grenade exploded.", Peterson said. "Is that true?"

"I won't with Grant at all that night. Didn't even see him. He was not in the bunker. It won't me running nowhere."

"Well", Peterson asked, "would Douglas make up something to get you in trouble?"

Jackson answered, "I never had no problem with him. No reason I know for him to make up something."

After a three-hour conference, Peterson realized two things: First, he could get no more from Jackson because Jackson had no more to give him other than the denial with no corroboration; and second, he had his work cut out for him in the toughest kind of case — a 'he said-he said' murder case with no strong evidence other than one eyewitness, and Jackson's wishing him dead.

This case was more difficult because the victim was a Marine officer, murdered while sleeping. The Corps looks after its own, and the military panel for the general court martial would consist chiefly of Marine officers. Furthermore, fragging of officers happened from time- to-time in South Vietnam, in both the Corps and US Army. Fragging was a problem, and the Corps had a history of dealing successfully with problems.

Things did not look good for Lance Corporal Ricardo Jackson.

David went back to his office and made a starter list of the things he needed to do to represent Jackson:

1. Prepare for Article 32 hearing cross-exam of witnesses.
2. Go to VCB, check out Douglas' hooch and scope out Douglas' ability to see anyone running from Speight's hooch. Where was he standing; where were the men when he saw them running.
3. Re GCM military panel make up for murder case — requires 12 when death penalty is at play unless the convening authority specifies lesser number due to physical circumstances or military exigencies. Object to any number less than 12. And request in writing the inclusion of enlisted members (at least 1/3 of number of the total number on panel.)
4. Attempt to get meteorological evidence concerning the storm conditions between midnight and 0500 on murder date — may undercut Douglas' eyewitness testimony.
5. Are there any witnesses other than the guys in the bunker and all of Alpha.? Probably not likely, but check it out.

When David completed this list, he knew he would be adding to it as trial prep continued. He also knew that he had to create as many issues at trial as he could which could be argued on appeal if Jackson were convicted. He also knew that it was entirely possible, maybe even likely, that Jackson would receive the death penalty if he were convicted of the murder of the lieutenant. David never had a case which needed his considerable skills more.

The Article 32 Preliminary Hearing didn't take long. It was conducted by Major Womack, with a court reporter recording the proceedings, so Peterson would be able to review the transcribed witnesses' testimony. Ratcliff, Jones, Parker, Walters, Evans and Douglas each testified consistently with the statements they gave to the NIS agents.

As expected by David, Womack found probable cause for all 3 charges. David continued to check off his to-do list. He found out that there was no meteorological evidence gathered at VCB or anywhere in I Corps of the conditions when Lieutenant Speight was murdered. All anyone in I Corps knew about the typhoon was that it rained like hell, the thunderstorm was unforgettable, and the wind was blowing so hard the rain came down sideways. He thought the members of the military panel had experienced the typhoon and would know the difficulty of identifying someone running, twenty or so yards away, only when it lightened.

David was exceptional at judging strengths and weaknesses of cases, and usually could accurately predict the most likely trial result. Any verdict had to be unanimous. David had no illusions that he could convince the entire panel that Jackson was innocent of all charges. He knew if he just one panel member was not morally certain of Jackson's guilt on any of the charges, that is, if just one panel member had 'reasonable doubt' of Jackson's guilt, and if that person had the guts to hold out against the pressure of all the other panel members who had no reasonable doubt, he could get a mistrial as to that charge, which would just lead to another trial on that charge.

But all of David's considerable instincts told him that there was just no way all members of the panel would acquit Jackson or have reasonable doubt of all charges. That meant Jackson's best-case scenario would be for the panel to find that there was not sufficient evidence that Jackson threw the grenade — that he was not the murderer. He could argue that point effectively because there was no evidence who tossed the grenade. But the remaining charges — accessory after the fact and conspiracy, well, David believed it was highly unlikely that Jackson would be acquitted of both of those charges. He never told Jackson, but David knew in his gut that Jackson was going to prison. He just hoped they dodged a guilty verdict to the murder charge, and the death penalty.

David filed his motion to have enlisted Marines on the military panel. It was granted, so one-third of the panel would be enlisted above the lance corporal rank of Jackson. Peterson began his final preparation of trial.

0800 Hours, Mon, 7 Jul 69
Third Mar Div Courtroom
Quang Tri
The Trial of Lance Corporal Jackson

The prosecution of Lance Corporal Ricardo Jackson began with the reading of the charges and the entry of the plea of NOT GUILTY to each charge. David's motion to not reduce the number of Marines on the panel was denied on the predictable grounds of military exigencies. The officers on the panel were a bird colonel, a lieutenant colonel, a major, two captains and a first lieutenant. The enlisted were two gunnery sergeants and one first sergeant. Except for the bird colonel, each enlisted man had more time in the Corps than each of the officers. David knew those enlisted men were what the Corps referred to as 'hard Corps.' They had been through it all. He and Jackson had their work cut out for them.

A corpsman testified, using photos taken at VCB of the murder scene and Lieutenant Speight's riddled body. It appeared from the position of the rack and the hole in the ply board deck of the hooch that the grenade had detonated directly under the middle of Lieutenant Speight's back, stomach or side, depending on how he had been sleeping.

The body was torn apart and even though the explosion probably caused the lieutenant's body to move upward, it then fell into the hole made in the ply board. The corpsman testified that the on-the-scene personnel had to crawl under the hooch to reach the lieutenant to search for a pulse, which they did not find. Even though the corpsman's testimony about what someone else did would normally be subject to an objection from defense counsel since the corpsman was not at the scene, David saw no reason to object. He wanted the government to move off the subject matter and pictures of the dead lieutenant as soon as possible.

David's prediction that Mike McMurry and Kevin Ross would call PFC Douglas last was correct. The testimony of five of the Marines in the bunker who heard Jackson's comment about wanting the lieutenant dead didn't take any time at all. In fact, David had planned to ask them no questions if they testified consistently with their statements to the NIS agents, which they did. They were on and off the witness stand in no time at all.

Kevin handled the direct exam of Douglas and touched all the points Douglas made in his interviews. Peterson had done all he could do to prepare for the cross examination of Douglas. He started his exam with an easy question:

Defense counsel: PFC Douglas, what time was it when you say you saw men running from the direction of Lieutenant Speight's hooch?

Witness: Sir, about 0300 hours.

DC: Did you hear the grenade detonate?

Witness: Yes sir.

DC: How much time was there between the grenade detonating and the time you allegedly saw the men running?

Witness: Just seconds, sir.

DC: Now, describe the weather conditions at the time you say you saw the men running.

Witness: Sir, I've never seen a storm like that before. The wind was howling and rain was coming down in sheets. The rain was coming down mostly sideways.

DC: As you are looking out from your hooch, the lieutenant's hooch is about thirty yards to the left of your hooch, right?

Witness: Yes, sir.

DC: So the men you say you saw running had their right sides to you, right?

Witness: Yes, sir.

DC: Which of the two men was closer to you?

Witness: Grant was closer.

DC: Describe Private Grant's build.

W: Sir, he's about six feet six inches tall, real big. He's the biggest man in in the platoon

DC: How far apart were the two men you say you saw running?

Witness: I, um, I don't know, sir. I couldn't tell.

DC: When the men were even with your hooch, who was in front?

Trial counsel: Objection, that question assumes a fact not in evidence, namely that one of them was in front of the other.

The Court: Objection sustained. Ask another question, Lieutenant Peterson.

DC: Were the men side by side when they ran by your hooch?

Witness: I don't remember.

DC: How far from you were the two men you say you saw running?

Witness: About thirty yards.

DC: There was no artificial light in the area was there?

Witness: Sir, I don't know what you mean.

DC: There were no streetlights or other lights shining on the area where you say you say you saw men running, were there?

Witness: Oh, no sir.

DC: Well if there were no lights, then it was dark when you allegedly saw the men running right?

Witness: Well, sir, it lightning all the time. I seen them when there was lightning.

DC: So, the opportunity — the only chance — you had to actually see to identify the men you saw running happened when lightning occurred, right?

Witness: Yes, sir.

DC: How many times did lightning occur when you say you saw the men running?

Witness: I don't know, sir.

DC: Just how long was there light when the lightning occurred?

Witness: I just don't know, sir.

David knew he could ask Douglas to explain why he didn't remember who was in front if either man was ahead of the other. He also knew that more questions may give Douglas a chance to explain the weak parts of his testimony. He knew that Kevin would ask Douglas questions on re-direct to shore up his testimony. He decided he had done the best he could do to undermine Douglas' testimony. He could point out those inconsistencies in his final argument. He hoped it was enough, so he told the court he had no further questions. After some redirect of Douglas by Kevin, and no further examination by David, the government rested.

David called Lance Corporal Jackson to testify. David decided it was best to cut to the chase in his direct examination of Jackson.

Defense Counsel: State your name, rank serial number and date of birth.

Witness: Ricardo Jackson, Lance Corporal, 6258042, 16 July 1949.

DC: When you were in the underground bunker, during the typhoon, on the night Lieutenant Speight was murdered, did you make the statement in the presence of the other Marines in the bunker who have testified in this case that you wished Lieutenant Speight was dead?

Witness: Yes, sir.

DC: Why did you make that statement?

Witness: Sir, Lieutenant Speight was not a good platoon leader. He made mistakes in the field. I didn't want to be in his platoon, and just said I wished he was dead as a way to not be in his platoon, Sir.

DC: Did you mean you wanted him dead?

Witness: No, Sir, no way. I just don't want to be in his unit.

DC: Why do you say he was not a good platoon leader?

Witness: Sir, on our first op in Dewey Canyon, on the way back to base camp, the lieutenant went up the same path we'd left on, even though he was told not to go there 'cause the VC may have put a mine on that path. He ordered us up the path anyway, 'cause it was quicker and, he said he had the red ass and needed to get to the base camp fast, and my friend Scully stepped on a

mine and lost his leg. And at an ambush on Apache Snow, he opened fire on the Marines at the other end of the ambush even though the firing lines had been set out. But I didn't frag him and don't know who did.

DC: When you left the underground bunker, after saying you wished the lieutenant was dead, even though you didn't want him dead, what did you do?

Witness: Went back to my hooch Sir.

DC: Was anyone in your hooch when you got there?

Witness: No Sir.

DC: Did anyone come into the hooch before the fragging?

Witness: No Sir.

DC: Did you leave the hooch before the fragging?

Witness: Only to go to the head to take a wiz — I mean to pee. The head is next to my hooch.

DC: Did you see anyone before or after the fragging either outside or anywhere else?

Witness: No, Sir.

DC: Did you throw, or help throw, or know who threw, the grenade under Lieutenant Speight's rack?

Witness: No Sir. No way. I'm innocent.

After asking Jackson questions about the arrangement of hooches at VCB, and having him identify the map of the layout Jackson had drawn, particularly as to the estimated distance of Douglas' hooch to the pathway on which Douglas said he saw the Marines running, David finished his questions of Jackson by asking him about his outstanding record at Parris Island, his Bronze Star and his receiving promotions quickly. David then told the court that he had no further questions for Jackson, and awaited cross-examination of his client.

Peterson thought Jackson had done as good a job as anyone could in answering Kevin's cross-examination. Jackson did not waiver declaring his innocence in the face of Kevin's cross-exam. Both the government and the defendant then rested

After both arguments, the military judge gave the nine-person panel instructions for deliberation, explaining the elements of each alleged crime, the definition of burden of proof, the definition of reasonable doubt and the other standard instructions.

The jury recessed for deliberation at 1500 hours. David knew from experience that the waiting time during jury deliberation could feel like an eternity, regardless of the actual length of the wait.

At 1610 hours, only one hour and ten minutes after being excused to deliberate, the panel informed the military judge they had reached a verdict. David thought the short deliberation time was a bad sign.

As the panel filed in, each of them looked at the defense table. David saw no compassion in their faces, and he thought the colonel, the highest-ranking officer, would be the panel foreman. He was right.

When the military judge asked the colonel if the panel had reached verdicts in each case, the colonel stood, and said "Affirmative, your honor." The colonel handed the verdict paper to the judge.

The military judge ordered Jackson to stand. David stood also. From the look on the faces of the panel members — each of whom glared at Jackson, David knew he and Jackson were not going to hear good news.

The Judge read the verdict sheet:

"How do you find the defendant, Lance Corporal Ricardo Jackson, on the charge of conspiracy to commit murder?" The colonel answered loudly, "Guilty."

"How do you find the defendant, Lance Corporal Ricardo Jackson, on the charge of accessory after the fact to the crime of murder?" The colonel again answered, "Guilty."

"How do you find the defendant, Lance Corporal Ricardo Jackson, on the charge of murder?" The colonel answered "Not guilty."

No death penalty! For that, David was relieved. Now the military judge would begin the sentencing phase. David had arranged for Jackson's squad leader to testify about his bravery during Dewey Canyon, why he was awarded the Bronze Star for valor, and what he was doing when he was wounded, for which he received the Purple Heart. His excellent SRB was put into evidence and reviewed by the military judge as he deliberated on the sentence.

After the mitigating evidence was presented, Kevin and Mike were offered the opportunity to put on aggravating evidence — evidence for a long sentence, but they chose only to argue to the court that the findings of guilty by the jury were sufficient basis for a lengthy sentence.

Having heard from both sides on sentencing, the military judge ordered Jackson to stand. David stood also as the judge announced the sentence: "It is the sentence of this court that for the crime of accessory after the fact to murder, you shall be imprisoned in the federal prison at Fort Leavenworth, Kansas, for a period of ten years, and you shall be dishonorably discharged from the Marine Corps and you shall forfeit all rank and pay. For the crime of conspiracy to commit murder, you shall be imprisoned in the federal prison at Fort Leavenworth, Kansas, for a period of ten years, to begin to run at the completion of the ten-year sentence for accessory after the fact, and you shall be dishonorably discharged from the Marine Corps, and you shall forfeit all rank and pay. Guards, take the convict away."

Not guilty of murder but twenty years! The trial judge granted David's request to talk to Jackson for ten minutes after sentencing, before he was taken to the brig. David did what he could to give the stunned Marine the run-down of the automatic appeal process, but it was like talking to someone in a coma. Jackson would be about forty-years old when he completed the sentences. Nothing David said registered, so he decided that he would talk to Jackson at the brig in a couple of days. But he knew he had little comfort to give his client.

0730 Hours, Thurs, 24 Jul 69
Marine Corps Base, Camp Pendleton, Ca
Staging Battalion

"Lieutenant White, do you know what your duties are as the executive officer of this staging battalion?"

The question was asked by the darkest Black man Woody had ever seen. He wore the silver railroad tracks of a Marine Captain, and the name tag "Barkley."

"Sir, I guess my job as your XO is to do what you, the commanding officer of the battalion, order me to do before we leave for Nam."

"Lieutenant, you and I are going to get along just fine. Have a seat and we'll set out the two-week training schedule for these 160 hard asses we've got to keep in line, before all of us go to war."

Captain Barkley was a former enlisted man, with a high school education, who had been in the right place, at the right time. He was the driver for what he called 'the grief detail' — the Marine officers and chaplains who went to the homes of Marine families, to tell wives they were now widows and to tell children their dads would not be coming home.

Barkley was stationed in Washington, DC where the practice was that if the deceased was a field grade officer — major, lieutenant colonel, colonel, or a general officer, the detail consisted of at least one field grade officer to accompany the chaplain. Each detail had a driver, and Barkley was often the driver. But he became more than a driver. He was frequently asked to accompany the officer and chaplain into the homes to which they were delivering this terrible news, and he was a comforting force, often helping with the children of the deceased officer. He had a way about him that made people open up to him and like him. Even he was hard pressed to define what he came to think of as his 'gift'. The Corps had a process to make an enlisted man an officer, and the officers Barkley drove around had the clout to make that sort of thing happen. Now, he was a captain, heading to Vietnam to be assigned to an intelligence position in MAC-V headquarters, in Da Nang.

Woody watched everything Barkley did and how he did it. This was Woody's first real command. He didn't count the training exercises at TBS where the new second lieutenants took turns leading squads, platoons and the company in combat field exercises. But at Pendleton, Woody was ordering enlisted men, whom he didn't know, to do physical training, march, and all types of things to keep them tired and busy.

On three different occasions, the company had 'saddled up' to be bused to Norton Air Force Base for the flight to Vietnam, and each had been called off. Woody no longer became frustrated when one order was countermanded by another. At OCS, the platoon would be ordered to 'fall-in' outside, in formation, with canteen and web belt on, and then the order came for no canteen or web belt. And back and forth. Woody of course never knew, but he suspected it was just part of the practice of keeping the candidates off balance. It worked.

But at 2300 hours on Saturday, 26 July 1969, the word came to get the gear and meet the buses on the parade deck. One-hundred sixty-two Marines got on the buses and started for Norton AFB. And this time, they were headed for South Vietnam.

When the bus Woody and Captain Barkley stopped at the terminal, Barkley pulled Woody aside. "Lieutenant, do you know what the Marine Corps protocol is for boarding modes of transportation?"

"No sir, didn't even know there was a protocol."

"Now, Lieutenant, the Marine Corps has a protocol for taking a crap, so you know they have one when it comes to boarding modes of transportation. And let's see if you can figure it out. Who gets on the plane first, the officers or enlisted?"

"Sir, I don't know."

Barkly continued. "Well, the protocol is that enlisted get on first, so the officers will be the first off, as would happen if they were in a car. But tonight, we're getting on first. We're not following that protocol. Do you know why?"

Woody answered, "No sir. Why is that?"

"Because we're getting ready to sit our asses in airplane seats for five hours to Hawaii for refueling, and then maybe fifteen to eighteen hours to Okinawa, depending on the headwinds. You and I are getting on first because there are two — only two — seats with extra leg room on that civilian passenger aircraft that is going to take us on this wonderful journey, and those seats are on the starboard side of the plane, at the front of the plane, right behind the galley. And I want the extra leg room for this flight. So — follow me."

Woody had no idea they would be flying a civilian plane to Nam, but it made sense. The military didn't have a lot of aircraft which could carry 200 or so men across the Pacific. Woody guessed some politicians back in DC probably had a bunch of airline stock and that Ike's military-industrial complex was alive and well.

And the plane had stewardesses. Good looking ones. Flirty ones — particularly with the enlisted. One last time of innocent flirtations before war.

Captain Barkley directed Woody to the window seat, so Barkley had a bit more leg room. Woody settled back as the plane was backed away from the terminal building. He put his seat in the 'up' position when the stewardess was giving directions about seat belts, seat in the up-right position during take-off, and where the flotation devices were, as if they could do them any good if the plane ditched in the Pacific. Woody was the antithesis of a nervous flyer. He figured he had no control, so why worry? He always fell asleep when flying, usually before the wheels were up. On the one helicopter insertion training exercise at TBS, his platoon had boarded a CH-46 chopper and flown 15 minutes to the landing zone in the Virginia countryside. Woody had to be awakened when the chopper made its descent, even though the ride had been a rough flight.

As Woody settled in, he thought it was a perfect SA time, which he learned about during summer school after his freshman year at

Wake. He had made a *D* in math and a *C* in biology and needed to pull up his grades, so he registered for Sociology 101 taught by Professor Accorsi. The class was held in the basement of the Z. Smith Reynolds Library, in the middle of the Wake campus. Professor Accorsi was a real hoot who made learning fun. Woody remembered two points the professor made. First, if you really screw something up, and someone is mad at you because of it, go straight to that person and just tell him, "I'm a sorry SOB for messing you up." Once you've done that, the professor pointed out, it makes it harder for the person to come after you.

The second thing Woody remembered was the importance of SA time at certain junctures in your life. As Professor Accorsi explained it, "There are times in your life, or there will be, when you've been on a path for a long time, you find yourself at a place where you are getting ready to take an entirely different path and you should use that opportunity for SA time — self assessment time. Think about where you've been, how you got to where you are, where you are, and where you're going."

Woody began the SA process. He was a high school, college and law school graduate, a lawyer licensed to practice in the courts of North Carolina, he was a second lieutenant in the United States Marine Corps — one of history's most elite fighting forces, he was a certified military lawyer, and he was heading to a war zone.

As the plane began its takeoff roll, he leaned back and closed his eyes. He wondered if his dad would have been proud of him. He'd never know that answer because of a 3 a.m. phone call on Wednesday, 8 October 1958.

Jerking Sodas and the Mill Run Valley Case
Woody's sophomore year at Rose High School in Greenville, North Carolina officially began September 2, 1958, but as far as he was concerned it started Friday, 15 August. That was when varsity football practice started. There were not many guards on the varsity squad Woody's sophomore year, so even though he was not a particularly good football player, he made the varsity team. Practices began in hot August with 'two-a-days', one at 6:30

a.m., usually without pads, and a practice at 5:00 p.m., usually with full pads and contact.

By October 3, the Rose High football team's record was 4-0, and 2-0 in their conference. Homecoming versus the arch-rival Washington Pam Pack was scheduled for October 9. On October 6, the coach called Woody into the coach's office before practice and talked to him. "White, you're not very experienced, but you need to pick up your game, because you're starting in place of Wade."

"Coach, I think that's great. What's wrong with Wade?"

"Well, Wade has mono, probably from kissing a girl who had mono. He's weak as a newborn puppy, and Doctor Aycock won't let him play. He may be out for the season. You're my new right guard, offense and defense. I'm counting on you."

"Coach, I won't let you down." Woody finished dressing out for practice and ran onto the practice field. He felt sorry for Wade, a little bit. Woody knew he could not get mono from kissing some girl, because he hadn't kissed any girls. He was not someone girls found particularly attractive, and he knew he was not, and never would be, cool like some of the guys. But he was excited about starting. He was sorry his dad would be in the VA hospital in Durham and couldn't see the game.

The next day was 'picture day'. A photograph company would take the pictures of every student at Rose High, and those pictures would be published in the Rose High Annual, <u>The Tau</u>. Before he went to bed, Woody picked out a tie to go with the one sport coat he owned.

There was only one phone in the White household, and it was located in the pine-panel den which was at the front of the house. It was a very small den, in a very small house. Woody's bedroom had twin beds, and you had to turn sideways to walk between them. His bedroom was only about five steps from the den. He slept with his door open, and he heard the phone ring. The bedside clock read 3:00. He wondered who would be calling at this hour.

Woody answered the phone. "Hello."

"Is this the Woodrow White residence?" It was a man's voice.

"Yes, it is."

"May I speak to Mrs. Frances White please?"

Woody told the man to wait a minute and walked to his mother's bedroom. She had heard Woody talking and was out of the bed when Woody got to her room and told her the call was for her. She brushed past Woody and reached the phone and said, "This is Frances White." Woody could not hear the other end of the conversation, but since he had cut on a lamp in the den, he saw his mother's expression as she listened. Woody saw her hand go to her mouth and her eyes close. She said "I understand. I'll be up there."

She hung up the phone. "Son, do you know Uncle James' number?" Woody did not so he looked it up and dialed the number. After a while, his Uncle James, his dad's oldest brother, answered and Woody handed the phone to his mom, who said," James, I just got a call from the VA hospital in Durham. The man told me that Woodrow has taken a turn for the worse, and he asked me to come to Durham. I need your help." His mother listened, and then said, "I'll be ready."

She looked at Woody. "Son, James is going to take me to the VA hospital. There is no reason to wake up Hailey now. You and she just need to go to school, like always." Fifteen minutes later, Woody's mother left with James.

Every instinct in Woody's 15-year-old mind and body told him his daddy had died. There was no other reason for the VA hospital to call in the middle of the night to say his dad had taken a turn for the worse. After his mother left with James, he went to his bedroom and tossed and turned until early morning. He told his sister Hailey that their mom had gone to see their Dad, and that was all he said. She didn't ask for any particulars.

Woody was in Ms. Greene's 8:50 Algebra class when the school secretary came to the door and spoke to Ms. Greene, who in turn told Woody he was needed in the principal's office. His classmates made the usual, "What's he done now" comments, but Woody knew. They had come to tell him his dad was dead.

Margaret, James' wife, was waiting in the principal's office and told Woody what he already knew. She took Woody and Hailey to their home while they waited for James and their mom to return from Durham. Woody noticed that within an hour of his getting back to the house, neighbors were bringing food. This was his first experience with someone dying, and he didn't know that when there is a death in the South, it is the custom for friends and neighbors to bring food. He thought it was a strange custom, maybe because he wasn't hungry.

James and Frances arrived about 11:30, and Woody's mother hugged him differently than she ever had. He knew his mother was a strong woman, but he also knew he was now the 'man of the house', although he wasn't sure what that meant.

After Frances and James had been there a few minutes, Frances told Woody to go with James to his dad's closet to pick out a suit for his daddy to be buried in. His uncle, who was a man of very few words anyway, said nothing as they walked to the bedroom closet. Woody picked out the one dark blue suit his daddy owned, a matching tie and a white shirt to take to the funeral director, who had arrived. James told Woody the funeral home did not need shoes. James looked at Woody as he turned to go to the den to see the funeral director and said, "Son, I'm going to look after you."

Woody asked him, "What does that mean?"

James didn't answer.

Woody got his answer on Thursday, May 21, 1959. The Rose High golf team, of which Woody was a member, had a match at the Greenville Golf and Country Club against New Bern High School. Woody was one down when he reached the seventeenth hole, a dog-leg right par 4. His second shot ended up about 2 feet from the hole, so he felt good about squaring the match and playing the eighteenth hole for the win. He didn't feel so good after his opponent hit a career shot through the trees at the corner of the dogleg and into the hole. An eagle 2! Woody lost 2 and 1.

James' car was at the house when a teammate brought Woody home. James and Woody's Mom were in the kitchen. A bottle of Jim Beam was on the kitchen table, and they each had a drink. James asked, "Aren't you 16 on June 6?" Woody told him he was. "What day of the week is that? A Saturday?" Woody nodded 'yes'. James continued, "Well, be at Dogs Head, the Carolina Grill, at 5:30 in the morning on June 8. You're working for me Monday through Thursday of each week Bring your lunch."

Woody asked, "What about Friday's?"

"I'm getting to that. Tomorrow, after school, go to Corner Drug, you know where it is, across from the courthouse. You'll be working for Mr. Small and Mr. Allred, doing whatever they say do, delivering prescriptions, selling *coffee, being a soda jerk, whatever. You'll work their schedule, every Friday, and they'll want you to work weekends, too."*

Woody wanted to ask James when he could play golf, or go to the beach, or whatever, but he now knew what meant when he said he would take care of him. He knew he needed to keep his mouth shut and get ready to work that summer.

The White family owned a very small construction company, doing some odd jobs — making a concrete patio, putting in some sidewalks, or putting in curbs and gutters when they won a state or city bid. On Woody's first day at work, the crew, mostly blacks Woody had known for some time, was pouring concrete curbs and cutters on Memorial Drive in Greenville. After just one day, Woody hurt everywhere, even his fingers. He was looking forward to Friday and working at Corner Drug.

The other soda jerks at Corner Drugs were older than Woody. One of them had been a basketball star at East Carolina College, which was located in Greenville. No one gave Woody a hard time, and learning how to be a soda jerk, stock guy, and delivery man was not challenging and beat putting in curb and gutters.

On the second Friday Woody worked at Corner Drug, he was serving a cup of coffee to Billy Wilkins, who was three years older than Woody. Billy had barely graduated from Rose High and wore the uniform and badge of a Pitt County deputy sheriff. Billy said he was a bailiff, but Woody had no idea what a bailiff did. There weren't many customers at 8:45 that morning. Woody looked out of the side door of Corner Drug and could see the south side of the courthouse, where people were lining up in two lines which reached into the southern entrance of the courthouse annex.

"What's going on at the courthouse?" Woody asked Billy.

"Haven't you heard? It's the trial."

"No, I'm been working so hard I haven't listened to the news or read the paper. What's going on?"

"Well, they're trying a colored guy for threatening and showing his pecker to a white woman at her house, out at that new golf development, Mill Run Valley. I'm one of the courtroom bailiffs. I've heard it all."

Woody asked, "What have you heard so far?"

"Well, warm up this coffee — at no cost — and I'll give you the short version." Woody filled up Billy's cup and made a mental note to put a dime

in the cash register to pay for the refill." The woman testified she was at her new house, alone. Her husband had come to town for something. The colored guy came to the back door which opens to a garage, said he was working construction on the new house next door, and asked for a glass of cold water. She testified she told him to wait at the door and turned her back to him to get the water, but he followed her in, told her he'd kill her if she fought him, then he unzipped his pants and showed her his pecker and tried to push her to the floor. She got away and ran to the front of the house, and he ran out the back door. The husband testified that when he came home, he saw the guy walking from the back of his house to the house next door. He asked his wife what the guy was doing at their house, and she told him he had threatened to rape her and that he showed her his pecker. The husband testified that he got his shotgun, locked the back door, and called the sheriff. When the deputy sheriff got to his house, the woman told him what she told her husband, and the deputy sheriff went next door and arrested the guy and took him to the jail."

Woody said, *"Damn, that is something. What is happening next? Has he testified? Who are his lawyers? Is he guilty?"*

"Hold on White. Not so fast. The woman has been testifying. When we broke for lunch, the solicitor — you know, he's the guy that tries the case for the State, told the judge he had a few more questions for the lady, so when he's through with her, one of the defense lawyers will cross examine her. Her husband already testified and was cross-examined by the defense lawyers."

"Will the guy testify."

"Nobody knows. His lawyers are Mr. Garrison and Mr. Cavanaugh." Woody knew both of them from the drug store. They usually came in for coffee, but he didn't remember either of them ever sitting and talking with the other lawyers or the businessmen who congregated for coffee and shot the breeze. Mr. Garrison and Mr. Cavanaugh always seemed busy, and with this case, Woody could see why.

"So, the defense lawyers, or one of them, starts asking her questions this afternoon, right?" Woody asked.

Billy replied, *"Yep, at 2pm sharp, or as soon as the solicitor has finished his questions. Let me tell you, that judge is all business. Those two lines you see, what the judge has done is have the clerk of court fix up 126 tickets, because he figured there were 126 seats in the courtroom, and so the first 126 people in line get in, and 63 go up the left staircase and sit on the left side of* the courtroom, and 63 up the right staircase and sit on the right side. If a spectator leaves the courtroom, he don't get back in, period. That judge is from Lexington, and he is all business, let me tell you."

Woody looked at the line snaking into the courthouse. "I'd like to go this afternoon. If I can get off work here, can you get me in, Billy?"

"Can I get you in? Damn, Woody, I'm one of the bailiffs. Of course I can get you in, at a front row seat, next to me, but as a trade-off, I'd would like to come over here about 12:30 when the judge recesses for lunch, and have you toast me one, no, make that two, of those chicken salad sandwiches and fix me a Pepsi — make that a chocolate shake, courtesy of Woody, and I can make it happen."

"So, I fix and buy your lunch and I'm in if I can get off, right?" Billy nodded. "How do you sleep at night, taking advantage of a young 16-year-old guy? Woody turned to Jordy, his co-worker on the morning shift. "Do you work this afternoon?

"Not scheduled, but if you want me to work for you, I'll do it. And you pay me MY wage rate, not yours, time and a half."

Woody said, "So let me see if I've got this right. To get into the courtroom this afternoon, I fix and buy Billy his lunch, and I pay you your wages time and a half, right?" Billy and Jordy nodded. "You guys are criminals, I'm going to call the sheriff to arrest one of his own men, but I'll take this deal. AND I'll remember it, too."

"Okay, Woody", Billy said. "But be sure to pee and take a crap if you need to before we go to court this afternoon, because that judge will not let you back in if you leave. I'll see you for my free lunch, about quarter to one."

At 1:45 pm, Woody and Billy entered the courthouse through the new annex entrance and went up the stairs on the west side of the courthouse, past the jury room, and entered the courtroom.

Woody had never been in a courtroom before. The Superior Courtroom for Pitt County was on the second floor of the courthouse, which had been built in the 1920s. Billy told Woody to sit in the chair outside the rail and told Woody the rail was what was called the 'bar' and that only court officials or witnesses could come inside the 'bar'. Woody estimated the courtroom was over one hundred feet long, and about sixty- feet wide and had floor-to-ceiling windows at each end. The judge's bench was at the north end of the courtroom. To the left of the bench was what Woody guessed was the witness box. In the middle of the room was a section with fourteen seats in it. "Is that where the jury sits?" Woody asked Billy.

"Yeah."

"I thought there were 12 jurors but there are 14 seats. What's the deal?"

"The judge has 14 jurors for the case, so if up to 2 get sick or can't continue, he will still have 12 and the case can finish. Now, you need to shut the hell up. Court is about to convene."

He looked at his watch. It had been his Dad's Hamilton watch, a wedding gift from Woody's mom. She gave it to Woody for his sixteenth birthday. It was 2 minutes to two o'clock.

He looked across the courtroom and saw the defendant, a large Black man. He was sitting behind and between his lawyers, Mr. Garrison and Mr. Cavanaugh. All three were seated at a long table, which had several files and books on it. There were two deputies sitting behind the defendant.

The solicitor's table was directly across the room from the defendant's table and appeared to be the same size as the defendant's. It also had files and books on it. Two men sat at the table. Woody recognized one of them but could not remember his name. He worked as an attorney for the county. Woody also recognized the other man, and knew his last name was Beaman. He was from New Bern, the county seat of Craven County, about 40 miles away, and was the solicitor or prosecutor for Pitt and Craven Counties. He was about 6'3"tall had on a light tan-colored suit, with a blue shirt, vest and a dark brown tie. Woody thought he must be hot as hell. While the courtroom was air conditioned, it was filled up with spectators and was beginning to feel warm. There was another man sitting behind the solicitor's table. Woody recognized him as a law enforcement officer, because he had been into the drug store, wore a pistol in a holster on his right hip, and everyone called him "Detective." Woody recognized the lady sitting behind the solicitor, next to the wall. Her last name was Leggett. Woody assumed she was the woman who said she'd been assaulted. He had seen her at the country club pool last summer. She wore a wedding ring, but there was never a man with her at the pool. Woody had seen her tease and flirt with some of the older boys at the pool. She had a beautiful body and had some of the older boys rub suntan lotion on her back. Woody could tell that the mothers at the pool with their kids did not think much of her. She was holding the hand of the man next to her right, who Woody figured was her husband. Her chair was canted so that she was looking straight at the jury.

When the courthouse bell-clock rang twice, the door across the courtroom opened. The high sheriff went to the middle of the courtroom, and commanded, "ALL RISE", and everyone stood. The judge walked from the door to the bench and when he was standing behind the bench, the high sheriff said, "Court is now in session." The judge directed the high sheriff to have the jurors come into the courtroom, and the sheriff went to the door behind the solicitor's table and disappeared. He returned in a minute, and held the door open for the fourteen jurors. Woody didn't know any of them. He also noticed that none of them were Black.

The judge directed Ms. Leggett to sit in the witness chair and addressed the solicitor. "Mr. Solicitor, does the State have any further questions of Ms. Leggett?"

"No sir, not at this time."

The judge looked down at a lady sitting in front of and to the left of the bench. Her back was to the jury, and she was typing on a small machine. "Madam court reporter, let the record reflect that at 2:02, the State announced it had no further questions of Ms. Leggett at this time. Does the defense have any questions of Ms. Leggett?"

Mr. Cavanaugh stood and told the court he had questions for Ms. Leggett and then sat down and began his cross examination.

"Does the front of your house face north, south, east or west?" Mr. Cavanaugh had a loud, growling voice which intimidated Woody. He wondered how Ms. Leggett felt.

Ms. Legget answered, "I don't know and what difference does it make anyways?"

Mr. Cavanaugh stood and addressed the judge. "Your honor, please direct this witness to just answer the question and not ask me questions."

The judge turned toward Ms. Leggett. "Ms. Leggett, you can't ask the defendant's lawyer any questions, just answer the questions, do you understand?"

"Yes, sir I do. I don't know which way it faces."

Mr. Cavanaugh's next question sounded like a rifle shot. "Well, do know what the sun is?"

"Objection", Mr. Beamon yelled as he stood to address the court. "Counsel is trying to belittle the witness."

"Overruled, but Mr. Cavanaugh, get to the point. This isn't a geography or astronomy class."

"Yes, your honor. Ms. Leggett, when the sun comes up in the morning, it shines on the back, the rear, of your house, correct?"

"Yes, sir it does."

Mr. Cavanaugh said, "Then you'd agree the back or rear of your house faces east, correct?"

"Yes, sir."

Mr. Cavanaugh continued, "As you face the front of your house, is there a house to the left of your house?"

Ms. Leggett answered, "Yes, there is. The Davenports live there."

Mr. Carlson continued. "The house to the right of your house was being built, wasn't it."

"Yes, sir. The defendant who assaulted me was working a it."

"How big is your back yard?"

Ms. Leggett answered, "I really have no idea."

Mr. Cavanaugh continued. "Have you met the neighbors who live behind you?"

"No, I have not."

Mr. Cavanaugh continued. "But you have seen the people who live in the house behind you, working in their garden which is next to the rear fence in your yard, correct?"

"Yes, sir, I have seen a woman working in that garden, and I guess she lives in that house, but I've never met her."

"And you have a flower garden at the back of your yard, next to the fence where the back-door neighbors have their garden, don't you?"

"Yes, but how do you know that!" Ms. Leggett asked. The judge reminded her to not ask questions.

"Ma'am, from where you're sitting to the back wall of this courtroom is a little bit further from your garage to the fence at the back of your yard, next to the neighbor's garden, where your flower garden is, isn't it?"

"Yes, sir, I guess so."

"And your garage opens to the back yard doesn't it, so when you drive into the garage the front of the car is facing the street, correct?"

"Yes."

"There is no garage door, is there?"

"There is no garage door."

"So if I'm standing at your flower garden, I can see into the garage and see the back door to your house because there is nothing obstructing that view, no garage door, no trees, bushes, or anything like, right?"

"Yes, sir."

Mr. Cavanaugh approached the witness box. "You can read the clock hanging on the back room of this courtroom, can't you?"

"Yes, sir, it is 2:10." Every spectator and the jury turned to look at the clock.

"Do you see the back-door neighbor in this courtroom? You may stand up to look at the audience."

Ms. Leggett stood up and scanned the courtroom audience for about a minute, and then answered. "No sir, I do not."

Mr. Cavanaugh walked back towards his counsel table, pointed in the direction of the first row on the right side of the court room, and made a motion with his hand for someone in the audience to stand up.

Everyone in the courtroom, including the judge and court reporter, looked at the woman who rose from her seat on the first row. To Woody, she appeared to be about five and a half feet tall. She had grey hair and what Woody thought was a kind-looking face. She was wearing a necklace with a gold cross.

Mr. Cavanaugh stood by his counsel table and addressed Ms. Leggett. "Ma'am, this lady who is standing is your back-door neighbor, isn't she?"

"Yes, sir, I believe she is."

"Ma'am, you know that your back-door neighbor is Rev. Clement, the minister at First Baptist Church, located on Ninth Street, and that lady who stood up is his wife, don't you?"

Ms. Leggett answered, "I think I heard that somewhere. Yes."

Mr. Cavanagh addressed the Court, "Your Honor, we would like to have these three photographs marked as Defendant's exhibits 1, 2 and 3 for identification."

After the photographs were marked by the courtroom clerk, the judge directed Mr. Cavanagh to show the photos to the solicitor, who examined them and said he had no objection to their use. Mr. Cavanagh then showed the three photos to the witness and asked his next question. "So if Mrs. Clement were standing in her garden, at the backyard fence and was looking toward your house, she would see what these pictures show, wouldn't she?"

"Yes sir."

"So when the defendant came over to your house to ask for water, if Mrs. Clement was standing in at her garden, she could see him and she could see him standing in the garage, and could see whether he went into your house, couldn't he"?

"Objection." Mr. Beamon was on his feet and practically yelled. "That calls for speculation by the witness."

"Overruled", the judge said, "From the questions and answers, it is clear the witness is familiar with her own back yard and garage areas and the neighbor's garden. Answer the question, Ms. Leggett."

Woody knew something important was about to happen, but he didn't know what it would be. The only sound in the courtroom was the ticking of the second hand on the clock which hung between the two floor-to-ceiling windows at the south end of the courtroom.

Ms. Leggett squirmed in the witness chair as if she were very uncomfortable. She had a tissue in her hands and was squeezing it. She looked to her husband and the solicitor. After about a minute, she answered the question. "Yes."

Mr. Cavanaugh stood at the bar, with his back to the standing Mrs. Clement, faced Ms. Leggett, and asked his next question. "If my client had come into your garage, rung your back door bell, and stood in the garage, given the distance from the fence to your back door, given that there was no garage door, given the fact that there were no obstructions in the back yard blocking the view of the garage and back door, then if Mrs. Clement was standing at the fence, working in her garden when the defendant came over to your garage and back door, she could have seen the defendant come to your back door, ring the doorbell, stand in the garage, take the glass of water from you, NEVER enter the house, and then return to the house he was working on, couldn't she Ms. Leggett?

Everyone in the courtroom looked at Ms. Leggett, who clearly was uncomfortable. After about a minute, Mr. Cavanaugh addressed Ms. Leggett: "Do you want me to ask the question again?"

Ms. Leggett shook her head back and forth "no."

Mr. Cavanaugh moved to the defense counsel table. "Ms. Leggett, my client came into the garage, rang the doorbell, asked for water, which you gave him, he never came into your house, never exposed himself to you, never threatened or touched you, finished the water, left the glass on the step, left the garage and went back to work. You made up this story about his actions because your husband would have been mad that you gave him water, now isn't that the way it happened?"

Woody noticed again there was not a sound in the courtroom, save the ticking of the clock. Ms. Leggett looked at Mr. Cavanaugh, said nothing, and then began nodding "yes." She also began to sob and her shoulders shook. Mr. Cavanaugh said, "Ms. Leggett, the court reporter needs to record your answer, not the movement of your head. My question is: My client is innocent of all the charges brought against him, isn't that correct?"

Ms. Leggett spoke in a whisper, "Yes."

Mr. Cavanaugh moved to the center of the courtroom and faced the judge. "Your honor, I move for a dismissal, with prejudice, of the indictments against the defendant."

The judge said and did nothing for a few seconds, and then addressed Mr. Beamon, the solicitor. "What do you say to Mr. Cavanaugh's motion to dismiss, Mr. Solicitor?"

Mr. Beamon's head was bowed, and in his hands. "The State dismisses the charges against the defendant, with prejudice."

The judge stood up. "In light of the testimony of the prosecuting witness that the defendant did not commit the crimes with which he is charged, and in light of Mr. Cavanaugh's motion to dismiss with prejudice, and in light of the statement of the solicitor dismissing the charges with prejudice, it is adjudicated that the charges against the defendant are dismissed with prejudice. He is free to go. Mr. Solicitor, this court will be awaiting a report from your office regarding any action you may take against Ms. Leggett as a result of her testimony in this case. Sheriff, adjourn court, please."

The high sheriff went to the center of the courtroom and announced that court was recessed. Billy stood up and directed Woody to follow him out. When they reached the street level, Woody thanked Billy and ran across Third Street to the side door of the drugstore. His head was spinning.

As he entered the store, Mr. Small, one of the pharmacists, said, "Woody, Dr. Haigwood called in another prescription for Ms. Bigelow, over on Second Street. You took one to her last week, remember, and you got lost. Think you can find it today?"

Woody laughed. "Yes sir, I can handle it."

As Mr. Small gave Woody the prescription, he asked, "Well, did you learn anything at the trial?"

"Yes, sir. I learned that I want to be a trial lawyer."

0730 Hours, Sun, 27 Jul 69
Above the Pacific Ocean
East of Okinawa
In Transit

"Lieutenant, Lieutenant White. "Woody heard someone calling his name, and felt his left shoulder being shaken. At first, he had no idea where he was. Then he heard the plane's engines and opened his eyes. He was staring at the partially unbuttoned blouse of Susannah, one of the stewardesses. There was enough showing for Woody to know that she had beautiful breasts.

For reasons totally unknown to Woody, Susannah had been flirting with him during the trip. On several occasions, he went to the plane's galley to get a cup of coffee, Susannah made it her business to come up beside him and press her breasts against his arm and make comments full of sexual innuendo. All Woody could think was that it was just his luck — this good looking woman was making a pass at him, which was the first time a women made a pass at him in his life, and she was doing it in a damn airplane at probably 35,000 feet high, in the presence of 161 Marines. Just what did she expect Woody to do, and where did she expect him to do it!

"Lieutenant, we will be landing on Okinawa soon. I wanted you to know that. And I wanted you to have this." Susannah handed Woody a piece of paper and returned to the galley area. Woody opened it and saw it was a note with the name, address and telephone number of a hotel in Naha, Okinawa, and a note Susannah wrote — "I hear marines love hand to hand combat. I'd like to try that with you at this hotel. Call. It will be worth your time."

'What the hell' was all Woody could think. The Corps had owned him since 30 September 68. He would be in Okinawa awaiting a flight to Vietnam for maybe 24 hours, and the Corps would not give him leave to get laid. He was hoping to have time to pee and couldn't even think about trying to get laid. He put the paper in his pocket, got up, stepped over the sleeping Captain Barkley, and walked around, getting the kinks out.

Woody's body clock was all messed up. He had left the Hamilton watch with his mom, in case something happened to him. The aircraft had crossed the International Date Line and several time zones, so Woody didn't know the actual time. He didn't' even know what day it would be when they landed.

The jet landed in 45 minutes, and Woody was directed to one of the largest buildings he had ever been in. He'd never seen so many Marines in one place in his life. He wondered if this was what Ellis Island looked like at the turn of the century, if everyone were wearing military green.

He found his assigned place and was bused to some building, where a medical team was locked and loaded to probe every orifice of his body, and stick needles taking out blood or putting in medicine of some description. Woody usually asked doctors what they were doing when they examined or treated him and was surprised that his questions often ticked off some of them, as if they were too important to answer a patient's questions. Woody was a little disappointed in himself, because when he noticed a doctor got ticked off at his questions, Woody thought even harder of another question, just for the sport of it. His mom would not have been proud, but he reasoned the doc's mom would not have been proud of her doctor son acting like he was better than the patient who was paying him for medical services. Every time that happened, Woody reminded himself to always treat clients with respect...once he had a client. But he had learned that in the Corps, he needed to keep his mouth shut, so he didn't ask what they were doing to him.

When the medical team had finished their work, Woody and Captain Barkley were bused to a barracks for officers, and Woody assumed the enlisted men were sent to their barracks. He was told he would be there the next 18 hours, and that he could go only to the PX, which was within a quarter-mile, the chow hall across the street, and the gym, for PT. No hand-to-hand combat with the stewardess.

1700 Hours, Mon, 28 Jul 69
Officer's Club, Third Mar Div
Quang Tri
Reasonable Doubt

Kevin Ross and Mike McMurry had been sitting at a corner table in the O Club for about thirty minutes. They had finished the prosecution duties for the day and were nursing their Budweisers. Neither said anything, which was very unusual for them.

Mike spoke up. "What's wrong with you, man. You're never quiet. What's up?"

"Well, you aren't exactly a blabbermouth yourself", Kevin replied. "But the fact is I'm having a hard time getting the Jackson case out of my mind."

"Me too", Mike admitted. "There are two things bothering me. First, the opportunity for Douglas to be certain of identifying the men running — maybe OK with Grant 'cause he was so big, but the other man — was so weak, I mean, saying you could see the man that far away well enough to ID him when the lighting flashed is hard to believe. I can believe he saw two men running, but to have a guy be found guilty and get two consecutive ten-year sentences on the testimony of one witness who said he ID'd him from thirty yards in driving rain only when lightning occurred, well, I can't buy it. I know the panel convicted Jackson, but I wonder if we charged and convicted the right man. And to top it off, Jackson was convincing to me in his testimony denying the charge. Not enough obviously for the panel, but he was convincing to me."

"I know. I've got the same concerns", Kevin said. "David did his usual masterful job in defending Jackson. I know he's rotating back next week, and that means Jackson won't have anyone in his corner. The transcript is being prepared and won't be ready for Suarez before he rotates back at the end of August, so his SJA replacement will decide whether to approve the conviction and sentence. It's hard to imagine that a new SJA would do anything other than recommend to the general that he approve the conviction, assuming there were no prejudicial errors. I don't believe we committed any prejudicial errors, and in some ways, it was an easy case to prep and try — 'he said/he said', and the panel decides"

Mike responded. "I agree. I just wonder if something was missed. That IO, was it Breckinridge? He went through the process pretty damn quick and ended after he talked to only six witnesses. He didn't do anything further."

"Yeah", Kevin said, "but we and the NIS agents talked — or asked several questions, to everyone in the company, and at the end of the day, there was only one man who was a useful witness for the government, and that was Douglas."

Mike picked up his Budweiser and took a big swig. "Well, the bottom line is that there is no one else who can do anything about it. Everyone here knows all about the case. In one sense, it's real easy to say it's over and let's move on, but it's hard as hell for me, and I guess for you, to let it go when we have these concerns. There is absolutely nothing we could do on our own, and anyway, we're so close to the case we couldn't see the forest for the trees. It would be great if we could get someone who knows nothing about the case to take a look, but I can't think who that'd be, so I guess we're stuck. Let's finish these beers and get some chow."

1700 Hours, Tues, 29 Jul 69
Officer's Club
Third Mar Div
Quang Tri
Welcome to Vietnam

On Tuesday, 29 July, Woody left Okinawa, again on a passenger jet, with stewardesses, and in a few hours, landed at Da Nang Air Base. It was one busy place. F-4 Phantom jets took off and landed frequently. Every type of chopper the Corps flew was in the air at one time or another. Woody and the men on his flight were directed to a building marked "Quang Tri/Dong Ha." He knew Headquarters Company, the Third Marine Division, was in Quang Tri, because his orders said so, but Dong Ha was new to him. He showed his orders to a gunnery sergeant who took one copy, returned the remaining orders to Woody and directed him to a seat in a passenger area. Woody placed his sea bag next to him, and it hit him for the first time that he was in a war zone, and that while he would not likely be in combat, there were plenty of other ways for him to get hurt, not the least of which was from a rocket attack on the Quang Tri base. He wondered if those attacks were frequent. From his training, he knew that the bigger bases, such as Quang Tri, were targeted with rockets which were fired without any particular target in mind, because those rockets did not have sophisticated guidance systems. They were fired in the direction of the base, and they hit wherever they hit.

After a 2-hour wait, Woody and 20 other Marines, 3 officers and 17 enlisted, were directed to the flight deck and told to board a prop plane. They boarded with some Vietnamese, two of whom had dogs. There was no stewardess on board.

The plane took off, and in about an hour, Woody heard the flaps being extended for the landing. The aircraft began its descent and landed safely. Woody got off the aircraft with his sea bag and went into the wooded building marked "Transit." He was approached by a warrant officer. Woody had learned at TBS that a warrant officer's rank is above the highest enlisted rank, and below the lowest officer rank. The WOs were usually specialists at something. A number of chopper pilots in the Corps were warrant officers.

"Lt. White, I'm WO Masterson with Legal." He extended his hand, which Woody shook. "Welcome to Vietnam. Are you ready to head to HQ?

Woody wondered if he had a choice. "Yes, ready to go." Mr. Masterton took Woody's sea bag and led him to a jeep, a type of vehicle which Woody had seen in war movies.

Woody noticed no one was riding shotgun, either figuratively or literally, and all Masterson had was a .45 caliber pistol. Woody hoped they would not encounter any bad guys on the way to the legal office.

Quang Tri was huge, at least the part Woody saw. They drove about 15 minutes before they arrived at a hooch, Woody's home for the next twelve months. Mr. Masterson directed Woody inside and followed him with the sea bag, which was deposited onto a bunk. There were 16 bunks in this hooch, 8 on each side. Mr. Masterson pointed out the head, which is Marine for "bathroom", and the showers, which consisted of canvas held up by 10 poles, with no roof. "This is the hooch for most of the defense lawyers. Come on, I'll show you the office and introduce you around."

The first building Mr. Masterson took Woody to was a large Quonset hut, with a sign reading "Division Legal". The Division Legal hut was air conditioned, and there were about ten desks, each being manned by enlisted men whom Woody assumed were Legal's admin staff. Mr. Masterson asked one of the men if the colonel was available, and after getting a nod, went to the door marked "Lt. Col Suarez, Division SJA" and knocked. Woody heard someone say, "Enter", and he and Masterson went in.

There was only one desk in the room, and the man you sat behind it didn't stand up when they entered the room. "Colonel, this is Lieutenant White, our new lawyer."

Colonel Suarez didn't look up at first, but just said "Hello" as he continued to write. He finally stood up but did not extend his hand. "Lieutenant, I think you'll like this group. Someone else will decide what your specific duties will be. I'm a short-timer, 29 days and a wake-up and I'm back to New Mexico to run for judge next year. Mr. Masterson, has he met Major Forrest?"

"No sir, I showed him his bunk and came straight here. Should I do that now?"

"Yes. Glad to have you here, Lieutenant."

As they exited the colonel's office, Woody spoke without thinking. "That was quick."

"Yep, not to be repeated, but the colonel is not a lot of fun, and his replacement will be welcomed with open arms, whoever he is. Let's go to Major Forrest's office across the room. Now, he is the military judge for special courts martials and he is the chief administrative officer for us. Normally there are two different people for those two billets, but we're short. He will decide whether you will be assigned to the trial or the defense team."

Woody commented, "Well, I've never tried a case before. Hope I have time to learn the ropes before I have to try a case."

"Well, if you've never tried a case before, they'll put you on the defense side."

"But I don't know jack about trying a case!"

"Exactly", Mr. Masterson said. "The government likes to have a good won-lost record."

Major Forrest's office door was open, but Masterson knocked anyway.

"Major, I've got Lieutenant White, our new lawyer."

Major Forrest stood up and came from around his desk and extended his hand. "Welcome to the Third Mar Div Legal, Lieutenant White. We've got plenty of work for you." Woody thought Major Forrest had the darkest, most lifeless eyes he had ever seen. They were almost evil-looking. He was bald, and the skin on his face seemed to be pulled back tightly. He attempted to smile, but just couldn't do it.

"Sir, I am looking forward to it. I'm sure there are some good men to work with."

"There are. Lots of assault cases, some murder cases, an occasional assault on officer case, and larcenies. Pretty typical of a front-line legal office." The major stood back a bit and looked Woody up and down. "I don't know, Mr. Masterson. Think he could take Bull?"

"Sir, my money would be on Bull. After all, he was All Big 10 defensive tackle his senior year at Iowa"

Woody was wondering what the hell was going on.

"I disagree", the major said, "I think Bull is a bit long of tooth, and I think Lieutenant White is one of those lean and mean guys. Lieutenant, are you a fan of arm-wrestling? Would you like a bit of competition with our legal office champ?"

Woody knew the only answer a Marine officer could give in that situation was "Yes, sir", but he sure didn't mean it.

"We can find out before chow. Lieutenant, when Mr. Masterson finishes introducing you, we go to the O Club at 1630 every day, and we work every day including Sunday, 0730 to 1630, breaking for chow at 1130 to 1230. You'll be in the defense shop. I imagine they've got a few new cases for you. Did you have any trial work before coming to 'Nam?"

"No, sir, not a bit. Just some moot court at Justice School."

"Well, it ain't the same, so good luck. As you know, defendants can choose to have the military panel or me, hear the case."

"Yes, sir. Thank you for that information." Woody thought he'd have no trouble telling his clients to have the jury decide their case. Major Forrest looked like a man who would convict his own grandmother and give her jail time. Not a lot of the milk of human kindness flowing in that guy's veins.

"Let's go, Lieutenant", Mr. Masterson said. "You'll need to meet the men in the defense shop, before you meet Bull, who is a prosecutor."

The defense shop was in a wooden building which was about fifty feet long and thirty-five feet wide with desks on both sides of the building. Woody shook hands with all of the lawyers, each of whom was very busy and didn't do much more than say, "Hi." The head of the defense was Captain Fred Conner whom Woody addressed as 'Captain'. Fred told Woody, "We're pretty informal here. The trial and defense lawyers are on a first-name basis, without regard to rank, except in the courtroom, in a trial. And we don't bother with saluting other company-grade officers, ok?"

"Yes, sir. I mean, yes. I'll remember", said Woody.

Fred continued. "You'll want to advise your defendants to have their cases before the military panel, not Major Forrest. He'd convict his grandmother and give her jail time. But — and this is a big but — the military panel we presently have consists of three Marines, a couple of first lieutenants who did well in combat and are on the way back home, and a major, Judge Roy Bean."

Woody stopped him. "Wait a minute. Judge Roy Bean was a hanging judge in the wild west around the turn of the century, wasn't he?'

"Right on, that's why we gave him that well-earned nickname. His real name is Major Bullock. You can't miss him. Neck about 22 inches, knuckles drag the floor, a real Neanderthal-type. He finds everyone guilty. But the lieutenants are good officers who don't appear to buckle in to Major Bullock. All in all, it's a fair group. We're all busy and we can help you out when you get started, but remember, each of has more cases than he should have — lots of crime out here, so most of your education will be trial by fire."

Fred continued. "Let's get over to the O Club, it is coming up 430 — I mean 1630. I still can't remember to use military time. The drinks are twenty cents, there is some good chili, and it is air conditioned. But before I forget, right after breakfast tomorrow, come back here. You've got your first cases. Now, let's go have a drink, or two."

The O Club was packed. It was nothing fancy, but it was cool, which was more than Woody could say for the defense shop or his hooch. Woody found out at TBS, and even at the Navel Justice School, that there was a real drinking culture in the Corps. There were also rules to remember, the chief of which was to not wear your cover in the O Club, or by tradition, you bought a round of drinks for everybody in the Club. The bar was horseshoe shaped, with about ten bar stools and then maybe twenty tables scattered in a room which had a low ceiling and no windows. Woody noticed there were leather cups on the bar. He knew they contained dice, and bets were made on the throwing of the dice with the loser buying the drinks. Since Woody didn't know the rules of that game, he was determined to stay away from the cups. The smoke hung heavy in the air. Many of the officers sitting at the bar put their cigarette pack and lighter on the bar, along with their right elbow, and then drank, smoked, and shot the shit.

The lawyers in the defense shop gathered in a corner and gabbed about cases. Then Major Forrest came over to Woody. A Marine who looked like a Big Ten football player stood next to the major. The major was the ringmaster for what Woody knew would be the shortest arm-wrestling contest in the history of the Corps. "Alright, I've got five bucks on Bull, in 15 seconds. Keep track of the bets, Fred. What say the rest of you?"

Bets were made and Woody tried to look like he was not concerned, for obvious reasons. But he felt the officers who were betting on him were not people from whom he would seek financial advice.

"All the bets in? Ok, outside", the major ordered. Bull and Woody sat facing each other at the end of a picnic table. Bull asked what the Third Mar Div record was, and someone said "three seconds." Bull boasted he would beat it by one second.

"Alright, Bull, Lieutenant White, take your positions. I'll give you the 'go' signal." Bull put his right elbow on the table, and held out his hand, which Woody thought was as big as a major league catcher's mitt." Okay, the combatants are in positions. Ready, GO!"

Woody couldn't tell which came first, Bull releasing his hand, or the 20 cold beers hitting his head and back as all the officers yelled, "WELCOME TO VIETNAM!!"

Woody stood up and shook his head like a lab coming out of the bay with a Mallard duck in its mouth. "Well, didn't see that coming. Anybody got a beer?" He was handed a Pabst Blue Ribbon, which he chugged in about 10 seconds, to the encouragement of the guys. Woody then crushed the empty can, tossed it into a trash can and asked, "Can I be in the front row when the next rookie gets here?" Woody had no way to know that he would be on the front row and welcome the next new lawyer with a vengeance.

When they retreated to the bar, Woody received a standing ovation. After a few drinks and chow, Woody started back to his hooch. Fred was with him. "By the way", Woody asked, "have there been any attacks on this base, rockets, or anything like that?"

"Not in about three weeks. We're at a place on the base where the bad guys will never be around us — way too many folks to go through and lawyers aren't high on their kill list. After all, they haven't read Shakespeare. Rockets — that's another thing. They can hit anytime, anyplace. If you hear them, and trust me, when they hit, even if they hit a mile away, you'll know it. There is a siren warning when there is incoming, so run to those sand bags." Fred pointed to a circular sand bag emplacement, above ground. It didn't look like it could protect anyone from anything, but Woody kept his mouth shut.

That night, at 2115, thirty-five rockets hit the base in twenty-five minutes — the longest twenty-five minutes of Woody's life. As soon as Woody heard the first one hit and the siren wail, he was hauling ass to the sandbags. He ran past Jack someone, another defense lawyer, who was just sauntering to the sandbags.

Five minutes after the last rocket and the 'all clear' two wails on the siren, Woody and Fred were walking back to the hooch. Woody said," Fred, I hope you're better at giving me pointers about representing defendants than you are at guessing about rockets. If you ain't, all my clients are going up the river."

1015 Hours, Wed, 30 Jul 69
Legal Office, Third Mar Div
Quang Tri
Woody's First Case

Woody didn't see any damage from the rocket attack the night before when he went to the chow hall on his first morning at Headquarters Company, Third Mar Div. After breakfast, he went to the defense shop, where Fred Conner gave him a brief explanation of Woody's first case, The Government vs. HM2 Al McArthur, a Navy Corpsman.

"This guy is charged with possession of 1300 pot joints, found in a sea bag in his hooch. Look at his record and you'll see he's decorated. You know, corpsmen are all a bit nuts, because of all the chances they take in the field to get to a jarhead who is wounded. This guy got the Bronze Star with 'V' for valor while out with 1/9, which they call the 'Walking Dead', 'cause of their high casualty rate.

"First, you need to review the spec, you know, the UCMJ specification under which he is charged and make sure you know the elements. Then talk to him, get his story. Maybe there were times he wasn't in his hooch and someone dumped the sea bag in the hooch to pick it up later. And, if you can get the officer who nominated him for the Bronze Star to testify, it may go a long way towards having 'Judge Roy Bean' and the other panel members set him loose. But don't bet the ranch. Bean hasn't found anyone not guilty yet, and he's heard about twenty cases in a month and a half." Fred told Woody how to get up with McArthur.

Woody's interview with McArthur, his first client, was conducted later that day at Woody's desk in the defense shop. There were no walls for confidentiality, but everyone was so busy, no one had time to listen to anyone else.

McArthur was about 5'11"and weighed about 180. He had a handle-bar mustache, which he could get away with since he was in the Navy. He was a HM2 — a hospital corpsman second class, the equivalent of an E-5 sergeant. The winged caduceus on his collar was the badge of corpsman.

Woody addressed McArthur. "Well, Doc, you're charged with violating Article 112a, the 'wrongful possession of marijuana, a controlled substance'. I read the file. There were 1300 joints in a sea bag in your hooch. What's your story, and by the way, whatever you tell me is confidential 'cause I'm your lawyer, but, if you testify, you can't say something in the courtroom that is different than what you tell me. You've got to shoot straight with me."

"I damn sure want to testify, Lieutenant. Those joints weren't mine, and the sea bag wasn't mine. We'd been on a three-day patrol. I came back, dirty as hell. Took off my utilities and went to take a shower. Came back, didn't notice the sea bag, which was under my rack. I hadn't been in the hooch for three damn days, and anybody could have put that sea bag there. Lots of people come through that area."

"Now Doc, why would anyone put their joints in your hooch?"

"Well, maybe they heard there was going to be a shakedown, you know, an inspection of their own hooch, and they needed a place to put the sea bag, and since I wasn't there, they put it way back under the rack in my hooch, where I wouldn't see it. We had an inspection, the sarge found it, and next thing I know, I'm charged. And I'm innocent."

"Will the officer who recommended you for the Bronze Star testify about your character?"

"Yes, sir, he said he would. His name is Fulp, and he is at our company HQ now. I'd like you to talk to him. Maybe it will help. I want to go to med school when I get back — if I get back, and can't get in if I have a conviction and a bad conduct discharge, which they would probably give me if they convict me. So, there's a lot on the line."

On Monday, 4 August, the military panel found McArthur not guilty. Woody had won his first trial. The doc would have a chance to apply for med school — if he made it back. Woody went to the O Club to celebrate.

"Lieutenant, come over here." The summons was from Major Bullock, aka Judge Roy Bean. He was in the corner of the O Club, sitting between the other members of the court panel, two first lieutenants. "Take a load off." Woody sat across from them and sipped his Bud. The major spoke, "We didn't do you any favors in letting the doc go, you earned it for him. Having his CO testify about the action in the field, and why he wrote him up for the Bronze Star, was a nice touch, but that was not why we found him not guilty. A pot head can be a hero. You did a good job of showing that anyone could have put that pot there, and there was more than a reasonable doubt the pot was his. So — you won one."

"Yes, sir. I guess I did."

Bullock continued, "Was that your first trial over here?"

"Sir, that was my first trial anywhere."

One of the lieutenants piped in, "Well, I guess that means you've only got one way to go, and that's downhill." All laughed.

"Yes, sir. I guess that is one way to look at it."

"Well, we don't want to hobnob with you too much. You might be accused of fraternizing with the enemy if you sit over here too long."

"Yes, sir, but I would like to ask a favor. Don't know the protocol of this, but if you feel like I'm messing up, I'd appreciate your comments on my trial work after a trial. I want to learn from my mistakes. No way to learn better than asking someone who has experience in these things."

"We'll see, Lieutenant. Have a good day." Bullock dismissed Woody, who went to join the other defense lawyers at a table across the room.

He was observed by the lawyers who had prosecuted Jackson.

"That's the new guy, Warren, isn't it?" Kevin asked.

Mike corrected him, "No, it's White. Went to Wake Forest. Did you hear that today he won his first case, and Roy Bean was on the panel."

"You're kidding, really! How the hell did he do that?"

McMurry answered, "I talked to the court reporter, Spivey, and he said White tried a real good case. Got Bean and the other guys to realize the pot the doc was charged with could have been left in the doc's hooch by anybody, so they found reasonable doubt and acquitted him. I believe that is the first time Roy Bean has been on a panel which found someone not guilty."

Ross looked at McMurry. "Well, you know we said we wanted to get someone else to help us take a look at Jackson's conviction. This guy knows nothing about the fragging or the trial — he wasn't here. He would be totally unbiased. Maybe he's not real experienced, but that may be good. Not as jaded, so maybe he'll have a little messianic spirit. But in fairness, we should first talk to Fred about letting us get help from one of his defense guys. Let's see if Fred can meet with us tomorrow, okay?"

"Sounds like a plan to me", McMurry agreed.

The next afternoon, Woody got back to the hooch from the O Club about 1800, after drinks at the club and some surprisingly good chow — steak and baked potato. Fred was in the hooch.

"Woody, I've got a new case for you, so let's go over to the courtroom. There's nothing being tried, and we can talk there."

When they got to the empty courtroom, Fred spoke. "Well, I'm giving you your first murder case. Here's what happened. An Apache named, I kid you not, Geronimo Abaya, who is with 2/9, came in from a week-long patrol, got too much beer or booze, had a .45, got in a shouting match with a Black guy, and shot him dead, in front of 20 or so witnesses. Now, have you noticed much racial tension here?"

Woody replied, "Yes, I have. Even in our area, the Blacks are giving each other the black power salutes, like those two athletes did in the Olympics in Mexico City last fall. And they wear these black, green and red — I guess they are bracelets, which sure aren't part of the uniform, and they can seem a bit surly."

"Surly is probably an understatement. Anyway, the blacks see this murder as a 'black-white" thing, and so, Geronimo has been placed in solitary for his own safety, at our brig here, but he will be sent to the brig in Da Nang after you interview him and give them the go-ahead to send him. Here's his SRB. Take a minute to look through it and tell me what looks helpful to you as a defense lawyer."

After examining the SRB of his first client charged with murder, Woody said to Fred, "Well, he came to the Corps because some judge gave him the choice of going to jail or enlisting. May have been good for the civilian world, but not the Corps, because he's had 5 or 6 office hours, and every time he made rank, he lost it because of his aggressive conduct. He dropped out of school in the eighth grade. He's had a few barracks fights. In one of the fitness reports, his gunny sergeant noted he was a strange-acting guy. I wonder if he was in his right mind when he killed the guy, you know, either too drunk to form the intent to kill, which may keep him from the death penalty, or just off his rocker. I don't know, some sort of defense of insanity or something like that, could make a difference. What does that sound like?"

"Woody, I think that is EXACTLY where you need to go. Good thinking. We have a form you can fill out that will start the wheels rolling on a psyche eval. I'll show it to you when we get back to the office."

Woody stood up. "Okay, thanks. I'd better get to work."

Fred motioned for Woody to sit down. "There's one other thing, and this is absolutely off the record, meaning you don't tell anyone, ok?"

"Yes, sir."

"Well, here's the deal. Last June, after a big op in Apache Snow, two Marines with 1/9, at VCB, were ID'd running from the hooch of a lieutenant where a grenade had just exploded, killing the lieutenant. The two guys were each charged with murder, accessory after the fact to murder and conspiracy to commit murder. No one is sure who actually tossed the grenade, so both were charged. David Peterson in our office represented Jackson, and did a damn good job, but Jackson was convicted of the accessory and conspiracy charges and acquitted of the murder charge. He got a dishonorable discharge, reduction in rank, and loss of pay in each case, and two ten-year sentences of hard labor back to back, at the federal prison at Fort Leavenworth. The trial transcript is being prepared and as you know, the SJA has to make an independent review of the trial record and give the division commanding general, who convened the general court martial, his recommendation as whether to approve the conviction. Grant, the other Marine charged, hasn't been tried yet.

"Here's where it gets sticky. The trial counsel were McMurray and Ross. For some reason, after the trial, and independently of each other, they began to believe that Jackson may not have done it, and a different man was with Grant. They have told me their concerns about the conviction only because they wanted me to talk to you about helping them and wanted my 'okay' since I'm chief defense counsel. See, the trial was probably as close to a 'free from prejudicial error' trial as you can have. You remember from Justice School that there are going to be errors in trials, but there will probably be no reversal for harmless error — an error that probably didn't change the outcome. On the other hand, reversal is probably required if the error was prejudicial — meaning something happened in the trial which was not legally acceptable, and which may, or probably did, affect the outcome. The amazing thing about this is that the two prosecutors independently came to the same conclusion in what was probably an error free trial, that the wrong man may have been convicted, they are top-notch, and their instincts mean something.

"They have been instructed by Colonel Suarez that as soon as the transcript and record have been completed and readied for submission to the CG for review, he will recommend approval of the conviction, without even reviewing the record or transcript. He wants to do that because he wants it on his record that he had something to do with the successful conviction of someone who murdered an officer, for use in his campaign material when he runs for judge next year, back in New Mexico.

"The trial transcript is being prepared but isn't finished, and McMurry and Ross are hoping it will not be completed before Suarez goes back to the States in about three weeks. That way, the new SJA will have to deal with it, and they're hoping they will be able to find something that would give rise to a reversal. NIS couldn't initially investigate because a typhoon hit, so there was a very quick investigation by a non-NIS guy, the XO of Alpha 1/9. They — McMurry and Ross, hope or think something may have been missed. Plus, they tend to believe the defendant's testimony, and they believe the one eyewitness didn't have a good chance to see the people he ID'd as the killers even though the eyewitness testimony was good enough for the military panel to convict.

"They know you don't know anything about the case, which is an upside, because a new set of eyes can be good in this. They've lived with it since they charged Jackson and Grant. It would be a good opportunity for you, but you won't get any slack in your work. Wouldn't be fair. If you'd like to talk to them, then meet them on the basketball court at 1700 hours tomorrow. If you work with them on this, don't meet in an office. Keep it among the three of you. Any questions?"

"Are McMurray and Ross doing anything wrong here? I don't want to get in trouble."

"Absolutely not. They aren't willing to hurt their careers, they're just trying to do the right thing. If they told the court reporters to type the transcript slowly so Suarez won't get a chance to see it, I don't know it, they ain't telling and I ain't asking. There is no trouble to get into here."

Woody had one more question, "Fred, what would you do?"

Fred sat back, thought a minute, and then answered, "Well I believe it is the right thing to do. Some stone may not have been turned over in the investigation, and in practicing law, you almost always do well following your instincts."

Even though it was hot as hell, Marines were expected to stay in shape, even if they were not slated for combat duty. So, at 1700, on the day after Fred told him what McMurry and Ross wanted him to do, Woody was on the concrete basketball court near the O Club, by himself. The two goals had chain nets. Woody was stretching and taking some jump shots when Mike and Kevin came to the court.

After introductions, McMurry started the conversation. "Fred told us he gave you the short version, enough for you to know what is going on generally. We thought we could meet here, so no one would think we were talking about the law. If you decided to proceed, we could meet periodically to talk about your progress, or lack of it. But let's start with your questions. I know you must have some."

Woody asked, "Do you think the conviction would be overturned if it were reviewed properly?"

Mike answered, "Probably not. We think we prosecuted a trial that was free from prejudicial error, but that opinion is based on what we remember doing in prep and at trial. We haven't really analyzed that. Our larger concern is that the investigation was handled so quickly — understandably so given that an officer was murdered — that something, or someone, may have been overlooked. Plus, due to a typhoon, NIS couldn't get to VCB for a couple of days, so the initial investigation at VCB was handled by a first lieutenant with no investigatory skills. He may have missed something. We're sure NIS did their usual topnotch job. Who knows? We hope we can have a chance to find out. That's really where we're coming from."

"So, if I agree to help, what would I do?" Woody asked.

Kevin answered, "You'll want to read the trial transcript. But, and this is important, you'd also need to look outside the trial and to see if something was missed somewhere and form your own opinions about whether Jackson may be innocent for the reason that something or somebody was overlooked. You would be free to re-interview those who testified. In fact, Kevin and I discussed this very issue, that if we could get someone to help us, we did NOT want to give our opinions or reasons, 'cause it may influence the person's opinion. We want you to approach this as much as possible on your own. The military panel was properly fulfilling its duty in finding that they believed the eyewitness and not the defendant. The word was that the murder victim, his name was Speight, was a poor commander. Alpha, 1/9, was in some bad stuff during Dewey Canyon and Apache Snow, a lot of officers got hit and Speight's platoon had a high number of WIAs and KIAs, but that isn't a reason to kill the platoon leader."

"I've got another question", Woody said, "What's the end game, the game plan, if the transcript isn't finished before Colonel Suarez rotates home."

"Good question", Kevin answered, "When the new SJA gets here, we can make a pitch to him to let us run every rabbit we can, to see if Jackson did not, or may not, have done it. It is a long shot, 'cause he may not let us do it, but it's the only shot we got, and we feel Jackson deserves it. Are you on board?"

Woody answered, "Yes, count me in. Where do we start."

0630 Hours, Wed, 6 Aug 69
Legal Office, Third Mar Div
Quang Tri
Geronimo and the Shrink from Everetts

When Woody told Fred he was going to help, Fred brought the file Lieutenant David Peterson had worked when representing Jackson. It was a large banker's box which, at first glance, looked like it contained about three hundred folders. Woody put it under his desk, behind some other file boxes, but pulled it out at 0630 hours on 6 August before anyone was in the office. The box contained the transcript which included the testimony of L/Cpl Jackson, and a file folder on which was written, *Speight murder investigation. Gov't Witnesses — prepared by 1st Lt. Donald Breckenridge IV* and which contained 6 pieces of paper, written apparently by the same person. Woody was told that Breckinridge had rotated back home, was stationed at Camp Lejeune, in Jacksonville, North Carolina, and was scheduled to be discharged at the end of the year.

One file contained the autopsy report, which Woody didn't need to read. The lieutenant was dead, and the cause of death was not in dispute. After he had taken stock of the contents of the box, he thought he should begin by reading the statements of the witnesses, followed by the trial transcript of their testimony. But before he could start reviewing the file in earnest, he had to first meet the Navy psychiatrist who was conducting the psyche eval on Pvt. Geronimo Abaya.

The Navy medical office was located about a quarter mile from the legal building. Woody hitched a ride and walked to the front of the building. The screen door and the wooden door behind it were both closed. Woody hoped that meant the office was air-conditioned. It was.

He saw several Navy enlisted men in the big room and asked for Lieutenant Hardison's office. He was directed to an office in the corner of the building. He went to the open door and saw a slight, brown-haired Navy lieutenant sitting behind a desk, writing something. A nameplate on the desk read *Lt. Aaron Hardison*.

A US Navy lieutenant is an O-3, the same rank as a Marine Corps captain, so he outranked Woody. "Sir, I'm Lieutenant White, here to discuss my client and your patient, Pvt. Abaya."

"Come on in. I'll be with you in a minute." Woody entered the office. There was a seat in front of the desk, but he didn't take it, because the lieutenant had not offered it. Woody looked around the room. There was a road map of North Carolina tacked to the wall behind the lieutenant's desk. The distinctive Esso gasoline logo, the white oval with red letters, was in the lower left hand corner of the map. The lieutenant was left-handed, and Woody saw what appeared to be a college class ring with a light blue stone on his left ring finger. The lieutenant also wore a ring on his right ring finger. It was gold and had a black parallelogram, in which there was a white star. Woody had seen a ring like that before.

After about 5 minutes, Lieutenant Hardison finished writing and looked up. "You're here about Abaya, right?"

Woody was a little pissed. Common courtesy would call for his being invited to sit down. Woody was in no mood for military courtesy, so he decided to not refer to the higher-ranked doctor as *sir*.

"I am."

"Have you met with him?"

"I have not. I wanted to meet with you first and complete my review of the file."

The doctor continued, "Lieutenant, do you know what schizophrenia is? Do you know what Thorazine is?"

"I do not."

"Well, schizophrenia is a very bad mental disorder, where the afflicted can't tell the difference between right and wrong, can't think clearly, can't act normally in social situations, can't and doesn't have normal emotional responses — though I don't know how anyone can have 'normal emotional responses' in this hell hole. Thorazine is the drug of choice, the best drug we have, to treat folks who are schizophrenic. It — Thorazine — is supposed to help reduce agitation and the psychotic actions of the patient. Lieutenant, have you ever seen a Shetland pony?"

Woody wondered what the hell a Shetland pony had to do with a schizophrenic Apache Indian. "Yes I have."

"Well, after I received the request for the psyche eval, the first thing I did was to meet Abaya. It took me 5 minutes to diagnose the schizophrenia. I ordered Thorazine. We are now giving that guy enough Thorazine to sedate a damn Shetland pony, and there is no impact, whatsoever. I'm ordering him to the psychiatric ward at the Naval Hospital in Philadelphia. This war is over for him. There should be an order entered which ends this murder case 'cause I'm medically discharging him because he's out of his mind. I don't guess you won the case, but you didn't lose it, either. Anything else?", Hardison dismissed Woody.

"Yes, actually. Why the map of the Tar Heel state?"

"I'm from North Carolina."

"Whereabouts?" Woody asked.

"Small place, you've never heard of it, Everetts."

"In Martin County, Williamston is the county seat."

Hardison looked up as his jaw dropped." How the hell did you know that?"

"I'm from Greenville. I'll bet you were a Phi Gam at Carolina, too?"

Hardison got up and came around his desk and extended his right hand, which Woody shook. "Damn, you are one perceptive dude. What gave it away?"

"Well, the class ring was a clue, and I know guys from Greenville who went to Carolina and joined the Phi Gams and wear that ring. One of my golf buddies, Dick Henderson, is a Phi Gam. Do you know him?"

"Know him! He was my little brother. Great guy, even better athlete. For three years, he was voted best athlete in Phi Gam. Good student. He went to dental school at Carolina. Have a seat."

Woody and his new friend, Aaron Hardison, talked about eastern North Carolina, common acquaintances, and Wake Forest versus the Tar Heels, for about 20 minutes. Aaron — they were now on a first-name basis — promised to come to the O Club for beers in a couple of days. As he was leaving, Woody turned and asked Aaron, "Have you even been around, or used, or know anything about, sodium pentothal, the so-called truth serum."

"Yes, actually, I was involved in a study program during my residency which involved our administering it to defendants at Central Prison, in Raleigh, of course with the permission of their lawyers and the State. We weren't trying to do anything but see how it worked. Why?"

"No reason, just wondering. Well, I'll buy you a beer when you come over."

Woody knew it was time to shoot some more hoops with Mike and Kevin and discuss his meeting with his new friend, the shrink from Everetts.

1000 Hours, Sat, 9 Aug 69
Legal Office, Third Mar Div
Quang Tri
Chesty

After Woody told Fred that Dr. Hardison had declared Geronimo unfit for trial, he prepared the form to have that murder charge on Abaya dropped for medical reasons. He then he resumed reviewing the trial file in the Jackson case.

He pulled out the file of interviews prepared by Lieutenant Breckinridge and also examined the NIS interviews of the same six men. There was no variance in the interviews given to Breckinridge and the NIS, and what they had to say didn't look good for Jackson. Each of those interviewed — both by Breckenridge and the NIS — said they were with Jackson in an underground bunker, bitching about the mistakes Lieutenant Speight made on Dewey Canyon and Apache Snow, mistakes which they felt resulted in some WIAs. The notes summarizing the statements of each witness were to the effect that Speight was an inferior platoon leader who didn't know the basics of combat and who should be replaced. But, more importantly, the interview notes of each witness written both by Lt. Breckenridge and the NIS agents had Jackson saying that he wished the lieutenant was dead, that he then left the bunker, and later, each witness heard the grenade detonate. The interviews by the XO and NIS included an interview with PFC Douglas, who said he saw Jackson, and Marine named Grant, running from the direction of the lieutenant's hooch after the grenade exploded. Douglas said that even though it was nighttime, and even though the rain and wind from the typhoon was furious at the time, he said he could identify each man when it lightened. Douglas also said that Jackson and Grant were always hanging out together. Woody checked the trial record and saw that each of those six men testified. He made a mental note to compare their testimony at trial with the notes from Breckinridge and the NIS agents.

He then turned his attention to the actual transcript of Peterson's direct exam of Jackson. He had not previously seen a transcript from a trial or hearing,

The defendant was sworn in and questioned by Defense Counsel (DC):

DC — State your name, rank, service number and unit.

Witness — Ricardo Jackson, Lance Corporal USMC, 1025078, First platoon, Alpha 1/9.

DC — Did you throw a frag grenade into the hooch of Lt. Speight at VCB on 15 June 1969, or were you present at the hooch of Lt. Speight at VCB when a frag grenade was thrown into that hooch killing the lieutenant?

Woody thought: Nothing like going right for the bottom line, no foreplay or anything. He wanted to remember that tactic.

Witness — No sir.

DC — Before the grenade was thrown, were you in a bunker with the six Marines who testified previously for the government, talking about Lieutenant Speight?

Witness — Yes, sir.

DC — When you left that bunker, where did you go?

Witness — Back to my hooch.

DC — Was there anyone else in your hootch?

Witness — No, sir.

DC — Did anyone come into your hooch between the time you left the bunker and the time the grenade exploded?

Witness — No, sir.

DC — After you got to your hooch, did you leave it?

Witness — Yes, sir, I went to the head, right before the grenade exploded.

DC — Did you see anyone in the company area when you went to the head or after the grenade exploded?

Witness — No sir, I stayed down, didn't know what was going on.

DC — Did you go to, or from, the Lieutenant's hooch with Private Grant or anyone else the night the lieutenant was killed?

Witness — No, Sir.

DC — Did you make a comment in the presence of those Marines in the bunker that you wished that Lt. Speight was dead?

Witness — Yes, sir, I did.

DC — Did you mean that?

Witness — No sir, of course not.

DC — Well, if you didn't mean it, why did you say it?

Woody was so engrossed in the transcript that he didn't hear the two men come stand by his desk, but he sensed them. He looked up and saw Warrant Officer Masterson with a captain, whom he didn't know, who was wearing stateside utilities.

Masterson spoke: "Lieutenant White, I want you to meet our new lawyer, Captain Charles Brooker."

Woody stood up and extended his hand. "Hello, Charles."

Brooker did not extend his hand and glared at Woody and then said loud enough for everyone in the defense shop to hear him: "That's CAPTAIN Brooker to you, Lieutenant."

Woody had two thoughts at the same time: This guy was a first-class prick, and Woody wanted to embarrass the prick by being a super Marine. "Yes Sir, begging the Captain's pardon SIR! It will not happen again, **SIR**", all the time, standing at his best straight-backed attention.

"Well, it better not. And Lieutenant, just so you'll know. I'm gonna be in the trial shop, I've prosecuted before, and I don't give deals, understand."

"Yes sir, the lieutenant understands the captain, Sir!"

Masterson spoke. "Well, I guess we best meet some other officers, Captain. Lieutenant, we will see you later, maybe at the O Club."

Woody answered, "Sure thing Mr. Masterson. By the way, Mr. Masterson, I don't think the captain can beat Bull."

Brooker took the bait. "Who is Bull?"

Masterson answered. "Sir, he is the arm-wrestling champ of Third Mar Div legal — never been beaten."

"Well" Brooker said, "we'll see about that."

As Masterson and Brooker left the legal office, Woody resumed reading the transcript, but he wanted to be sure to get a front row at the arm wrestling, with a mug of Pepsi — this prick needed something syrupy to go with the beer.

Woody had to hand it to Major Forrest. He played the Brooker versus Bull arm-wrestling match almost verbatim to Woody's experience. Woody had appreciated his own 'initiation' because it helped make him feel that he was 'one of the guys' of Third Mar Div Legal when he was hosed with the beer. He wondered how Brooker would act.

They found out that Brooker was a different breed, because when 22 mugs of beer, and one mug of Pepsi, hit Brooker, he came up swinging at Bull. It took Major Forrest to pull rank on Captain Brooker to get him cooled down. Brooker stormed off towards the shower and everyone else went back into the bar.

In a few minutes Brooker returned, clean and wearing his new jungle utilities. He also was wearing a shoulder holster, with his.45 pistol in it. He was the only person in the bar with a firearm. No one said anything about it, but just glanced at each other, thinking — what the hell is he going to do with that thing!

Then Brooker asked a question that stopped everyone in their tracks. "Is there any way I can go on a LP?"

Fred looked at him as if he were crazy. "What do you mean, a LP?"

"You know, a listening post, where two guys go out from the base, find a good place to hide, establish a listening post to listen for the Cong or the North Vietnam Army, and report their position so the enemy can be wiped out. We learned all about them at TBS, don't you remember?"

Fred answered. "Yeah, we all know what a LP is but just wanted to know if that was what you were asking about. It's real easy to get killed in one of those LPs, 'cause if the bad guys find you, you are outnumbered and will get wasted. That's nuts."

Woody was looking at Brooker's face when Fred responded to Brooker, and noticed that his eyes were darting around the room, that he had a big upper lip, and even though the O Club was air conditioned, there was sweat on his upper lip and his brow. His hands were twitching, too. And then it hit Woody where he had seen someone look and act like that: Humphrey Bogart as Captain Queeg in the movie *The Caine Mutiny*, in the scene when Queeg was testifying and rolling the ball bearings in his hands. Brooker went to the bar to get a soda. The guy didn't even drink beer!

McMurry spoke up, "Who does he think he is, Chesty Puller? He wants to try to win four Navy Crosses like Puller did in WWII, and he doesn't care about his own ass, which means he doesn't care about yours either. He's a guy you need to stay away from. We need to knock him down a peg or two, and I've got just the plan." McMurry laid out his plan for the following Friday, while 'Chesty' was at the bar, ordering his Orange Crush.

As the bar crowd thinned, Woody told McMurry that he wanted some of him one-on-one basketball for $5.00 tomorrow afternoon. He was ready to talk about truth serum and the Shrink from Everetts.

The next day was Sunday, and Woody had a new case to prepare before he met McMurry for hoops at 1730 hours, because the trial of this case was set for the next Saturday. Nine days between assignment of case and the trial of that case! Woody thought the Corps' trial schedule gave a whole new meaning to the concept of 'speedy trial'.

PFC Charles Battle — Woody thought his client at least had a good name for a Marine — was charged with larceny, a violation of Article 121 of the UCMJ. The file contained to following charge:

In that PFC Charles Battle did, at Vandegrift Combat Base, in Quang Tri Province, the Republic of South Vietnam, on or about 3

August 1969, steal a tape deck, of a value of approximately $125.00,
the property of Lance Corporal Michael Pollard.

The case file contained a report from NIS which disclosed that
Battle was seen leaving Pollard's hooch carrying a tape deck at a time
when no one was in the hooch; that Pollard reported to NIS that his
tape deck was missing; that NIS found the eyewitness and NIS
obtained a search warrant for Battle's hooch and found the tape deck,
and Battle was then charged. When Woody had finished reading the
file, he made arrangements to have Battle report to his office.

Woody had just entered the door to the trial lawyers' office when
Chesty yelled out. "Hey. White, I bet you're here to make a deal on
Battle, 'cause I heard you were assigned to defend that scumbag. Well,
I'm prosecuting, and there ain't no deal. I'm going for a bad conduct
discharge — don't need thieves in the Corps. And one more thing —
you need to pay attention at this trial, and you will learn exactly how
to get a conviction with a search warrant. It's my specialty."

Woody decided to play along with the bastard. "Yes, sir, the
lieutenant will pay attention and learn from the captain. Thank you,
sir!"

He saw McMurry, made a hand gesture as if he were dribbling a
basketball, McMurry nodded, and Woody left to get his workout gear
on to shoot hoops.

"What is with this guy, Chesty?" Woody asked McMurry. "He's a nut
case. First, he volunteers to go on an LP, then he is so damn
unprofessional — yelling at me like that in your office. You ever met
anyone like that?'

"Yep, and that guy turned out to be a psyche case, busted out of
the Corps. Frankly, if Chesty keeps it up, as chief trial counsel, I'm
going to do what I can to get him sent to another unit. I can't discuss
the details with you, but he has caused a number of issues within our
trial group. We were good to go before he got here, but he stirs the shit
pot so much it stinks all the time. It's tough enough being here without

having that kind of situation. Anyway, what's up? You got something for me?"

Woody replied, "Yes I do. Turns out I met a Navy shrink about a psyche eval in a murder case — you know, the Apache who killed the black guy. We actually grew up 30 miles apart, if you can believe it. Small world. He acted like he was better than I before I told him we were kinda neighbors. Had mutual friends, and so on. Anyway, I just casually asked him if he knew anything about truth serum, and it turns out he does — had some study work with it during med school at Carolina, with some prisoners at Central Prison in Raleigh, which is near Chapel Hill. He wanted to know why, but I just told him I was curious. I have the gut feeling that he would help us by conducting a truth serum exam, assuming he can get some of that med. By the way, have you heard when Colonel Suarez rotates back home?"

McMurry smiled, "Funny you should ask. We just got the word from WO Masterson that the colonel's orders to rotate back home just came in. Going away party in a few days. His replacement comes, or is scheduled to come, in the next few days."

"Who is the replacement? What do you know about him?

"Well, he's from Tyler, Texas, the eastern part of Texas. He's a reservist bird colonel, and he is a county prosecutor. That's probably not good for us, you know, a 'law and order' kind of guy, you know 'the jury has spoken' and that's that."

Woody asked. "So, how do you plan to talk to the new SJA about Jackson to convince him to let us do what we can for Jackson?"

"Well, he'll want me and Kevin, as chief trial counsels, to give him a stat report on all the cases. At the end of that report, I'm going to just lay it out, and hope he is the kind of guy who puts a premium on taking a real good look at justice. I'll tell him what we've done, and what you're doing. I hope he'll be ok with all of it and give us his blessing to move forward, not only with the truth serum, but maybe also with a legit polygraph. Of course, Jackson could pass both the truth serum and a lie detector with flying colors and the colonel could still recommend approval of the conviction and sentence to the commanding general. At the end of the day, the CG makes the legal call. Polygraphs and truth serum tests are not in the legal playbook.

"What did you mean, legit polygraph? Has there been an illegitimate polygraph done?"

McMurry stopped dribbling. "Yep. During our trial prep, Lt. Peterson, Jackson's lawyer, came to us, told us he was convinced Jackson didn't do it in spite of Douglas' statement, and asked us to have a polygraph test run, with the agreement that the results would not be disclosed to anyone, and of course they aren't admissible. He wanted Jackson to take one, and since it couldn't be used even if he passed, we had nothing to lose. I guess Peterson, who is a damn good lawyer, thought if he passed it would sway us in some fashion. Well, from Jackson's position, it went over like a fart in a church. Showed he was lying about not being involved. But — and here's the rub — the exam was a farce. Do you know anything about the polygraph?"

"Not really. Why was it a farce?"

"Well, what I know about the polygraph can be written on a note card with space left over, but the idea behind it is that they measure pulse, maybe blood pressure or perspiration — in other words, how the examinee's body physically reacts when he is asked, and when he answers, the questions. I guess the idea is that if his heart rate jumps, or his blood pressure pops up, or whatever, he may be lying. But the questions have to be correctly formulated, correctly asked and to the point, and the examiner can't be out of control. I guess someone can get a bump in the BP if they're being yelled at, even if they are telling the truth when asked if they killed someone. The examiner was a gunny sergeant from Mississippi — a brown noser admin guy. Don't know who picked him, or if he had qualifications to conduct the test, but I was there. He was terrible. Made me sick to my stomach the way the gunny conducted himself and the way he framed his questions. I couldn't have passed it, and I wasn't at VCB when the fragging took place. So, we need to try a legit polygraph. After that — I don't know."

Woody thought a minute, "Well, maybe we're making some progress. But I need to finish my prep for a case Saturday. Captain "Chesty" has bragged all over the place that he is going to kick my ass in this larceny case, and the bad news is that a first year law school student could prosecute and win the case., I just hate losing to a blowhard like him even though it is impossible for me to win the case."

"Well", McMurry said, "off the record I hope you pull it out. He needs to come down a notch or two. By the way, did you hear what we have planned for him this Friday noon, with the siren?"

"Yes, and I'm looking forward to it."

1130 Hours, Fri, 15 Aug 69
Legal Office, Third Mar Div
Quang Tri
Siren at High Noon

The first time Woody heard the siren at HQ was about three seconds after the first rocket hit the base at Quang Tri, on his first night in country. It was the unit's way of warning the men of the HQ, Third Marine Division, to get in their foxhole or bunker during the incoming.

Woody had been in country for a couple of Fridays and knew that at noon every Friday, the siren was tested just to make sure it worked.

On Friday, 15 August, everyone but Chesty Brooker, who was spending his first Friday in Quang Tri, knew the siren would be tested at noon.

When the lawyers started gathering for chow at about 1130 hours on Friday, they started talking up the possibility of there being a rocket attack on the base. One of the trial counsel said, "You know, it has been about three weeks since rockets hit the base. Plus, it's coming up on a full moon and they seem to like to hit us then." Another lawyer piped up: "You know, I don't know how many rockets they hit us with last time, but I thought the incoming would never stop."

This went on for about five minutes before Chesty spoke, "Do you really think there is a possibility we may get hit? You know if you're in an area where shrapnel hits, you can get the Combat Action Ribbon." If anyone had a doubt as to whether Chesty was nuts, they no longer did.

The trial and defense counsel had one hour for lunch, and since the chow hall for their area was near their bunking areas, they were usually heading back to their hooches by 1145 hours, to take a load off before resuming work at 1230 hours. One of the trial counsel suggested again it would be a good day for the bad guys to hit them.

Almost every lawyer had a fan, with green blades, hooked on the foot end of his rack. It got so hot that guys would lay down, take down their utility trousers (nobody wore skivvies) to their boots, and let the fans cool their private parts. There was no effort for privacy in the Corps. Chesty and all of the trial counsel had assumed this position by 1150 hours on Chesty's first Friday in Vietnam. They kept up the talk about the possibility of incoming.

The siren began with a low growl and then grew louder. At the first growl, McMurry yelled, "INCOMING!! I think it's gas. Get your gas masks", and then he started running for the above-ground bunker, the go-to place for legal when there was an attack. Everyone in the hooch followed him. Chesty was on his rack when the siren started its growl, with the fan blowing on his privates, and his utility trousers down at his feet.

Chesty rolled out of his rack and started stumbling for the above-ground bunker. He was trying to pull up his jungle utilities as he ran, but was losing that battle, in part because he was using only one hand. The other hand was holding his officer's.45 caliber pistol.

Chesty fell into the bunker with the other lawyers, all of whom were laughing at Chesty's efforts to get to the bunker. The siren stopped after about thirty seconds. Chesty had finally pulled up his utilities and was looking to the sky, holding his pistol. "Chesty, what the hell are you gonna do with your.45, shoot down the rocket?" As the lawyers made their way back to their hooch, they noted that Chesty's reaction to the episode was not that a joke had been played on him. Rather, his reaction was summed up in his question: "Do you think any rocket will ever hit in our area?" He wanted that CAR.

0800 Hours, Monday, 18 Aug 69
Courtroom, Third Mar Div
Quang Tri
US Government vs. Battle

Woody had entered a not guilty plea for PFC Battle. The ASJA, Major Forrest, was presiding as military judge. 'Judge Bean' and two lieutenants were the panel deciding guilt or innocence. Chesty called his first witness, a private named Swanson. After having the private give his name, rank, service number and unit, Chesty began his questioning.

"Private, did you see the defendant, PFC Battle, on 3 August 1969, at Vandegrift Combat Base, with a tape deck?"

"Yes sir, I did. He took a tape deck into his hooch."

"Later that day, did you hear a tape deck had been stolen."

"Yes sir, I did. I went to my CO and reported what I saw."

"Did you later talk to NIS Agent Wilfong?"

"Yes sir, I did. I signed a paper he typed up saying that I saw Battle go into his hooch with a tape deck."

Chesty approached the witness box, "Is this the paper you signed?"

"Yes, sir, it is."

Chesty addressed Major Forrest, the trial judge, "The government moves to introduce the affidavit of Pvt. Swanson as Government's Exhibit 1."

After reviewing the documents, Woody had no choice, "No objection, your Honor."

"It is received as Government's Exhibit number 1. Proceed Captain Brooker", the judge instructed.

Chesty walked back to the prosecution table. "Private Swanson, come down from the witness chair and look at this tape deck on this table. Is this the tape deck which I have marked as Government Exhibit 2, the tape deck you saw the defendant with?"

"Yes, sir, looks like it."

"Your honor", Chesty addressed the court, "we move for the introduction of Exhibit 2, and have no further questions of Private Swanson."

Woody stood up. "Your honor, no objections to the introduction of the tape deck as an exhibit and no questions of Private Swanson."

"Very well", the judge announced, "Does the government have other witnesses?"

"Yes sir, we call NIS Agent Nifong."

After Agent Nifong was sworn and identified himself, Chesty began his questions. "Agent, did you have a meeting with Private Swanson, who just testified, on 3 August 1969, at VCB?"

"Yes, sir, I did."

"Did you prepare this affidavit signed by Swanson, which has been introduced as Government's Exhibit 1?"

"Yes, sir I did."

"What did you do after you prepared the affidavit?"

"I took the affidavit and Swanson to an officer who was assigned judicial duties at VCB, and told him that I believed the affidavit was legally sufficient for him to issue a search warrant which permitted me to search the hooch of PFC Battle."

"Agent Nifong, did that judicial official issue a search warrant?"

"Yes, sir he did."

"And is this document, which I have marked as Government's Exhibit 3, the search warrant that was issued?"

"It is."

"After obtaining the search warrant, what did you do?"

"Sir, I left the office of the judicial official who issued it and went to the hooch of PFC Battle and executed the search warrant. PFC Battle was there, the tape deck was there, so I secured possession of the tape deck and placed the defendant under arrest for larceny of the tape deck."

"Agent, has this tape deck been in your possession continuously since the day you obtained it from the defendant's hooch?"

"Yes, sir, it has. It has been in our evidence locker until I personally brought it to this courtroom today, and it has not been tampered with. That tape deck, Exhibit 2, is the tape deck I obtained from the defendant's hooch."

Chesty announced, "No further questions of Agent Nifong your honor."

Woody stood up. "The defense has no questions of the agent."

The judge spoke. "Very well, Agent Nifong, you are excused. Captain Brooker, any further evidence."

"No, sir, the Government of the United States of America rests."

Woody immediately stood up. "Your honor, I must say that was the best presentation of the obtaining and execution of a search warrant perhaps in the history of jurisprudence, and it was, just as advertised on number of public occasions by Captain Brooker, a veritable model of how to do it. Having said that, the Defense makes a motion for directed verdict of not guilty."

Chesty jumped from his chair. "What do you mean, directed verdict. You just said it was a perfect search and seizure."

Major Forrest intervened. "Captain Brooker, please have a seat. Lieutenant White, on what basis do you make your motion." Woody was looking at the judge when he was asked that question, and he sensed the judge knew exactly why he had made the motion.

"Well, your honor, the elements of the crime of larceny include the element that the property allegedly stolen belonged to someone who did not give permission for the defendant to take the property. In this specification, the government alleged the tape deck belonged to a Marine named Pollard. The Government, through Captain Brooker, rested its case without presenting evidence that the tape deck belonged to anyone, much less Pollard."

The judge looked at Brooker. "Do you have a comment, Captain Brooker?'

Brooker didn't respond for a few seconds, then he stood up." Your honor, the failure to call Pollard was just an oversight, and I would like to call him now. He's right here", pointing to the front row of the courtroom.

Woody had remained standing. "Your honor, I wrote it down, because I wanted to learn from Captain Brooker how to try a case, because he told me he was going to show me how it is done. And just a minute ago, he said, 'The Government of the United States rests'. I have it written right here. That means, he's through with his evidence. I can show it to you Captain Brooker. I abbreviated Government, but here it is. Here, Captain Brooker, do you want to see what I wrote when you said the government rested?"

Brooker took a step toward Woody, whose trial desk was less than five feet from Brooker's. His right fist was balled up. He was ready to throw a punch.

"GENTLEMEN," the judge yelled to get their attention, "we will take a break. I want both of you in my chambers. Captain Brooker, you go first, and then, Lieutenant White, you follow."

The judge's chambers were not much larger than a walk-in closet of a rich woman who loved dresses and shoes, but it did have a desk and chair, at which Major Forrest sat. He addressed Captain Brooker first. "Captain, you made an aggressive move toward Lieutenant White in my courtroom. I want to assure you that should that occur again, I will personally obtain the appropriate specification naming you as defendant. Understood?"

Brooker was contrite. "Yes sir."

"Now, Captain Brooker, I am giving you the opportunity to state your case why I should not grant the motion to dismiss made by Lieutenant White."

"Well, sir, it was just an oversight. We all knew whose tape deck it was. The specification listed it. I just think the ends of justice will be met if I am permitted to reopen my case to call Pollard to ID the tape deck. He's here, sitting on the front row."

The judge looked at Woody. "Lieutenant White, what do you have to say about the request of Captain Brooker?'

"Well, sir, I just don't know how freely I can talk. After all, he is a captain, and I'm just a second lieutenant, as the captain has frequently reminded me. I'm afraid if I speak frankly, I could get in trouble."

Brooker spoke up. "No, no way. You speak as freely as you want, Buddy. I won't hold anything against you. We're all Marine brothers."

Woody looked at the judge. "Your Honor, may I then be assured that I can speak freely and without repercussions."

"Absolutely, you can."

Woody turned and faced Brooker. "You know, when I first met you, I extended my hand in friendship, and called you by your first name. You didn't shake my hand, and you ordered me to call you 'Captain'. You are the only officer in legal who insists that I salute you, even within our little area. You don't ask that of any other lieutenant. When this case was assigned to me, you publicly made a point, both in your office and at the chow hall, that you were the best, you were going to kick my ass, and you were going to show me how to try a case. And now that you've screwed up the Government's case, you're all 'BUDDY-BUDDY'. But most importantly, you want me to turn my back on my responsibility to my client, and let Pollard testify it was his tape deck, and then the military panel would convict unless they are brain dead. You want me to forget the lessons I learned from the dean of my law school at Wake Forest, that we owed all our responsibility to our clients, no one else, that we could not turn our back on the client, even if he were guilty. You want to be my 'good buddy' so I can bail you out. Well, here is my answer, sir." Woody came to attention. "Hell no sir", and did as crisp an about face as he could and left the room.

Brooker didn't come to the O Club that night. Woody was congratulated on winning the case, even though his client was guilty as hell, and he didn't have to buy any drinks — that was taken care of not only by the defense shop but also by the prosecutors. As they left for the chow hall, Mike McMurry walked beside Woody. "Brooker has requested to be transferred to First Division legal, in Da Nang. His request has been granted. He will be someone else's problem in two days. And, I've got some news about our case. We need to shoot some baskets tomorrow at 1700."

1700 Hours, Tues, 19 Aug 69
Legal Office, Third Mar Div
Quang Tri
There's a New Sheriff in Town

Woody had to admit that McMurry had a decent jump shot and could handle the ball pretty well. They played a little one-on-one, worked up a sweat, which only took five minutes, and then stood under the goal. No one else was on the court.

McMurry spoke. "Suarez is having his going-away party tomorrow night and Masterson told me he will be on a flight from here at 0700 the next day. I guess he's going back to New Mexico and show he's a hero and run for judge. The new colonel is supposed to arrive sometime tomorrow afternoon. I doubt he will go to the party if he is here. Kevin and I plan to meet with him when he tells us he wants to see us. After I give him a report on pending cases, I'll tell him what's going on about Jackson. I'm going to shoot straight with him though, meaning we think the trial may have been error free, but we nevertheless have concerns and want some time to explore everything — even following stuff that happened outside the trial. We just hope he'll let us run the rabbit. If he doesn't, then the transcript and record will go to him and he'll do whatever he thinks the situation warrants in making his recommendation to the commanding general. I hope our talk to him will encourage him to tell the general the case is not yet ready for recommendation and give us time to do what we need to do to get to the bottom line."

Woody said, "Well, thanks for keeping me posted. Let me know what I can do.

Masterson addressed both Mike McMurry and Kevin Ross: "Colonel Sullivan will see you now". The trial counsels had prepared a list of pending cases with explanations of the status of each case as a report to the new ALJ: Was the investigation complete; the anticipated date of the trial; difficulties in contacting and interviewing witnesses who were in the field — as thorough a rundown as they could prepare.

The colonel stood when they came into his office and walked around his desk to shake their hands. "Captain, Lieutenant, I'm pleased to meet you. Take a load off and sit." He talked in a flat twang. McMurry thought that at least he was cordial and not too formal, which could be unusual for a bird colonel.

Colonel Bill Sullivan sat behind his desk, which was barren. He put his feet on the corner of the desk and sat back in his seat. "Either of you men chew?" He was digging his fingers into a pack of Red Man chewing tobacco as he asked the question. He pulled out the dark brown strands of Red Man, made it into a ball, and popped the ball in his left cheek and then offered the bag to McMurry and Ross, both of whom declined.

"Probably not a nastier or more unhealthy habit known to man, but, god, I do love it. Got started on a day when I was playing golf in early November. Either of you play golf?" They shook their heads. "Well, in east Texas, where I'm from, the wind blows like a banshee, and if the temp is down just a bit, it can get as cold as a well-digger's ass in Alaska. One such day, I was warming up hitting some wedges, freezing my ass. My best golfing buddy, my dentist no less, came out and started hitting shots next to me. He heard me griping about the weather, reached into his bag, pulled out a toboggan, told me to put it on, which I did, and he then handed me some Red Man. He told me to take just a small bit, put it in my left cheek, don't swallow, and in 30 seconds I'd think I was standing next to a fire. He was right. Been chewing ever since. They even have spittoons in our county courtroom, but I don't chew in a courtroom. That's kind of a sacred place, if you know what I mean.

"I'm told you two are the top prosecutors of the Third Mar Div and have been for several months. I guess you brought a status report on the cases, right?" They nodded.

"Well, here's the way I see it. I'm a bird colonel, an O-6. Each of you are O-3s. You work for me. I've been told you know what you're doing, individually and jointly, that you are top notch trial lawyers, excellent administrators, and keep track what is going on. Don't be falsely modest — is that an accurate assessment?"

McMurry and Ross each nodded, 'yes'.

"Well, good. I respect a man who is confident about his work. I don't micromanage people who work for me. I let them do their job. They can come to me with a problem and I'll fix it if it should be fixed and if it is in my power to fix. Don't come to me with a problem without at least two possible solutions. If you mess up your work by being stupid or negligent, I'll be on you like white on rice. I'm probably the most informal bird colonel in the Corps, with people I trust and like. Any questions about my MO?"

"No sir", McMurry said and Ross agreed.

"Good. I don't need to know about the routine stuff — you're paid to handle it, and by all accounts, you're doing a good job. Is there anything unusual you need, or want, to tell me about?"

McMurry answered. "Yes, sir, there is. It will take a few minutes. We prosecuted a Marine named Jackson, with 1/9, for murder, accessory after the fact to murder and conspiracy to murder his platoon leader, a lieutenant, who was killed by a frag grenade. A Marine named Grant is also charged with the same offenses, but he hasn't been tried. Jackson was convicted on the accessory and conspiracy counts and acquitted on the murder charge. The record has not been completed for the SJA's review and recommendation to the CG, but, frankly, the trial probably has no reversible, prejudicial error. After the trial, we each, independently, came to the conclusion we may have charged, tried, and the court martial panel may have convicted, a Marine who didn't do it. And we concluded for the same reasons. The reasons we…"

Colonel Sullivan held up his hand, and McMurry stopped. "I don't need to know the facts. You tried the case. You've got a gut feeling you convicted the wrong man. What was his sentence?"

"Ten years on each count, to run consecutively, at Leavenworth, loss of rank and pay, and a dishonorable discharge."

"What have you done about this up to now?"

"Sir, we felt it would be good to get a different set of eyes on this 'cause we're so close to the forest we can't see the trees. After the conviction, a second lieutenant lawyer, fresh out of Justice School, reported for duty and was put in the defense shop. He appeared to know what he was doing in a couple of cases, and because he knew nothing about the Jackson case, we asked him if he'd like to help, on his own time. We cleared that with the head of the defense shop."

"So to sum up," the colonel said, "you two tried a man whom you think may be innocent, based mostly on your gut instincts. You want as much time as I can give you for a chance to see if you can find something justifying your gut feelings, and you've got a rookie helping you, right?"

"Yes, sir, that sums it up perfectly," Ross replied.

The colonel was silent a few seconds, and then spoke. "In my second year of practice, I represented a guy charged with stealing a car. It was found on the street in front of his house. It was stolen between 10pm and midnight the night before — the owner knew that time frame. My guy told me he was in an illegal poker game from 9pm until 2am, walked home and didn't notice the car when he got to his house. But — and here's the rub, he didn't know the real names of any of the guys at the poker game who could support his alibi. He could describe them, and knew their nicknames, but not their real names. His alibi was that he was at an illegal poker game, with five guys he didn't know before or after the game. His goose was at least in the oven, even if the oven hadn't been turned on to cook it. But then, a detective working another case, whom I had a case against and whom I treated fairly and with respect, heard about my case and mentioned to me that one of his witnesses in some other case had been in a poker game the night the car was stolen, didn't know anyone, but knew the game lasted from 9 to 2. The detective arranged a lineup for his witness in the other case to view six guys, one of whom was my man, and that guy ID'd my man as being at the poker game. The DA dropped the case against my man. I understand we can't be too tight-assed with the justice system, so unless you guys did something really stupid by doing something you should not have done, and it doesn't seem like you have, I'm going to give you some time, though not a lot, 'cause my boss, the Commanding General, will be interested in finalizing a case because an officer was murdered. What is the name of the lieutenant helping you?"

McMurry gave the Colonel Woody's name. "Both of you go get Lieutenant White, and let him know he's not in any trouble. Ya'll come back with him in the next 30 minutes. I've got some papers to push, and I really love doing that." McMurry and Ross laughed at the sarcasm. They liked their boss.

"Lieutenant White, where'd you go school and law school." The three lawyers were standing in front of Colonel Sullivan's desk. "And all of you have a seat."

Woody sat down and answered the colonel. "Sir, I went to Wake Forest College and Wake law school."

"Are you a Baptist?"

"No, sir, and if I ever thought about being a Baptist, those mandatory chapels twice weekly cured me of that."

The colonel leaned back in his chair and put his feet on his desk. He wore what Woody called 'chucker boots', which he had seen before, worn by Sheriff Andy Taylor on the popular Andy Griffith tv show. The colonel had put on a cowboy hat which was tilted back on his head. He reached in his pocket and pulled out his Red Man and took some to add to the chew that was already puffing out his cheek. "Lieutenant White, would you like a chew?"

"Actually, I would sir. Thank you."

McMurry piped up. "How did you get started on chewing?"

"Well, one day during Christmas break, my senior year in college, we were hitting balls to loosen up for a golf match. Our driving range faces north, and there was a cold wind blowing from the north. I told my buddy that I was cold as hell and he said to try these, and he handed me a toboggan and a pack of Red Man. He said they would warm me right up, and he was right. Don't use it a lot, but every now and then, it's ok."

Everyone laughed and looked at the colonel. Woody looked around. "What's wrong?"

The colonel answered, "Nothing, Lieutenant, but I think you and I are gonna get along just fine. Now, what's the plan?"

"Well, I need to talk to Lance Corporal Jackson. Haven't done that yet 'cause I wanted to get familiar with the entire file. I need to go over the testimony against him and talk to him about the witnesses who testified. I need to compare their before-trial interviews with their testimony, and I need him to trace his steps for me the night of the murder. I probably need to get out to VCB to see the area — kinda get a feel for the place. Then, I'd like to get a doctor to give him some truth serum, sodium whatever it is, and see what his answers are under that, and then give him a polygraph. And there could be some step I should take that won't show up until it shows up."

The colonel spoke up. "How are you gonna get him shot up with truth serum in Vietnam?"

"Sir, I had a murder case and met a Navy shrink — psychiatrist, who has actually done that before, and I'm pretty confidant he'd help."

The colonel put his boots back up on his desk and leaned back. He thought for a minute or so. "You know, I'll say it again. This is a long shot. But the plan sounds like a good one, given the limitations of being in a war zone, and given the fact it was a good trial and a reasonable verdict. You know, when I meet with the division CG, he'll for sure want a status report on this, and I can stretch it out a little bit — you know, in good professional conscience, I can tell him the transcript is being finished and we're making sure the record is perfect for the appeal. But there will come a time when, as his SJA, I've gotta tell him to approve or reverse the conviction, and my guess is that he ain't gonna be impressed with truth serum, a polygraph, or gut reactions, as reasons to free a man convicted in an up-an-up trial —

assuming no prejudicial error — of the fragging of a Marine lieutenant while he was sleeping. But I'll give you three some rope to do some work on this. There is no need to put or keep me in the loop on this project. I suggest you move with dispatch, 'cause I don't know when the CG will want my recommendation.

"I promise I'll tell him what you have done, but I can't recommend that he overturn the conviction unless there is some legal meat on the 'free-Jackson bone', so to speak, when I give my report. Unless there's something else, thanks to all of you. That's all."

It always felt hotter when you left an air-conditioned building, and all three lawyers were sweating within moments after leaving the colonel's office. McMurry spoke. "Well, that could not have gone better. You need to get over to the brig ASAP, introduce yourself to Jackson and start the process. To keep control of this, we need to meet daily, even if it turns out we don't have anything to discuss. Is that ok?"

Woody nodded, but his mind was elsewhere. He was wondering how his meeting with Jackson would go.

1300 Hours, Thur, 21 Aug 69
Third Mar Div
Quang Tri
Woody's First Trip to the Brig

Woody decided he needed to meet with Jackson sooner rather than later, even though there were parts of the trial file with which he was not totally familiar. He hoped he could form a bond with Jackson in order to maximize Jackson's opportunity to help.

Mr. Masterson drove Woody to the brig which was about a mile from Legal. "You ever been to a brig, Lieutenant?" Masterson asked. Woody shook his head. "Well, be prepared for a lot of noise — can't do much to shut up a man in prison. It will smell to high heaven — each man gets one shower a week. The so-called 'interview room' is secure, but you hear all the going's on like you were in a cell yourself. The guards escort your client to the room and stand outside, ready to help you if you need it. Believe it or not, some of those guys go after the very lawyers who are trying to help them. They come into the meeting without cuffs or shackles but can be restrained in seconds if they get out of line. You should be safe. What's the guy charged with?"

Woody had agreed with McMurry and Ross that no one else should know what Woody was doing, even though they had the colonel's blessing, and the last person he would tell would be Mr. Masterson. The warrant officer was a godsend to everyone in legal — he knew where to get stuff, and how to get things done, better than anyone. But he dearly loved to shoot the bull, and there was no way Woody would trust him to keep quiet about what Woody was doing. "I'm seeing a Corporal Gaskins charged with larceny." It was true that

Woody had a client named Gaskins in the brig, who was charged with larceny, so he had his cover. "I'll expect to be with him for a couple of hours."

"Well, just get someone at the brig to give me a call if you can't hitch a ride and I'll come get you."

The brig area was much bigger than Woody had envisioned. It was constructed of cinder block, with walls about forty-feet high. There was both barbed wire and concertina wire stretched at the top of the walls. There were guard towers at the four corners of the brig fence, each manned by a Marine with a M-60 machine gun on a tripod. It was quite a powerful weapon, definitely a deterrent to an escape attempt. There were spotlights positioned at each corner.

Woody entered the brig building through a steel door and went to the admin office and told the corporal on duty who he was and who he wanted to see. The corporal told a PFC to get Jackson, and Woody was shown to a room which had one table, two chairs and a window on the door. There were two Marines outside the door, both of whom looked like they could have played in the line for the Washington Redskins. Neither wore side arms or had a rifle, so if they were overpowered, the prisoners wouldn't get the weapons. Each had nightsticks about two feet long. Woody had no doubt they could handle any problem. He hoped he would not need their help.

He knew he would not need their help when the door opened and a man who was only about five and a half feet tall and who weighed maybe 140 pounds came into the room. Jackson looked like he was in the ninth grade. His face was pock-marked with acne, and he had the biggest nose Woody had ever seen this side of Karl Mauldin, who had starred with Steve McQueen in one of Woody's favorite movies, *The Cincinnati Kid*. Jackson looked at Woody but just stood at the closed door.

Woody spoke. "My name is White. I'm your defense lawyer. I need to talk to you. Have a seat."

Jackson didn't move. Woody knew this part of the meeting would be difficult, because Jackson didn't know who he was, and the only man Jackson knew from the defense legal shop had been his lawyer, Lieutenant Peterson, who had rotated back to the States. There was no one Jackson knew who could introduce Woody to Jackson as a man he could trust. Woody knew Jackson had to be one scared guy, half a world away from family and facing 20 years at Leavenworth. Woody had given a lot of thought as to how to gain Jackson's trust, and could only hope his plan would work.

Woody spoke. "There are three people in the world who think you may be innocent and who want to try to prove it. I'm one of those people. The other two are the Marine captain and the Navy lieutenant, McMurry and Ross, who prosecuted you. You've got absolutely nothing in the world to lose by talking to me, and you've got everything in the world to lose if you DON'T talk to me, because I need your help if I'm going to help you."

Jackson moved away from the door, toward the table, but stopped about 5 feet away from the empty chair. "What can you do for me?"

"Well, for starters, I can tell you that when I got in-country after your trial, the officers who prosecuted you came to me to ask my help in seeing if maybe they had charged and convicted the wrong man, that I've read some of the trial transcript, that I've got some ideas to work on that may help you, and that the Staff Judge Advocate for the Third Marine Division, a bird colonel, knows and approves of what we are doing. You are now my client, and you and I need to talk."

Jackson moved to the table, pulled out the chair, sat down, and looked at Woody. His eyes started to fill with tears, which flowed down his cheeks. "I did NOT kill that lieutenant."

"Did you hear the grenade explode?" Woody had earlier decided to cut to the chase in the interview.

"I did, but it was thundering and lightening that night, and raining like hell so I didn't go see what was going on."

"Where were you when you heard the grenade."

"In my hooch."

"Was there anyone else in the hooch?"

Jackson moved his head slowly back and forth. "No sir. I don't know where everyone was then. It was late, we'd come in from an op and were on stand down because of the storm. Some guys got some beer from somewhere, and there was some weed some guys had they were smoking in a underground bunker. I left the guys in the bunker and was in my hooch when the grenade exploded."

"So, you were in the bunker with the other guys before you went to your hooch?"

"Yes, in the underground bunker."

"Who was in the bunker when you left it?"

Jackson named Radcliff, Jonesy, Parker, Walters, Evans and Douglas, who were the same men named by the witnesses as being in the bunker when Jackson left. Woody had read and re-read the statements of the men taken by the NIS and by the IO, Lieutenant Breckinridge. "What did you say about Lieutenant Speight when you were in the bunker?"

Jackson put his hands in his face. His body heaved as he sobbed. "I was really pissed at that lieutenant. He fucked up — -sorry, sir, I didn't — "

Woody held up his hand and told Jackson to not worry about cussing and to keep talking. "I — all of us talked about the screw-ups he got us into, on Dewey Canyon and Apache Snow. We were in the field…"

Woody spoke. "Lance Corporal, I don't care what happened in the field. That can't be changed. And whatever mistakes he made, he didn't deserve being murdered. But what I want to know is what you remember saying to those men in the bunker about the lieutenant."

"I just said that the lieutenant was a shitty officer, that he should not have been in a command position, that we tried — or the staff sergeant tried — to give him some pointers about what not to do, and what to do, that he got the platoon in bad spots and got guys killed and wounded, and that I wished he was dead. Then I left the bunker. What they said in court was true — I did say I wished he was dead, but I didn't mean it."

Woody had another question. "About the Marine, Douglas, who testified he saw you and Grant running from the direction of the lieutenant's hooch after the grenade exploded, did you see him that night after you left the bunker?"

"No sir, he was wrong, I was never with Grant that night."

Woody continued his questioning. "Did you get along OK with Douglas? Was there ever any trouble — anything at all — between the two of you? I'm trying to figure out any reason why he might lie about seeing you?"

"No sir, he and I never had a problem. But he didn't see me 'cause I wasn't with Grant."

Woody had more questions. He had to get a picture of Alpha's area at VCB. He remembered Mr. Cavanaugh's asking questions about directions to the lady who said she had been assaulted in the Mill Run Valley case. "I haven't been to VCB yet. If I stood in the front of your hooch, where is the bunker, the lieutenant's hooch, the head and Douglas' hooch?"

"The bunker was to the left, then next to it is a hooch, then the head, then my hooch, and about fifty yards away was Douglas' hooch and away from that was the lieutenant's hooch. They was on the other side of the little walkway."

"When did you know the lieutenant had been killed"?

"Well, everyone knew the next morning. Someone said one of the officers had been named the investigation officer, kinda like the detective in charge, and he was talking to people to find out what went on. The word was that Grant had done it. He was a mean guy, and he talked bad about the lieutenant all the time."

"Lance Corporal, help me with this. If Douglas was right when he said he saw a white guy running with Grant after the grenade exploded, and if wasn't you, who do you think it was?"

"Sir, I don't know. There were some other white guys in other squads in First Platoon and some white guys in second and third platoons. I didn't know them well. Grant was a scary guy who could have made someone do something they didn't want to do. I don't know. I've tried to think who might have done it and can't come up with a name. But it won't me!"

Jackson continued. "Lieutenant, did you know that all six of those guys who testified against me got to rotate back home right after the trial, even though none of them had pulled their tour? It's almost like they got rewarded for testifying."

"Jackson, that didn't happen. The Corps doesn't work that way. Never happened. Let me ask you this: Do you have a problem in taking a polygraph — a lie detector test?"

"I had one, right after I got charged. I flunked — or the gunny who gave it said I flunked. He was yelling at me and asking stupid questions.

"Have you heard of sodium pentothal? Truth serum?"

"No, sir. What's that?"

"A doctor puts a needle in your arm and the truth serum goes into your veins. It — I think this is right — it does something to your brain that causes you to lose what are called your inhibitions, the things which you have that guard you from saying something which would get you in trouble." Woody had seen Jackson's SRB and knew he completed the tenth grade, so he hoped this basic explanation would suffice.

"Lieutenant, I'll do whatever you say to show I didn't kill that lieutenant, 'cause I know that what I say after they give me that truth serum will be that I didn't do it."

Woody stood up." Okay, Jackson, that's all for today. I'm not sure when I'll be back. Oh, there is one other thing." Woody gave Jackson a sheet of paper and pencil. "Draw me a map of the area at VCB we talked about."

When Jackson had finished the drawing, Woody told Jackson to hang in there, that he was doing all he could do and would let him know what was going on as it developed. He had to report to McMurry and Ross.

Woody stopped by the prosecution shop after he left the brig, and he, McMurry and Ross went to the empty courtroom. Woody filled them in on his meeting with Jackson and told them that he agreed with them that Jackson certainly was convincing when asserting his innocence.

Woody continued, "About the polygraph, is there a risk if we give him a legit polygraph and he still doesn't pass?"

McMurry answered, "I don't think we have anything to lose. It would not have been admissible at trial but if he passes the polygraph AND if we dig up some other stuff, it may mean something to the colonel and the general, but that's a big 'AND'. We know a guy who can do it for us. He is totally honest. We deal with him as prosecutors, and he's a straight shooter. He's with NIS. He investigates and if he thinks the guy is innocent, he tells us, and if the evidence isn't too strong, we usually follow the recommendation that we drop, or don't take up, the prosecution. We've gotten some blowback from some commanders, but so far, no one has pushed us too hard when we follow Graham's recommendation — that's his name, Jack Graham. I believe he'd do it for us. Want me to ask?"

Woody asked, "Yes, and if we find the truth serum, should we do a test?"

McMurry chimed in, "I think it would be a mistake to not play every card we can think of playing. This is like most murder cases, in that it really isn't complicated, in a way. We have someone killed. We have someone charged. There usually are no witnesses, only circumstantial evidence and not a lot of that. In this case, Jackson was convicted chiefly by Douglas' eyewitness testimony of what he said he saw when it lightened when the typhoon was raging. A lot of cases like this have a big chance to have the wrong outcome. We need to present everything to the colonel, so he can present it to the general when he makes his recommendation, even if it is a long shot. I'll get up with Graham. If he will do it, he can do it in the courtroom where it will be quiet. I'll see him tomorrow. Woody, why don't you contact your shrink buddy to see if he can round up some truth juice in this hell hole. Time is probably running short on us, so let's move."

Woody left the courtroom and felt elated and depressed at the same time. He was glad to be taking some action, but he was depressed, because even if Jackson passed the polygraph, and even if his answers while he was under the sodium pentothal were truthful that he didn't do it, those results probably would not cause the colonel to recommend to the general that the conviction should be reversed. Even if the Colonel recommended reversal, there was no guarantee the general would follow the recommendation.

In fact, Woody had a hard time imagining a general overturning the conviction of a Marine for the murder of an officer, in an error-free trial, just because the prosecutors thought he may be innocent, and just because a lie detector test and truth serum, neither of which could be used in court, might show him to be innocent. But they had nothing to lose by giving it their best shot.

0835 Hours, Fri, 5 Sep 69
Courtroom, Third Mar Div
Quang Tri
Polygraph

Jack Graham had been a NIS agent for ten years. His first tour had been in Da Nang, where he spent much of his time investigating drug traffic. He believed that of all the bad which would come from a war that was probably un-winnable, the use of drugs by servicemen might be one of the most devastating long-term. No matter how good the confidential informants were, no matter how excellent the investigations were, there were just not enough people to catch the bad guys, and there were too many bad guys. Jack was from Maine and felt the fight against drugs was like trying to sweep back the tide with a broom during a Nor'easter.

After his first tour, Graham volunteered to return to Vietnam, and negotiated placement near the front. There was plenty of crime to be investigated, there were fewer drugs than in Da Nang, which was a metropolitan area, and he really wanted to deal with and get to know first-hand some of the Marines on the front lines.

He had seen McMurry and Ross prosecute, individually and jointly, a number of cases, and was very impressed with their zealous and substantial prosecutorial skills. He was equally impressed with their sense of fairness, and their liberal use of common sense. When they explained their interest in the Jackson case, he readily accepted their offer to help. He wanted to know if Jackson was in the brig at Quang Tri or Da Nang.

Ross answered, "He's in the brig here. Lieutenant White, whose is helping us, interviewed him at our brig."

Graham asked, "What did he say his impressions were — guilty or maybe innocent."

Ross replied, "He thought he may be innocent. Understand, White is still wet behind the ears, but he's got a lot of common sense and is good in the courtroom."

Graham thought a minute. "Well, there is an interview room at the brig, but it is so loud — you can hear all the inmates raising hell. I need a quiet place to conduct the exam. What do you suggest?"

McMurry answered. "How about the courtroom? We can do it when no one is there. We can get some guards to escort him. We don't usually get involved in the transporting of Marines, 'cause we prosecute them, but we can figure it out. What else do you need other than the courtroom which we'll secure so we won't be bothered?"

"Get some Pepsis and some kind of snack. I want this guy to be at ease as much as possible. That will give us the best chance for a valid test. Let me know when you can set it up. I need about 8 hours' notice."

"Lance Corporal, do you know why you are here?"

"Yes sir. Lieutenant White told me I'm gonna take a lie detector test. I already done one, though."

Graham leaned back in his chair. He and Jackson were alone in the courtroom. Jackson's handcuffs and ankle shackles had been removed at Graham's request. There were guards standing outside the courtroom. "Yeah, but this one is going to be different and done right. The other one was messed up. You with me?"

"Yes, sir."

Graham spent the next few minutes trying to get Jackson to forget where he was, and what he was facing. He offered Jackson a Pepsi, and some Nabs, which he scarfed down. He asked Jackson about his parents, where he grew up, what sports he played in school, his first date — everything he could think of to get Jackson in a comfortable frame of mind. He took notes of Jackson's answers. Graham told a story about him and some high school classmates throwing eggs at the Spanish teacher's house, and Jackson was grinning. Graham felt it was a good time to get down to business.

"Here's how this works. Before you're hooked up, I'll tell you the questions I'm gonna ask after you get hooked up and you will give me the answers, before you are hooked up, so you'll know the questions, and I'll know the answers, before the test. There will be no surprises, understand?" Jackson nodded. "When you're hooked up, the machine tells me how your body reacts when questions are asked and answered. The theory is that you respond one way when you tell the truth, but another way when you lie. Again, since you and I will know what I'm asking and what you're answering before we start the test, there are no surprise questions on this exam. Understand?"

"Yes, sir, but that ain't the way it happened last time. He yelled at me and I didn't know what he was going to ask."

"Well, remember I told you this one will be done right. Here are the questions." Graham started with asking Jackson his date of birth, names of siblings, and other softball questions. When he had ten questions left, he looked at Jackson when asking the most important question of the exam: "Did you throw or help throw a grenade into the hooch of the lieutenant Speight?" He then asked if Jackson had gone to boot camp at Parris Island, if he had ever driven a car, and then he finished with questions about Jackson's childhood.

Graham wrote down Jackson's answers and asked Jackson if he were ready to be hooked up. "Yes sir."

The application of the devices took a few minutes, during which time Graham got Jackson to talk about everything BUT the exam. When he finished hooking Jackson up to the machine, he asked him if he were ready to proceed, and when Jackson nodded 'yes' Graham began with the first question.

Graham never looked at the machine when administering a test. After all, the machine would record the results. He felt there were advantages in his looking at an examinee as the questions were asked and answered. The expressions on the face of the examinee could be significant to an experienced polygraph examiner, such as Graham. He made mental notes of how Jackson looked as he answered questions, and Graham was very careful to look at Jackson for the several questions before the most important question was asked.

The exam took about 25 minutes, about a minute per question. Graham never rushed an exam. As he was being unhooked, Jackson asked, "How did I do, Mr. Graham."

Graham stopped unhooking Jackson and looked him in the eyes. "I have no idea. I did not look at the machine as I was asking the questions. It takes some time to interpret the results — maybe 4 or 5 hours, and then I'll report the results to Lieutenant White, who can tell you what he wants to 'cause he's your lawyer. But you could not have been more cooperative with me, which helps make the results, whatever they are, be valid." Graham wanted to tell Jackson that polygraphs had not been, and probably never would be accepted as determinative of guilt or innocence. That was White's job, and Graham surmised White had already told Jackson that fact. He went to the door to let the guards know he was through. After Jackson was placed in shackles and handcuffs, he was escorted back to the brig.

Graham had not been honest with Jackson when he said he was not looking at the machine during the test, because he had glanced at the machine as Jackson answered "no" to the question about whether he killed or helped kill the lieutenant. Graham knew that Jackson's body reacted the same way during that answer as it did when Graham asked him to confirm his date of birth. Graham also knew that this data would probably not be enough to keep Graham from going to federal prison for 20 years.

0800 Hours, Wed, 10 Sep 69
Office of the Staff Judge Advocate
Third Mar Div
Quang Tri
Advance Team Deployment

"You boys want some coffee? My wife sent it to me. She got the beans from a place outside of Texas. Hope she didn't get it from Cuba. It is strong as a mule's kick, and wakes you up like an incoming rocket, but I love it. It'll put hair on your chest."

McMurry, Ross and Woody White declined Colonel Sullivan's offer. They had been summoned from their offices by WO Masterson, who said the SJA wanted to see each of them ASAP.

"OK, boys, I normally don't like to drink alone, but since it's 0800 and I'm drinking coffee, I can handle it. Have you boys ever heard the word 'Vietnamization'?" All three lawyers stated they had never heard it. The colonel continued. "Well, this war kept one President from running for reelection, kept a candidate from winning the presidential election, and is a real albatross around the neck of the winner of that presidential election. President Nixon is desperate to find a way out of 'Nam, I guess 'cause he wants his presidency to mean more than a losing war. So, and I have this on good authority, in a couple of months, he is going to start a drawdown of US troops, called "Vietnamization", or something like that. What that will mean is that the South Vietnam army, the ARVN, is going to start fighting, and dying, on a larger scale for their country, and the US is going to reduce its force and hopefully its wounded and KIA until all we have is a bunch of advisors, just like we started with before we got bogged down.

"What that means on a practical basis is that more Marines are going to begin rotating back to the States, or Okinawa, or wherever, and fewer and fewer replacements will be coming to Vietnam. Well, you can't just turn this troop flow on and off like a faucet, so we're gonna start moving our office, along with some other mainly admin offices, back to Oki, and eventually the entire Third Mar Div will be gone from Vietnam and on Okinawa. One of the things happening with all of this — remember I said fewer troops will be coming into country — is that Oki is beginning to sink into the ocean 'cause Marines with orders for 'Nam via transit at Oki, are stuck there since they aren't rotating here. And because their stay in transit is normally short, and because the troops are normally kept on a short leash when they're in transit for here, they don't get in trouble and they don't normally need many lawyers, judges, etc. to deal with them. Well, they aren't on a short leash now. The Marines are getting in trouble, so legal and some admin staffs there now are just under-manned to handle the increasing load.

"I'm tasked with coming up with two defense attorneys, and two trial attorneys, to go to Oki, kinda as an advance team, to take stock of what needs to be done for the crisis they now have, and, importantly, to set up the Third Mar Div legal office so we can be up and running when the rest of our office gets there. I don't want to be hunting for my desk when I get there. Captain McMurry and Lieutenant Ross, ya'll have been in country a long time and deserve to get to leave early. Lieutenant White, you ain't been here long, but I've got confidence in you, and so you're deploying with McMurry and Ross. There are those who will take issue with my selection of you, a relative 'newbie' but they don't have the eagles of a bird colonel on their collars and I do. I have total confidence in the three of you. Lieutenant White, who do you recommend I name as the other defense counsel?"

"Lieutenant Ross Jefferson, Colonel. He knows his stuff. I like working with him, and it sounds like it will be important for the lawyers in the so-called 'advance group' need to get along."

"Jefferson it is, then", the Colonel replied. "Here's the deal. You three, and Jefferson, along with Masterson, will be leaving here in about two weeks. You're going via landing craft, down the Cua Viet River, out to the Gulf of Tonkin, onto a ship, and to Oki. There will be other personnel, from other units, leaving when you do. Once you get to Oki, you'll take charge of dealing with setting up the legal shop and dealing with the multiple issues of deciding who to charge with what and when to try them. There are two military judges on Oki, one who was scheduled for here, and one for the First Division in Da Nang, but they're staying put. They do have some limited court personal, such as reporters. So you will be a skeleton crew, but it will work for the short-term. You will set up our offices at Camp Courtney — trial shop and defense shop, admin shop, etc. Kinda along the arrangement we have here, 'cept there won't be a need for an incoming rockets siren, thank goodness. Any questions so far?"

The three lawyers were too stunned to come up with questions. They realized and appreciated that the colonel was putting so much trust in them. They also realized they would be out of harm's way in a week or so. It was hard to take it all in.

"Here's two other things," the colonel said. "First, our legal shop is going to know ya'll are gone, so no problem in just telling them you're being deployed to Oki. If they ask you if the deployment is permanent or temporary tell them, you don't know. DO NOT, DO NOT, tell them about 'Vietnamization', and the pending division move in a couple of months, and don't communicate the phrase 'Vietnamization' or your deployment to your families. Let everybody think this a temporary duty assignment move.

"Second, moving an entire division five miles is a big deal. Moving it across the ocean to another land is a much bigger deal. The commanding general will have this division deployment at the top of his hit parade list and will be less concerned about keeping his finger on the pulse of the review of the Jackson murder case. I can, and will in good conscience, let him know that the move, and particularly moving all of you as the advance team, will result in the slowing down of that Jackson review process, if he asks me. This will give you some extra time for this Jackson project. I'll try to pull in some favors to get

Jackson moved to the brig on Oki ASAP. Y'all got a lot to do, so get doing it. And, send Jefferson here, I want to tell him this myself. And White, tell Jefferson that when you all get to Oki, he owes you at least five Kobe beef dinners and some Orion beer for selecting him. OK, dismissed."

"Is the O Club open, and isn't it five o'clock somewhere, so we can start celebrating?" asked McMurry. He, Ross and White were walking slowly from the SJA's office back to their respective work areas. Each was lost in his own thoughts about their good fortune. White realized he had to get out to VCB before he shipped to Oki and was at first at a loss as to how to make it happen. And then he realized he knew just the man to handle this, so he told McMurry and Ross he'd catch up with them later.

Sinclair Wright was an E-8, a First Sergeant, and First Sergeants in the Corps were called 'Top'. Wright was assigned to the admin office of the Third Mar Div. Woody knew Top could arrange a hop to VCB, so Woody could see the layout where everyone slept and where the fragging was committed. He remembered that Mr. Cavanaugh's cross exam of the alleged victim in the Mill Run Valley case centered on knowledge of the 'lay of the land'. He didn't think he would unearth any clues at VCB, but he just wanted to get the picture of the area in his head.

"Top, can you help me get to and from VCB, need to be there only about two hours, max?"

"No problem, lieutenant. We have convoys and choppers going out every day. If you can be here at 1000 hours tomorrow, I can make that happen. By the way, I hear you're on the advance team for legal on Oki."

"That's right. Good news travels fast. What can you tell me about Okinawa?"

Woody had talked enough with First Sergeant Wright to know that he had been in the Corps for about 30 years, so he'd probably served in both WW2 and Korea, and had probably made some of those horrific landings when Marines island-hopped across the Pacific, as ordered by MacArthur. Although First Sergeant Wright was enlisted and Woody was an officer, and therefore in the chain of command Woody was superior to Wright, both Woody and Wright knew that Top, with 30 years and the next-to-highest enlisted rank, was more important to the Marine Corps than was Woody, so Woody deferred to him.

"Well, it is part of the Ryukyu Island chain. I can tell you that on April Fool's Day of 1945, I was on a landing craft that took me to the Oki shoreline to take on the Japs. I was told that we were on the largest amphibious assault force in the Pacific during WW2. It took us almost three months to take that island. It was bloody as hell, lots of hand-to-hand combat. The Army was there too. We got the word that FDR had died about three weeks after we hit the beaches, but that didn't change anything we were doing. We'd never heard of Truman. We heard that some Japs committed hari-kari by jumping off cliffs into the sea when they knew they'd lost. Wish they'd done it before we got there. We liked Truman after he ordered those two A- bombs dropped on Japan in August 'cause we were getting ready to invade their Motherland. Thank goodness he ordered that. No telling how many people would have been killed if we'd invaded Japan."

Woody had another question. "Top. How many island landings did you have during WW2?

After a few seconds, First Sergeant Wright answered. "Five. Tarawa, Saipan, Guam, Iwo and Okinawa."

"Can I ask you one more question?" Top nodded and Woody continued, "With all that killing not only on landing, but once you got onto an island — the Japs were so brutal — how did you keep on fighting, knowing that you could be dead the next minute?"

Top sat down and had a faraway look on his face. "Well, Lieutenant, the only way we made it was to make our minds think that we were already dead — that it had happened so we couldn't do anything about it. So we weren't afraid of dying 'cause we already were dead. Kept us going, strange as that sounds."

Woody could not even imagine what that had been like. At OCS, the candidates were shown a film clip about the Tarawa landing, and the beaches were literally red with the blood of Marines who fell. Woody wanted to change the subject.

"Do you know anything about Camp Courtney where legal will be?

"It's a nice place. Overlooks the water. There's an air base on Oki, at Kadena, and bombers — B-52s — take off from there to hit North Vietnam and South Vietnam, as well as other places we won't talk about. The Corps has a great training area at Camp Schwab, up north from Courtney. So, it will be a good place for us. And there are plenty of bars with girls for the troops, too, if you're into that kinda thing."

"Do you know anything about the ship we'll be on? Are we going to climb up those cargo nets to get on board?"

"Actually no, lieutenant. The ship is the *Dubuque*, named after a city in Iowa. It has a well deck, so you don't have to go up the ropes."

"What's a well-deck?"

Top answered, "The *Dubuque* has a ballast system, and as I understand it, the stern of the ship opens up, the ballast keeps the ocean out, and they drive the landing crafts into the belly of the ship, the doors close, and we're done. It's a neat way to get a bunch of Marines from or onto a ship. There are two scary parts. You'll be going up the Cua Viet River in the landing crafts, and the bad guys could have RPGs or small arms fire with range to hit you, and I don't imagine there will be air cover. The second problem is that if the ocean swells are high when you get to the *Dubuque*, the boat master of the LC has to time the LC going into the ship without being thrown up into the roof of the stern by a swell. But those guys know what they're doing. Look at it as an adventure, Lieutenant."

Woody thanked Top and returned to the legal office, to work on packing his files for the deployment before he went to VCB.

The next day, Woody took a chopper to VCB. As he looked down, he saw the rugged, battle-scared landscape of the northern area of I Corps and was thankful he wasn't assigned grunt duty. He wondered if he could have handled leading men in combat.

Once he was at VCB, it was easy enough to find the area where the lieutenant was killed. Woody was pleased that Jackson's sketch was accurate. As stepped off by Woody, the lieutenant's hooch was one-hundred twenty feet from Jackson's hooch. As he faced Jackson's hooch, there was a head ten feet to the left of Jackson's hooch, and it was about 90 feet from Douglas' hooch to the path where Douglas said the two men were running. Woody wondered if there was anyone other than Douglas who saw men running after the grenade explosion.

As best he could figure, there was no one at VCB when he got there who had been there when the lieutenant was killed, so he got on the next chopper heading back to HQ, and finished packing his files for deployment to Okinawa.

1800 Hours, Tues, 23 Sep 69
Down The Cua Viet River, To The Tokin Gulf,
and Into the Pacific
Deployment to Okinawa

On Tuesday, 23 September, Woody, along with McMurry, Ross Jefferson, WO Masterson, and others from the admin staff, along with some Marines Woody had never seen, were transported, sea bags and files, from their hooch areas to the Cua Viet River, where they loaded onto a landing craft.

Woody had no way to know if this LC had been used in WW2, but since it didn't look new, and since the Corps used gear until it rotted or fell apart, Woody imagined that twenty-five, or so, years earlier, there had been Marines on this LC who were getting ready to land on one of those many islands in the Pacific where the Japanese army waited for them. It gave him both chills and a sense of pride that he didn't think would be replicated in his life.

Top had been right. There was no air cover — at least that Woody could see — as the LC went down the Cua Viet River. Even though it stayed in what seemed to be the middle of the river, it looked to Woody like the LC was not out of the range of small arms fire or RPGs from the shoreline. There were no seats in the LC, so Woody crouched below the bulwark which he hoped afforded some protection from any small arms fire.

Woody could tell they had left the calm of the Cua Viet River when the LC started rolling in the swells of the Gulf of Tonkin. Woody soon saw the lights of the *Dubuque*, and was glad the swells weren't too high when they got near the stern of the ship. The lights from the ship became brighter when the well deck was opened. The boat master sailed the landing craft into the ship like he was parking a Cadillac in a garage. Then it hit Woody: He was out of the war zone, and probably would not be sent anywhere until he rotated back to the States next summer.

Woody was directed to his bunk area. He took the lower bunk, and it turned out that no one else was assigned to his sleeping area, which suited him fine. The officers were shown their officers' mess, and treated to a great dinner of steak, baked potato, salad and ice cream, all served by Filipino stewards, on linen tablecloths. Quite the change from the chow hall at Quang Tri.

The ship first headed south, to Da Nang, where Woody saw Eisenhower's military industrial complex at work. What appeared to be the trailer or transport part of tractor-trailer trucks were being off-loaded from the cargo holds of ships by huge cranes. The trailer sections were all marked *Sealand*. Woody wondered if it was too late to buy stock in *Sealand*, whatever that was, when he got home. No one ever knew why they sailed to Da Nang, probably because there was no need for them to know. After about a half-day, they lifted anchor and headed to Okinawa.

It took about five days to reach Okinawa. It was the easiest five days Woody had in the Corps. He had no men to give orders to or to be responsible for, and he never received an order to perform any duty. The ship had a decent library, and for the first time in his life, Woody read for the pure enjoyment of reading. He realized there was some irony in reading *The Caine Mutiny* while at sea, because in that timeless classic, Herman Wouk wrote a harrowing scene of a mine sweeper in WW2 in the middle of a typhoon while at sea.

However, the best thing about the trip was the food. Woody never regretted his decision to join the Marines, but he wished the Corps took some lessons from the Navy about chow.

The ship docked in Okinawa about 1000 hours on Monday, 29 September, and there were buses to transport the Marines to Camp Courtney.

The Third Division legal office was located at Camp Courtney, in a large Quonset hut, overlooking the most beautiful blue-green water Woody had ever seen. Woody had never seen water so green and blue at the same time. The building, which had a few desks and chairs, was large enough for both the prosecution lawyers and the defense lawyers to be in the same room, but at opposite ends and far enough apart so each could conduct business more or less confidentially. There was plenty of room for staff. There was also a large office at the end of the building which they agreed would be suitable for Colonel Sullivan.

A few hours after arriving, they were joined by some lawyers who had been previously posted on Okinawa. Under the ordered chain of command, McMurry was the CO of the legal office until Colonel Sullivan arrived. They met, found out what was pending by way of cases and defendants on the island, decided who would do what, decided the smaller building next to the Quonset hut would be the courtroom, and ordered the necessary furniture to set up their offices, the courtroom and Colonel Sullivan's office. After discussing the number of pending cases, the lawyers realized they would probably work harder on Oki than they had in Vietnam, a burden they were happy to undertake.

Woody was busy sorting the cases for trial or guilty pleas when the shrink from Everetts appeared at his door. "Well, when did you get here, and how is the shrink business on this glorious island, Doc. You look like the cat who swallowed the canary. What's up?" Woody said as he got up to shake hands.

Aaron Hardison was happy to see Woody. "Well, I caught a flight on a C-130 and got here yesterday and think there will be plenty for me to do to help the mental welfare of Marines. More than enough. And I've got some good news. I found some sodium pentothal in the OR at the aid station clinic down the road. I can't get the drug for a couple of weeks, so when Jackson gets here, let me know and I'll set it up. The sodium pentothal is a barbiturate and is kept under lock and key to minimize misuse or theft. I've got to write on the drug records exactly how much is used and why it is being used. This ol' redneck ain't willing to lose that medical degree from the greatest school in North Carolina because of not being transparent, so I'm telling it like it is."

Woody, replied, "Well, while I am gratified you have what we need and have found a way to use it, I take great umbrage at your erroneous assessment of your school's standing in the Tar Heel state. I'm not even sure it is in the top three in the State, and it definitely is behind the Deacons.

"I don't know if Jackson is on Oki now. Our colonel said he'd try to pull some strings to get him here ASAP. I'll check periodically with the brig and keep you posted. I can't imagine they'd prioritize the transport of a prisoner, but we'll see."

Woody continued. "Are you OK with my having a court reporter at this procedure, to tape-record and transcribe everything. I think we need a record of what happened to show the colonel and maybe the general."

Hardison replied, "Absolutely no problem. In fact, it is such a good idea I'm surprised a guy who got his law degree from that dinky school in Winston-Salem even thought of it. But, I need you to tell me what you want me to ask him."

"Already taken care of, Doc. I've typed the questions and here's a copy." Woody handed the list to Aaron. "I'd like you to review them and suggest any changes you think are in order."

After glancing at the list, Doc gave it back to Woody. "It's a good idea to have some no-brainer type questions, such as his DOB, full name, mom's name, etc. which he and I can discuss before I stick him. In fact, when we had that experience at Central Prison in Raleigh, one of the things I remember is that we give them the no-brainer questions after sticking them, listened to the answers, and watched the subject react, to get an idea when they are far enough under the influence to get to the nitty gritty in the questioning. Does that sound OK?"

"I'll redraft with those type questions and get them to you."

"Woody, I've got a last question", Doc said, "How big is this guy so I can be accurate on the dosage?"

"I'll find out. He's not a big guy — no more than 140 pounds, except for his nose, which is huge. But I'll get him weighed before we do this."

1330 Hours, Sat, 11 Oct 69
The Aid Station
Camp Courtney, Okinawa
Truth Serum

Dr. Aaron Hardison was nervous as he prepared to stick a needle into the antecubital vein of the right arm of Lance Corporal Jackson. He had not stuck a person with a needle since his first year of med school, but the entire episode, of being in an OR, injecting sodium pentothal into the vein of a Marine inmate who had been convicted of accessory after the fact to murder and conspiracy to commit murder, as armed guards waited outside, was as surreal an experience as Aaron had ever had.

Part of the process required putting Jackson at ease as much as possible. Hardison asked Jackson, "What do they call you?"

"Sir, they call me 'Nose'."

"Why in the hell do they do that?" Hardison asked, laughing, and Jackson joined in. Woody had been right — Jackson had one of the biggest noses he'd ever seen, and it probably looked even bigger because Jackson was so skinny. Jackson was on a gurney, on his back. Aaron followed the standard procedure of placing a tourniquet around the bicep area of Jackson's right arm, but he wasn't sure it was necessary because the veins in Jackson's arms almost popped out.

Aaron continued the conversation as he swabbed the arm before the stick. "Corporal, you're going to get a little buzz on, almost like you had a few too many beers at the E Club. I'll be asking you some questions. Just answer the questions and all will be fine. You will feel this stick, and then we'll start." Hardison hoped Jackson didn't see his hand shaking as he placed the tip of the needle in the vein, but he actually made a smooth stick, and Jackson didn't wince at all.

"Lance Corporal, start at 100 and count backwards, please." Aaron remembered from his experience at Central Prison in Raleigh that when the patient began counting slower, or skipped numbers, it meant that the sodium pentothal was hitting the patient's system. When Jackson took about 8 seconds to get to "93"and followed that with "67", Hardison knew he needed to adjust the sodium pentothal flow and start asking questions.

He nodded to Woody that it was time to start the questioning. Woody had asked Corporal James Greevy, the senior and most-trusted court reporter, to go to the OR with him. He explained what was going to occur and obtained Greevy's word that this would remain confidential. Woody even had Greevy wear a surgical gown, as if he were an assistant, so the guards wouldn't be suspicious. The guards had been told Jackson was going to have an unspecified outpatient procedure. Greevy moved his tape recorder and his stenographic machine next to the gurney in such a way that the guards could not see him or his equipment. Woody had not told Jackson that the session was to be recorded. He wasn't sure about the ethics of not disclosing that fact to his client, but he knew a record of the interview was essential for the presentation to Colonel Sullivan and the general. Besides, he thought Jackson would be out of it and wouldn't notice Greevy.

Aaron slowly asked all the questions Woody had given him. Woody thought Hardison had been accurate when he told Jackson he would probably feel like he had a few too many beers, because that is what Jackson sounded like. Jackson's replies were given slowly, and he was thick-tongued, just like a drunk. But he answered that he had not been at the lieutenant's hooch and had not been present when the grenade was tossed under the rack.

Woody had asked Jackson these same questions several times, in several different ways, in every interview he had with Jackson, who had answered them, every time, the same way he answered them under the influence of sodium pentothal. Woody was as convinced as he could be that Jackson did not kill Lieutenant Speight.

After Hardison had finished the questions, Woody asked Aaron a question. He had previously instructed Greevy to record this question and Hardison's answer, but Woody had not told Aaron that he was going to ask him a question, because he wanted Aaron's answer to be what the law called a 'spontaneous utterance', a knee-jerk answer which sometimes was given more creditability than other answers. "Do you think Jackson is telling the truth, as he knows it to be under the influence of the sodium pentothal, that he did not murder or help murder the lieutenant?"

Aaron replied, "Well, I didn't know you would ask my opinion, but it is my medical opinion that this man has been given an amount of sodium pentothal sufficient to release his inhibitions so that his answers are truthful, as he knows the truth to be, and that he believes he did not kill, and was not involved in the killing of, Lieutenant Speight."

Aaron told Woody it would take Jackson about 30 minutes to come out of the buzz. Woody did not want Jackson to know Greevy had been recording the session, so he asked Greevy to take his tape recorder and steno machine back to the office and begin transcribing the session, since time was of the essence.

When Jackson came out from under the influence, Dr. Hardison helped him sit up. Jackson looked at Woody and asked, "What happened?"

"You had truth serum, just like I said. It is Dr. Hardison's opinion that you were telling the truth about having nothing to do with the killing of the lieutenant, and that is what I will tell my boss, the SJA. You'll be taken back to the brig. Remember you can't tell anyone what happened here. If you are asked why you were brought to the hospital, tell them it is none of their business, unless you want to be a wise-ass and tell them you had a penis reduction operation."

Jackson laughed to himself, and shook his head, looked at Woody and said, "Thanks".

Woody said, "I don't know when we'll know something, but it will move as fast as I can make it move. I will keep you posted."

Woody walked over to the door and asked the guards to take Jackson back to the brig. As they were putting Jackson in handcuffs and leg irons, Dr. Hardison spoke to them. "This man will need to have some chow before he is placed back in the brig. Make that happen, and that's an order, understood?" They both came to attention, saluted, stated they understood, and removed Jackson from the OR.

Woody and Aaron were alone, and Woody spoke. "Who in hell would think two rednecks from eastern North Carolina would find themselves halfway 'round the world giving truth serum to a convicted felon trying to find enough information to convince a general to let him go?"

"It boggles the mind", Aaron responded. "When do you think you will take all this to the commanding general?"

"Well, I don't know if the CG is back on Oki — probably not. He'll probably be among the last to leave 'Nam. Colonel Sullivan isn't here either. I guess when he gets here — and I have no way to know when that will be — we'll meet with him, and the CG will want to him to report soon. So, we'll see."

Hardison was quiet for a minute. "What do you think will happen?"

"I don't think the general will be impressed with the results from the polygraph, or the truth serum, or with the so-called "gut reactions" of the prosecutors, and will ask the colonel, as the SJA, to give his legal opinion on whether the conviction should be upheld. The colonel has got to say that it was a trial free from prejudicial error, and since there is no legal reason to not affirm the conviction, the general will sign the paperwork, and Jackson will start his two ten-year sentences at the federal pen at Leavenworth."

"Well, Woody, you've done the best that can be done for Jackson. No one can ask for more, giving him a chance he would not have had but for you, Mike and Kevin. Even if it doesn't work out, I hope you can take some satisfaction from the effort the three of you undertook. I know from my training and experience, self-esteem is critical to good mental health. Let me know if I can help."

"Thanks, Doc. That means a lot coming from you. I'll keep you posted."

1130 Hours, Fri, 17 October 69
Legal Office, Camp Courtney A
Americans Oppose The War

Of all the amenities offered on Okinawa, including no incoming, Woody most enjoyed the opportunity to keep up with national affairs back in the USA by reading the timeless *Stars and Stripes* military newspaper, and magazines such as *Newsweek* and *Time*. Woody and others found out, on 17 October 69, that two days earlier there had been huge marches across the US, and in some European countries, protesting America's involvement in South Vietnam.

While Woody, and most of the lawyers with whom he privately discussed US involvement in Vietnam, felt the war was a losing cause, they all resented the marches. It made them feel very unappreciated. They had put their necks on the line, and just because they were now safely in Okinawa, they guessed there were hundreds of thousands of American servicemen and women who were still in harm's way, and there was resentment that those participating in the marches were able to go home after the marches, have a martini, grill a steak, and make love to their wives or girlfriends, when Marines and soldiers were eating C-rats in a foxhole wondering if it were their last meal. Woody was trying to get better at letting go of things he could not control, as hard as that was.

1114 Hours, Wed, 29 Oct 69
Legal Office
Camp Courtney, Okinawa
The Gang's All Here

Woody was at the legal office, working on the defense of a Marine charged with assaulting another Marine at the enlisted club. There had been numerous assaults among the restless, young Marines. But there was no mistaking the arrival of the rest of legal from Quang Tri — they were a raucous group as they entered the building.

After the many handshakes and slaps on the back, Colonel Sullivan spoke to Mike, Kevin and Woody, "How 'bout showing me around. Let's see what you've got laid out for us."

After the tour of the office space, and after showing the colonel his own space, the colonel spoke. "Gentlemen, you have not disappointed me. This is a job well done. I know there's lots of organizing in assigning cases for those who just arrived, but they are ready to work out of a war zone, so don't mind loading them up. I think we'll be up and running in no time at all, due to the good work all of you have done. By the way, about that Jackson matter, the general sent word that he wanted to meet with me in the next two weeks — not sure when yet, for my recommendation. Where does that stand?"

Woody filled the colonel in on the polygraph and the sodium pentothal test results. The colonel thought a moment, then spoke. "Well, I will certainly review them, but I really don't imagine those things — as important as they are — will carry much weight, but we'll see. I'll keep you posted on the meeting. Again, thanks for the good job in transitioning us from Nam to Oki. Well done."

1420 Hours, Fri, 31 Oct 69
Legal Office, Camp Courtney
Happy Halloween, The Corps Has Screwed Up

Woody's mind was on Jackson, so he was having a hard time concentrating on the case of PFC Tilley, who was charged with the run-of-the-mill bar fight, when he heard Mr. Masterson addressing the lawyers in the prosecution section of the building, a few cubicles away. "Gentlemen, the colonel wants to see all second lieutenant lawyers in the courtroom. Now!" Woody wondered what the hell that was about. Then Mr. Masterson came to the defense end of the shop and made the same announcement.

When all the second lieutenant lawyers in the Third Marine Division legal office were seated in the courtroom, the colonel came in. He was wearing his cowboy hat, casually tilted back on his head. WO Masterson, in his most formal voice, brought the group to attention. This was unusual, because even though they were still Marines, the relationship among the lawyers and the colonel was more professional than military. Something was going on.

Colonel Sullivan just looked at the group for about 10 seconds, and then ordered, "Ready, seats", which was the command to sit down given at OCS and TBS. Woody was thinking of Yogi Berra: It was deja'vu all over again.

"Gentlemen, the Marine Corp was founded at Tun Tavern, on 10 November 1775, so it will be 194 years old in ten days. We are proud warriors, and we don't screw up often. But, and don't you agree Mr. Masterson, this latest news could be the biggest screw-up in the glorious history of the Corps?"

"Yes, sir, no doubt sir."

Woody knew every other second lieutenant had the same thought — what the hell is he talking about?

"Yes, Mr. Masterson, to paraphrase Sir Winston Churchill, never in the history of the Corps have so many, who deserve so little, received so much." Now Woody was totally confused.

"Gentlemen, I have received a message from SecNav, the Secretary of the Navy, our boss, that defies explanation, specifically that each and every one of you is being promoted to the rank of O-3, Captain, without ever being a first lieutenant. Mr. Masterson, this means what?"

"Sir, it means the newly promoted captains must plan, execute and pay for the promotion party to end all promotion parties."

The colonel continued. "And whom should I appoint as the commanding officer of this mission?"

"Colonel, there is only one man with the temperament, attitude, demeanor, and most importantly, the experience, who knows the terrain, the native population, and the objective. The Bagman is your man!"

The Bagman was Cary Boudarant, from New Orleans. Every day after work, Bagman would leave the legal office at Courtney and hitch a ride to the nearest bar, where, it was believed, he would get to know the local females in a Biblical sense, and drink some brown whiskey, Bagman's words for bourbon. Bagman dragged back to work the next day, a little hungover, and was asked how he was doing, he'd reply, "I'm in the bag today." Woody had never heard that phrase before.

There were smiles all around. CAPTAINS IN THE UNITED STATES MARINE CORPS! After discussing this good fortune, the consensus was that they must have been given credit for the three years they spent in law school, even though many of them — Woody was not the only one in this category — enlisted during, not before, law school. None of them wanted an explanation, though. No reason to overturn that apple cart.

Their commanding officer, the Bagman, was soliciting advice for the party, and there was no dearth of ideas. Woody just wished he were in a better mood for what was sure to be a once in a lifetime experience.

1830 Hours, Sat, 8 Nov 69
The Big Time Bar
Naha, Okinawa
Walleye, the Stripper and the Snake

"Tell me who the Bagman guy is, who set up this party. This is one wild deal." Hardison had to yell in Woody's ear. The band, such as it was, knew how to be loud, but couldn't carry a tune in a bucket. And no one gave a damn. The enlisted men from the legal office were drinking and eating on the officers' money, which probably made it taste better.

The new captains had received the silver 'railroad tracks' — two parallel silver bars — of a captain, earlier that day. They were all having a good time, except for Woody, who was drinking a soft drink. He was driving, and Kadena Air Base was between The Big Time Bar and Camp Courtney. The last thing Woody wanted to do was to get charged with driving after drinking on an Air Force base.

Woody pointed to Bagman, who was surrounded by the "hostesses", who, Woody guessed, were women Bagman had spent time with. Woody answered Aaron. "He's the guy with all the gals around him, blond hair, with the shit-eating grin on his face."

Hardison stood up. "Well, I must thank him. This is one hell of a party. And the beef — what the hell is it. I've never had any beef that good. What is it?"

Woody answered, "It is called Kobe beef. We heard about it as soon as we got here. Some of us spent our first two nights here going to restaurants, eating Kobe beef, drinking Orion beer, and then getting massages. What I was told is that they keep the cattle in stalls, feed them grain, and don't let them out to pasture, so there is no muscle, just good tender beef."

Hardison sat back down and looked at Woody. "Wait a minute. Tell me about those massages."

"Well, it wasn't a big deal. We went to these massage parlors, took a steam bath, and then went into a room. These Okinawan women who gave me massages, I had two, both women were about five feet tall and weighed maybe 200 pounds and were about 50 years old. No sex, no nothing, just a great — and I mean great — massage."

A roar went up. Woody and Aaron turned to the so-called stage, which was about 5 feet by 5 feet. The band had stopped playing, and a sound system had been turned on and was playing some slow song Woody had never heard. The spotlight hit the curtain, and out stepped an overweight, naked woman, with a real snake — Woody thought it was a boa constrictor, coiled around her neck.

Woody first saw a naked woman at the King County fair, when he was a sophomore at Wake Forest. There was nothing about that event which Woody found even remotely erotic or appealing, and he felt the same way this night.

But the stripper had one admirer. "Who the hell is that guy?" Hardison asked. Woody looked at the stage and a man, who was about 5'6" tall, was dancing around the stripper, and, like Bagman, he had the shit-eating grin of a drunk man getting drunker.

"That's Walleye, or that's what we call him. Name is Walter Francisco, a first lieutenant admin guy with our office. His eyes look like they are about to pop out of his head — they bulge. That's the way they always look, it's not just because he's drinking. He says he can see 180 degrees without turning his head. I didn't know he was such a heavy drinker, but I'm glad he's having a good time. Looks like everybody is."

"Captain White. That kind of has a nice ring to it, doesn't it?" Woody turned and saw the colonel was speaking. Aaron excused himself.

"Yes, sir, I guess it does. Doesn't mean I'm a better lawyer, just got some more rank."

"I thought you were a scotch drinker, but I've never seen someone mix scotch with a soft drink, which is what it looks like you're drinking. In fact, it makes me sick to even think about drinking scotch with a soft drink."

"No, sir, I'm not drinking tonight. Just not in the mood."

The colonel motioned Woody to move over to a corner of the bar. "Woody, I know you've got a lot on your mind about Jackson. I have read the reports from the sodium pentothal administration and the polygraph. I told you boys from the git-go that I'd give you the chance to prove the wrong guy had been convicted, and I have. And you, McMurry and Ross, and particularly you, have done much more than anyone could expect to help out this guy. It has always been a long shot, but, if you hadn't tried, there would have been no shot at all. You didn't do this to get the experience, you did it for a much better reason — to help. But you have received a bunch of valuable experience from your efforts, and it will stand you in good stead in the future."

The colonel continued, "You need to learn an important lesson: take time to have a good time every now and then. You're a Captain in the greatest fighting force in the history of mankind, and you worked hard to achieve that rank. Reward yourself. And one more thing. You will lose more cases than you'll win. You cannot, and I mean this, let a defeat in one case linger any longer than after the courtroom door hits you in the butt when you leave after losing a case, 'cause if you let it bother you, I guarantee you, it will make you screw up your next case, or not do your best in your next case. It took me too long to learn that lesson. You can and should learn from those losses, many of which you will lose because the facts weren't with you. Do not let them drag you down."

The colonel continued. "We meet with the general Tuesday, and then we'll know. I really think you should go, but we've discussed that, and I respect your decision to stay back at the office while McMurry, Ross and I meet with him. Now, go have a good time, and thanks for the party. Bagman should get some kind of medal for this, maybe the bronze star for drinking."

"Thank you Colonel, I'll do all I can to follow your advice, because I know it is good advice. It's just hard to deal with it now, because I think I know where we're going to end up with Jackson. But thanks for reading the reports. Let me know if you have any questions. I'll be around the office tomorrow catching up on some work."

Around 2200 hours, Marines started leaving the bar. Woody was ready to go, so he rounded up Hardison. He also noticed that Walleye was listing like the Leaning Tower of Pisa, so he decided to give him a ride home, and let him get his car tomorrow.

"Let me give you a ride, Walleye. It'll be safer."

Walleye slurred. "Hell no. I can drive myself. I don't need any help." Walleye was having a hard time walking and talking at the same time, and Woody was worried about his safety, and that of others, if Walleye drove himself. But his efforts to get Walleye to give him his keys only made Walleye more belligerent, so Woody backed off and decided he'd just follow Walleye back to Camp Courtney.

There wasn't much traffic, so Woody and Hardison didn't have trouble following Walleye's beat-up red with a white top 1958 Chevy Bel Air. Walleye's driving became worse when they reached the road which snaked through Kadena Air Base.

Woody said, "Would you look at him. He's moving all over the place, like he was Gale Sayers in the open field against the Lions on Thanksgiving Day. He'll never make it home."

Woody had no sooner uttered those words when the blue light and siren from an Air Police jeep filled the night. "Oh hell's bells. He's had it. I'm going to lay back a bit and see what happens. I haven't been drinking, but those Air Police may not like Marines, and while I'm brave, I ain't stupid."

Walleye managed to stop the vehicle, but it didn't bode well for him that the right front and rear tires were over the curb. Woody and Hardison were about 25 yards back. Woody cut off the engine and lights. The two Air Police approached Walleye's car, one on the driver's side and one on the passenger's side. Woody could hear one of the officers order the driver to get out of the car. When nothing happened, the officer on the driver's opened the driver's door.

Woody could not believe his eyes. Walleye fell out of the car, landing at the officer's feet. "Well, I guess the officer had probable cause to stop him with that wild driving, and now, it'll be hard to say he didn't have probable cause to arrest him. I need to help him if I can. You wait here."

Woody got out of his car and walked towards the Air Police. Aaron heard Woody announce himself as a Marine captain named White, and he asked if he could speak to the Air Police. After about 10 minutes, Woody turned toward his car and waived Aaron to join them. When Aaron got to Walleye's car, Woody said, "These kind gentleman seem to understand that it is not unusual for someone to get too drunk at a promotion party, so they have agreed to cut Walleye some big-time slack and not arrest him. But we've got to pick up his sorry butt, put it in my car, move his car to that parking lot over there" — Woody pointed across the street — "and drive him back to Courtney and throw his sorry ass in his rack. We thank the Air Force for this courtesy."

The taller of the two Air Police replied, "Don't worry about it Captain. Congrats on your promotion. My brother is a grunt with the Corps' First Division, out of Da Nang, so I'm kinda kin. Drive safely." Aaron drove Walleye's car to the parking lot, and then Woody and Aaron hauled Walleye onto the back seat of Woody's car and headed back to base.

0730 Hours, Tues, 11 Nov 69
Office of the SJA, Camp Courtney
Time to Meet the General

Woody, McMurry and Ross arrived promptly at the colonel's office at 0730 hours on the Tuesday after the party. The colonel had his usual office attire — cowboy hat tilted back, and he was wearing his 'chucker boots'. The colonel directed the three lawyers to take seats and poured them each a cup of coffee.

"Boys, ya'll remember your history. On this day, the eleventh hour of the eleventh day of the eleventh month, in 1918, the so-called 'war to end all wars' came to a close. Too bad they didn't tell that to Uncle Ho and LBJ.

"Well, the first thing you need to know is that except for Woody, who's not going, we are not meeting with General Jones. Even though he is the Commanding General, he is passing this off to his second-in-command, General Hugh Dowda, who will be making the decision. I can fill you in about him on the drive to his office.

"I've re-read the transcript from the truth serum episode. I also re-reviewed the polygraph report. All of them are favorable. And I appreciate the affidavits from you two" — the colonel nodded to McMurry and Ross — "stating your feelings about Jackson's innocence. After all, the bottom line is that one witness ID'd Jackson, at night, in a storm, from about thirty yards, or whatever it was, only when it lightened. Not the strongest of cases, but strong enough for the panel to convict. All of this will certainly be considered since you were the lawyers who tried him. But at the end of the day, I'm the general's lawyer, and he wants legal advice from me about whether there were any prejudicial errors during the trial that would cause, or should cause, a reversal. I've reviewed the entire record, and there aren't any. I will present all the information to the general, but I'll have to tell him that notwithstanding the post-trial efforts by you three, it's a good conviction and he should approve the conviction. I commend all of you. This won't make any of you feel better, but if I were charged with a serious crime, I'd want any one of you to represent me.

"Woody, I know you aren't going with us to meet the general, and I understand. I'll tell you the same thing a judge told me in a criminal trial during a recess: 'Unless you pull a smoking gun out of your ass and put it in someone else's hand, your client is gone'. I'm telling you that because once I DID pull a smoking gun out of my ass. I stumbled onto something at the last minute, and put it in the hand of the chief prosecution witness and got my man off. Do you think there are any more cards you can play?"

Woody answered, "No sir, I'm afraid there aren't."

Woody was wrong.

There was one more card, hidden in plain sight.

The colonel concluded the meeting. "Well, Mike, Kevin, it's time for us to go. I'll drive. You boys make sure your zippers are zipped and your gig-lines are right, so we can show that general how squared-away Marine lawyers are."

Woody went back to his workspace. He passed by Ben Harvey, a lawyer who had come to the Third Division a few weeks after Woody. Ben knew what Woody and the trial counsels were doing, and admired them, but he didn't hold out much hope for Jackson based on what he knew about it. He'd heard the meeting with the general was today. He thought about walking over to Woody, who was about 10' away, to console him, but figured there was nothing he could do for, or say to, Woody that would help, so he began concentrating on case prep for a Marine charged with smoking pot, which was a very serious charge in the Marine Corps. He heard Woody once more — probably for the last time — drag out the banker's box which contained the Jackson trial folders.

"Men, have either of you ever heard of General Dowda." The colonel was driving the vehicle assigned to the SJA office. It was about a five-minute drive to the CG's office, and it was a beautiful day, except McMurry and Ross knew it would probably not turn out to be a beautiful day for Jackson. They told the colonel they didn't know anything about the general.

"Well, I think he is one of the Corps 'up-and-comers'. Probably commandant material. In WW II, he was on the 'Canal, won the Navy Cross for, basically, saving his platoon. Then, on Iwo, he was awarded the Silver Star, but it was almost awarded posthumously. What happened was that he walked past a hidden spider hole, and a Jap popped out of the hole and was about to shoot him in the back, when the General's — who was then a lieutenant — platoon sergeant, who was behind the general, blew the Jap away. It was almost like John Wayne as Sgt. Stryker in the movie *The Sands of Iwo Jima* when The Duke got shot in the back. The general and that sergeant have been together ever since, and the sergeant is now General Dowda's first sergeant, his Top.

"He stayed in after the war and was scheduled to go to the first class at the Army War College in Carlisle, Pennsylvania when it resumed in '50. You boys know what Carlisle is famous for? Jim Thorpe went to college there, one of the greatest athletes of all time. At any rate, the general didn't go to the War College, he went to Korea. He got placed on the staff of God Almighty himself, Douglas MacArthur, and Dowda helped the general plan and implement the landing at Inchon, in September 1950. Probably one of the greatest military maneuvers in history. But I believe the true mettle of General Dowda is this: MacArthur awarded Dowda the Bronze Star with the combat V device even though Dowda never left MacArthur's command center on the ship and was never in harm's way. I'm sure he deserved the Bronze Star, but not the combat V device 'cause he was never in combat. MacArthur was giving out ribbons like he was the candy man at Halloween. Dowda had to accept it, of course, and he wore the combat V, until Truman fired MacArthur for, among other things, being insubordinate to him. That was the fourth best thing Truman did."

McMurry spoke up. "What were the other three things Truman did that were good, Colonel?"

"Dropped two bombs on the Japs and ended the war. Made Israel a nation state, or led the movement. And he began the process of integrating the services. Harry was one stud, in my opinion. And Dowda is a real leader. Let me tell you about something that happened at one of his duty stations after he made general. There was a lance corporal in his office, an admin guy. Without asking, he made what was described as a beautiful wooden name plate for the general's desk. The problem was that the general didn't like that kind of thing. He said if they don't know who the hell he was is by the time they're standing at his desk, a name plate wouldn't help. He told his Top to remove the name plate. Top told the general the lance corporal had busted his butt making it, was proud of his handiwork, and would be crushed if it were removed. Here's what the general did — told Top to call the lance corporal to his office right then, came out from behind his big desk when the Marine came in, shook his hand, told him to have a seat next to him, told him it was the most beautiful nameplate he had ever seen, and that he was honored to have it. Then, now remember this is a general talking to a lance corporal, then the general said he'd be honored if the lance corporal would give him, the general, permission to make a gift of it back to the lance corporal, and of course the lance corporal said 'yes'. So, the general got a pen, signed his name, and wrote something like 'from one Marine to another, I'm proud to serve with you', and gave it to him. Don't you know that lance corporal would run through a brick wall for General Dowda? Quite a guy.

"Now, when we go into his office, we're there to answer questions. Don't speak unless spoken to, and shoot straight with him. He may ask each of you if you think it was an error-free trial and if there was sufficient evidence for the military panel to find guilt. You know there was no error and there was sufficient evidence to convict, so I'd suggest you answer 'yes'. Don't know if he'll ask you to give reasons for your gut feelings of innocence, but don't be afraid to look him in the eye and speak from your heart. We're here."

They parked on a horseshoe driveway in a space marked 'visitor' and walked into the office and were told to wait for the general to finish some business.

Woody didn't know why he had re-opened the banker's box which contained the entire Jackson file. He'd been through it a hundred times. He thought he knew the front and back of every piece of paper in this file — there were over a five-hundred documents. He thought there was no way he'd missed anything. He was picking up files, and looking at documents, but not really seeing anything. His mind was on Jackson and what he would say to him after the general approved the conviction and sentence.

General Dowda was about 5'8" tall, and a very unassuming man, except for the star of a brigadier general on each of his collars. He was reserved but immediately put the colonel, McMurry and Smith at ease. He asked McMurry and Smith how it was they came to join the Corps and seemed genuinely interested in their stories. After a few minutes, the colonel spoke up.

"Would the General like me to give my report on this Jackson case?"

The general replied, "Colonel, I really do appreciate your adherence to the somewhat antiquated military custom to refer to senior officers in the third person, as you just did, when you're in their presence. But to me that custom seems awkward in practice. It is almost as if one is asking questions of a corpse laid out for visitation. Let's do this on a first name basis: My first name is General, and your first names are Colonel, Captain and Lieutenant. I'll be more comfortable. So, tell me about this case. I want to know everything there is to know."

As the colonel, McMurry and Ross began to inform General Dowda of the facts of the case from the trial, their post-trial misgivings about the conviction, the two polygraphs, and the truth serum results, Woody was returning the investigation officer's file to the banker's box when he saw, for the first time, a card he could play.

"SON OF A BITCH!!!" Woody yelled so loudly that Ben Harvey jumped out of his chair 10 feet away in his cubicle.

"WHAT THE HELL HAPPENED, WOODY?"

"SON OF A BITCH!" Woody was standing up, holding the IO's file. He looked at Ben. "You go right now and call the colonel at General Dowda's office. Tell them to tell the colonel that there is an emergency message from Captain White!"

"What the hell do you want me to tell them the message is?"

"You tell them to tell the colonel that Captain White found that smoking gun and is on the way and to not let the General sign the papers." Woody ran from the legal office to his car. Ben found the number for the general's office and placed the call.

"Colonel Sullivan, I do appreciate the report. It was concisely given. And gentlemen" — the General nodded to Mike and Kevin — "I appreciate your candor and your efforts on behalf of this lance corporal. And Colonel, please express my appreciation to Captain White. But, at the end of the day, I've got to look at this as a legal matter, and as a legal matter, we've got a murdered lieutenant, six witnesses including an eyewitness against the defendant, a military panel who weighed the evidence and then convicted the defendant even though he testified denying the offense, in a trial that was free from prejudicial error. So, Colonel, if you'll give me the paperwork to approve the trial and conviction, I'll sign it and we can be done."

As Colonel Sullivan was walking to the General's desk, there was a loud knocking on the office door. "COME", the General ordered.

Top stuck his head in the door. "General, there is a urgent message for Colonel Sullivan from a Captain White."

General Dowda looked at Colonel Sullivan, who shrugged his shoulders as if to say he didn't know what it was about.

"Well, what's the message, Top?"

"He said to tell the colonel that a Captain White has found that gun the colonel was talking about and to ask the general not to sign the conviction approval, and that he is on the way."

"Thanks, Top." The general then turned to Colonel Sullivan. "Colonel, what the hell is going on here. I've given you and your men plenty of time to go through this issue and now we get a mysterious message from another of your crew. What does that message mean?"

Colonel Sullivan came to attention. "General, when we left the legal office, I told Captain White that — well, General, may I state exactly what I said?"

"Colonel, I think you BETTER do that. What the hell did you tell him!"

"General, I told him that unless he pulled a smoking gun out of his ass and put it in the hand of someone other than Jackson, that you would approve the conviction, and Jackson was on the way to Leavenworth."

The general leaned back in his chair and nodded to Colonel Sullivan to sit back down. His elbows were on the arms of his chair and he steepled his fingers. "So, I'm supposed to believe that after all these many months, and investigations, and polygraphs, and whatever, that "the smoking gun" to free Jackson has just now been found, right?"

Colonel Sullivan again came to attention and faced the general. "Sir, Captain White is an excellent officer and attorney. I don't believe he has it in him to waste the gen — your time, with something frivolous. I would hope you'd give him a chance to tell you — to tell all of us — what he found."

"Colonel, I write your fitness report. This event and your judgment about these matters will be part of that fitness report. Are you willing to run the risk that your report may be bad if White comes up with something that falls flat?"

Colonel Sullivan seemed to stand even more erectly at attention, as if he were being inspected at OCS. "Yes, sir! Absolutely."

General Dowda just looked at Sullivan for a few seconds, nodded for him to sit, and spoke to Top. "When this Captain White gets here, show him in, please."

General Dowda picked up some papers on his desk to read, and Colonel Sullivan, McMurry and Ross just sat and wondered what the hell Woody had come up with. Each of them hoped this was not a wild-goose chase, but none of them could imagine what Woody found that could help Jackson.

There was a knock at the door. "COME", the general ordered.

Top opened the door. "General, Captain White is here." He stepped back and Woody appeared in the doorway, holding a file.

"Front and center, Captain", the general ordered.

Woody crossed the room and came to attention about three feet in front of the general's desk. When he came into the building, Woody removed his cover as required, and therefore did not salute the general. General Dowda waited a few seconds before speaking.

"Captain, the colonel told me what the message meant. I've got a second hand on my watch. You've got 60 seconds to state your case about this so-called 'smoking gun', starting now."

Woody's mind raced for about 10 seconds. Then he realized just how to say what the general needed to hear. "Sir, an officer named Breckinridge interviewed government witnesses who testified that Jackson said before the lieutenant was murdered that he wished the lieutenant was dead. The main witness in this case said he saw two men running from the lieutenant's hooch right after the grenade exploded. He ID'd a man named Grant, who has not yet been tried, and Jackson, the convicted Marine, but given the weather conditions

— that typhoon had hit, and the fact it was nighttime, the opportunity for positive ID was low. The investigation officer wrote what six witnesses told him and put those six interview sheets in this witness file I have, but on the inside of the file, he wrote — looks like the same handwriting to me — the names of SEVEN, NOT SIX witnesses he interviewed. He did not include the interview of the seventh witness whose name is written on the inside of the folder, a Marine named Corporal Jason Singletary. We don't know what Singletary said, but he may have said Jackson didn't do it. I noticed for the first time today there were the names of seven, not six, witnesses, even though I've handled this file beaucoup times since I got in country."

The general was silent a few seconds and then spoke up. "Captain, there could be any number of explanations why the interview sheet is not in there. He may not have interviewed this seventh person — what's his name?"

"Singletary, sir, Jason Singletary."

"This Singletary may have given the same story the other witnesses gave, and this investigation officer decided it was not important to add to his witness file, or, it could have fallen out of the file, who knows? You've brought me a problem you want me to deal with, without any hope that it will really help me decide this issue. I don't want folks bringing me a problem without a solution. What is your solution to the mystery of this so-called missing seventh witness?"

Woody knew from the sarcasm in General Dowda's voice that the general was running out of time and patience. Woody knew that he needed to come up with a plan that had a practical way to address the mystery.

"General, I think you should take such steps as are necessary to locate Singletary, interview him or have him interviewed, and have that interview made available to you. Then you will know everything there is to know about whether to approve the conviction. If he's on this island, frankly I think he should immediately report to this office and should speak directly to you about it so you will know firsthand what he said to that IO. After all, you're the one making the decision.

If he's stateside, a NIS agent can interview him and forward the interview to you. That's what I'd do."

General Dowda leaned back in his chair and again steepled his fingers and looked at Woody, who continued to stand at attention.

"Captain White, when you were at TBS, you remember they had a military protocol class which dealt with the way you address superior officers when speaking to them, don't you?"

"Yes, sir."

"Captain White, don't you remember being instructed that when you were in the presence of officers of superior rank that you referred to them in the third person?"

"Yes, sir."

"Well, you haven't done that today, with me. Why not?"

"Sir, I do hope I have not offended you, for several reasons. My failure to follow that protocol is certainly not a show of disrespect. But frankly, I find it very awkward to speak to a person by referring to that person in the third person. It's like I'm standing next to the coffin at a visitation and talking to the deceased. So I guess I didn't learn that lesson well, Sir, and I hope my failure to do that right does hurt my efforts — our efforts, for Jackson."

When Woody gave his explanation, a small grin came across the general's face and he chuckled. At the same time, Woody heard laughs from the colonel and the trial counsels. He wondered what that was about but continued to stand at attention.

General Dowda leaned forward and picked up his phone. "Top, I need you in here. And bring a legal pad with you." He looked at Woody. "Stand at ease, Captain, and let me see that witness file."

Top came into the office and stepped next to the general's desk. "Top, drop whatever you're doing. I need you to handle this as fast as humanly possible. Find out if a Marine named Jason Singletary, a corporal, is on Okinawa and report that to me. Thank you."

General Dowda stood up. "Captain White, I appreciate your ballsy approach to this issue. You came up with a plan of attack which made sense, which can be immediately implemented, and which will achieve the objective of at least finding out what Singletary knows. You've earned the opportunity for this office to follow this trail to its end. Gentlemen, let's move to that table." Colonel Sullivan noticed that because the table was circular, there was no 'head' of the table.

The general brought the file and a legal pad with him. "Okay, let's assume we find this Singletary, and let's assume he has something to say that is exculpatory — I think that is the right word — for Jackson. We still have a murdered Marine lieutenant and a Marine named Grant waiting trial for murder. By the way, why was Grant charged?"

McMurry answered, "Sir, Grant was easy to pick out, 'cause he was the tallest and biggest man in the platoon, or at least the tallest and biggest of the black Marines, and, he had a cast on his left arm, which we think was caused when he intentionally broke his wrist to stay off the line. He was easy to identify when he was running from the lieutenant's hooch."

The general said "Well, if you are right, and this Jackson was not involved with Grant, then we still have an accomplice or co-conspirator who hasn't been charged. Who might that be, and what do we do about getting him in the process? Anybody."

McMurry spoke. "Sir, there were thirty-three men in first platoon, Alpha 1/9, on the night of the murder, eleven of which, including Jackson, were white. Singletary was one of those eleven. We and the NIS interviewed those eleven, as well as the rest of the men in Alpha. Unless Grant got someone from another unit, which is unlikely, it is probably one of those eleven, but we don't have a clue as to which one. When we interviewed Singletary and Jackson, they denied having anything to do with the murder or knowing who did it, as did the rest of the platoon."

Top came back in. "General, we've located Singletary. He's a corporal, with first platoon, Delta Company, and they're training at Camp Schwab."

"Top, we don't have time to go through regiment, battalion, and company to get to his platoon. We can explain jumping outside the chain of command later, if anyone asks, which they won't. Right now, I want to talk to Singletary's platoon leader and if you can, patch him through to this phone. If you can't, I'll go where I have to go to talk to him. And give the training area coordinates to the chopper pilots and tell them to immediately head up there to Schwab to pick up

Singletary. I need to talk to the platoon commander before the chopper picks up Singletary.

"Gentlemen, correct me if I'm wrong on this summary — and speak up, I don't like 'yes men' around me. First, Singletary may not have even been interviewed by the IO. Second, if he were interviewed, the sheet may have simply been misplaced. Third, if he were interviewed, he'll remember what he said. Fourth, if he says, basically, what the other witnesses said, I have no choice from a legal perspective but to sign the approval of the conviction. Fifth, if he says something that either clears Jackson, or casts doubt on the conviction, then I'll consider not approving the conviction — but no guarantee of that. Sixth, if he points a guilty finger at someone else, we can investigate that and hold the decision on whether to approve or reverse the conviction. Do any of you have anything to add or change to those possibilities?"

Each shook their heads 'no'.

Top opened the door." General, I have Singletary's platoon leader, Lieutenant Barringer, on the phone, patched through to your phone."

General Dowda picked up the phone. "Lieutenant Barringer, this is General Dowda. Can you read me? This is no joke, you understand? OK. The CG's chopper is on the way to your training area. Not sure of its ETA. It needs to bring a corporal named Singletary — Top gave you his full name — back to my office. Now, this corporal is going to be pooping in his pants when he's ordered to get on a chopper with two general's stars on the nose. You tell him, loud and clear, first, he is not in trouble, second, no one in his family has died or is in trouble, third, he has not done anything wrong, and finally he is needed on an important administrative matter. Now Lieutenant, I'm going to ask Singletary what you told him, and I want you to know that I will be a very unhappy Marine general if he doesn't tell me exactly what I just told you to tell him. Understand? One more thing. When is your unit scheduled to return to Courtney? Well, just tell Singletary to bring his gear with him, and we'll get him a ride back to barracks, since the rest of the platoon will be back later today. He can get a head start on the beer. Any questions? OK, thank you lieutenant. I appreciate your help."

As soon as the general put the phone in the cradle, Woody heard the 'whop-whop' of the chopper's blades as it warmed up for the take off to the training area at Schwab, which was north. He had no idea how long it would take for the chopper — he guessed it was a Huey — to make the round trip. He'd driven north to Schwab once, to see a crime scene in an assault case. It was a long, beautiful drive in the hilly area north of Camp Courtney. Woody could only imagine what it had been like to fight the tenacious Japanese army on such terrain.

The general stood up. "Gentlemen, I still have a Division to help run, and since we've done all we can do until these pieces of the puzzle start falling into place, would all of you please give me this office. Top will call you when we need you. Thanks."

The colonel, Mike, Kevin and Woody left the general's office and went to the front yard of the HQ building. They were lost in their own thoughts, wondering what Singletary would have to say. Colonel Sullivan pulled out his ever-present Red Man and packed a chew into his jaw. "Woody, want some of this?"

"No, sir. I'm hyped-up enough but thank you for offering."

Woody didn't know how long they had been out of the office when he heard, and then saw, the chopper coming from the north. It was riding a tailwind, moving like a bat out of hell. It passed over the HQ building and reversed direction so it was heading north, into the headwind which would help the landing.

Once the blades stopped, a Marine in full combat gear jumped from the chopper. He just looked around, but then Woody saw Top walking to the landing pad to escort Singletary back to the building. The lawyers headed for the front door of the HQ building and were escorted back into the general's office. The general was seated at the conference table and he directed them to take their seats. Within a minute, Top opened the door, accompanied by Singletary, who didn't have his combat gear. Singletary looked around and saw the star of a brigadier general, the silver bird of a colonel, and the railroad tracks of three O-3s. He had a bewildered look on his face and had to be wondering — What the hell is going on!

The general rose from his chair and walked over to Singletary and extended his hand. "Corporal Singletary, I'm General Dowda. I'm proud to meet you. Come in and have a seat."

Singletary moved very cautiously. Just a few minutes ago, he had been training with his platoon at Schwab, and now he had a ride on a general's chopper and was shaking hands with a general in a room with more brass than he'd seen in one place at any time in the Corps. This had to be a surreal experience for him.

After Singletary was seated, next to the general, General Dowda spoke. "Corporal, I know they don't serve Pepsis in the field at Schwab, do they. Top, would you bring the corporal a Pepsi with ice." Top said he would do so, and General Dowda spoke to Singletary.

"Where are you from, son?"

"North of Pierre, South Dakota, sir."

"Is that near Lake Oahe?"

"Yes sir, it is." Singletary broke into a grin.

"That is beautiful country. I went pheasant hunting in that area once. You ever pheasant hunt, Corporal."

"Oh, yes sir. I love to pheasant hunt."

"What kind of shotgun did you have?"

Woody was amazed. General Dowda was talking to a Marine who was initially scared out of his skives to a Marine who was now smiling and talking about shooting shotguns for fun. Singleltary had inhaled the Pepsi and appeared more at ease. General Dowda was ready to get down to business.

"Corporal, your platoon leader, Lieutenant Barringer, what did he tell you when he said you'd be coming down here to meet with us?"

Singletary told General Dowda what Barringer had told him and it was exactly what the general had ordered. Lucky for Barringer, Woody thought.

"We're here — these officers are lawyers, because we have some questions about the murder of Lieutenant Speight at VCB right after Apache Snow. You were with Alpha 1/9 then, weren't you?"

Woody was looking intently to Singletary and noticed that when General Dowda said "murder", Singletary's body stiffened somewhat. Woody had learned that body language could sometimes tell as much or more than what a witness was saying.

"Uh, yes sir, I was."

"Did you go on Apache Snow?"

"Yes, sir."

"That was a tough operation, wasn't it."

"Yes, sir." By now, Singletary was squirming. Woody guessed he was realizing why he had been brought to the general's office, and he didn't like the position he was in.

"Corporal, you were interviewed by a lieutenant named Breckinridge about that fragging, weren't you?"

Woody could tell that Singletary was now becoming very uncomfortable. He was rubbing his hands together and was nervously looking around the room. He did not answer the general immediately.

The general leaned toward Singletary. "Corporal, I believe Lieutenant Breckinridge talked to you about the fragging. Your name is written by Lieutenant Breckinridge on the inside of this folder" the general held up the folder — "as a witness. Now, I need you to tell me what you told Lieutenant Breckinridge, and remember, whatever you tell us you told him, as long as it is the truth, will NOT, I repeat NOT, get you in trouble. I give you my word as a General Officer of the Marine Corps. Understand?"

Singletary nodded and addressed the general. "Sir, Lieutenant Breckinridge had me stand at attention right there in company headquarters and he gave me a direct order to not tell anyone else what I told him about that night, and I have obeyed that order. I didn't even tell the two lawyers and the detectives who came to VCB to talk to all of us, because the lieutenant had ordered me to not tell anyone what I told him. The order didn't sound right but, I followed it"

"Well, Corporal, my general's star outranks Lieutenant Breckinridge's first lieutenant's bar, and I'm ordering you to not follow his order, and to tell us what you told him about the fragging. Understand?"

"Yes, sir. This is what happened, and this is what I told the lieutenant. I'll never forget it. On the night the lieutenant was killed, I don't know what time it was. I didn't keep up with time in Nam, 'cause it don't matter. I was asleep and had to get up to go take a piss — -uh, sorry, sir.

"That's all right, Corporal. I've taken a piss or two myself."

Singletary continued. "The head is right next to my hooch. I was leaving my hooch going to the head and saw Nose leaving the head and heading back to his hooch, which is on the other side of the head. He didn't look at me, don't think he saw me."

The general looked around and spoke up. "Who is 'Nose'?"

Woody answered. "Sir, Lance Corporal Jackson has a honker, a nose, that would put Jimmy Durante to shame, about like Karl Malden's nose."

"Malden, was he the actor with Steve McQueen in *Cincinnati Kid?*"

Woody replied, "Yes, sir."

"Well, I guess he would be hard to miss. So, Corporal, what did you see?"

"Sir, as soon as I went into the head, I heard the grenade explode. I looked up and saw Grant and Garland Greenfield running from the area of the lieutenant's hooch, right toward me. They was close to me, I saw their faces when it lightened. Grant and Greenfield ran past the head and my hooch to their hooches, which are on the other side of the bunker, past where I was."

McMurry spoke. "General may I ask Corporal Singletary some questions?" The general nodded. "First, how far were Grant and Greenfield from you when you saw them running?"

"About fifteen feet."

"Second, how long was it from the time you saw Jackson go into his hooch to the time the grenade exploded?"

"Sir, just a second or two."

"Once Jackson went into his hooch, did he come out when you were in the head?"

"No sir."

"After you saw Jackson go into his hooch, was there enough time for him to run up to the lieutenant's hooch before the grenade exploded?"

"No sir. No way"

"How far is it from your hooch, when you were coming out to go the head, to Jackson when he was coming out of the head?"

Singletary looked around the office, pointed and said," About as far as here to that wall over there."

"Was Jackson facing you when he left the head?"

"No sir, I was looking at the left side of his face. It was Nose. Can't miss him."

McMurry spoke," General, that wall looks to be about fifteen feet away, which means Singletary was much closer to Jackson than Douglas was to the men he saw running, who he said were twenty or thirty yards from him."

General Dowda slid his legal pad to Singletary and gave him a pen. "Draw a map of the lieutenant's hooch, Jackson's hooch, the head, your hooch, and the hooch for Grant and Greenfield. Oh, and that bunker."

When Singletary had finished, Woody spoke up. "General, may I see that." The general slid the legal pad to Woody. "That is EXACTLY the map Jackson drew for me, except I didn't ask him to draw Grant's hooch. It's in my office if you need to see it. And I went out to VCB to see the place for myself, and that is the layout."

Everyone was quiet for a few seconds, absorbing all this information. The silence was broken by Singletary who was trying to sob without making a noise, but his body was shaking. When he looked up, tears were running down his face. He looked at the general. "Sir, when I heard Jackson had been charged, I knowed he was innocent. I knowed Greenfield was with Grant. I wanted to say something to somebody, but Lieutenant Breckinridge, he gave me a direct order. I was afraid to speak up. I didn't know what to do." He continued sobbing.

"Corporal, look at me!" General Dowda had gently grabbed Singletary's shoulders. "Son, you did exactly the right thing. All Marines are taught to follow orders, even if — make that particularly if — we don't understand them. That's just the way it is. This is not your fault. When you were talking to Lieutenant Breckinridge, was he taking notes?"

"Sir, I think he wrote some stuff down, but then he stopped. He didn't show me what he wrote."

General Dowda sat back in his chair. "Corporal, do you have any idea why Lieutenant Breckinridge gave you the order to not tell anyone Jackson was not with Grant?"

"No, sir. I didn't see much of any lieutenants, including him, sir, but he was…"

"He was what, Corporal?" the general asked.

"Well, sir, it was like we was back in the States the way he wanted us to look at VCB. He'd get on someone because of their haircut, or boots were messed up, or something like that. It's like he forgot we was at a combat base and was busy cleaning our weapons after patrols and didn't have time to polish our boots. I remember, one-time Lieutenant Breckinridge charged Jackson with an office hours offense, you know, Article 15. I think Jackson was filling sandbags — we did that all the time — and he was wearing a T shirt and his utility cover, but he didn't salute the lieutenant which normally you gotta do when you're outside and got your cover on. The hearing officer tossed it out, and I heard from some guys that Lieutenant Breckinridge got razzed by other officers about his charge against Jackson being thrown out. I guess even the officers didn't like him being so tough on Jackson. Maybe the lieutenant was upset with Jackson."

General Dowda said, "Corporal, you've been a great help. You followed orders like you were supposed to even though you wanted to speak up on Jackson's behalf. You did nothing wrong. Colonel Sullivan, what is the next step?"

Colonel Sullivan answered. "General, I'd like to get the corporal to sit down with one of our court reporters so his information can be transcribed and recorded, and so the corporal can sign the statement as an affidavit."

"Good idea, Colonel. Corporal Singletary, we'll drive you down to legal, and after you give the court reporter your statement, call Top and we'll get you and your gear back to your barracks so you can get started on the beer. And I'll have my office give you a call so you and I can go skeet shooting. We have enough shotguns for you to pick a good one. Thank you, Corporal, for your help. You're dismissed."

While General Dowda walked Singletary to the door, Woody called Legal, got Corporal Greevey on the line and told him what he needed to do when Singletary arrived.

The general spoke. "Well, this is something! As hard as it is to believe, we may have a rogue IO, who interviewed Marines who said Jackson left that bunker saying he wished the lieutenant was dead, and then interviewed one Marine who ID'd Jackson as the man with Grant, at night, from thirty yards or so, when it lightened, with a typhoon howling. Then the IO interviewed another Marine, Singletary, who said Greenfield, not Jackson, was with Grant, and then the IO didn't include that interview sheet 'cause he was pissed at Jackson. This is hard to believe. Colonel Sullivan, have I summarized this correctly?"

"Yes, sir."

The general continued. "Captain McMurry, and Lieutenant Ross, if that IO, Breckinridge, had included his interview with Singletary just as Singletary told us today, even with what the other Marine said about ID'ing Jackson, what would you have done as trial counsel?"

McMurry answered. "Well, General, to analyze the situation and then answer the question, eyewitness cases are tough, 'cause humans are talking about what they remember they think they saw in a split second or so. To me, Singletary, not Douglas, had the better chance to see Jackson. They were running toward him, not past him, as they were with Douglas. Singletary was much closer to Grant and Greenfield than Douglas was to the guys who were running. I believe Singletary is the better, more believable witness. His reaction today is pretty good evidence of that. I'm not saying Douglas is lying, I'm just saying he didn't see the right man. But we'd investigate, probably have lawyers assigned to both Jackson and Greenfield, then we'd see the level of cooperation, if any, came from either of them. We could not charge both of them and Grant, because there were only two people, so that would make it more confusing. If we charged Jackson, we'd tell his attorney what Singletary said. We'd have to do some serious thinking about this. We could talk to other Marines in Alpha 1/9 and see if we could connect dots between Jackson and Grant, or Greenfield and Grant. If we decided to charge Greenfield, we'd try to squeeze him to testify against Grant. Getting the death penalty off the plate may bring him around, and a conviction of the murder charges, versus the accessory and conspiracy charges, is more important to the government. Also, if we had both stories, we may ask the SJA to help decide. I think a decision on that issue is above our pay grade."

"So"the general continued, "where the hell is Greenfield. Anyone got an idea?"

When no one knew, the general went to the office door and asked Top to come in. "Top, we need to find another Marine in Alpha 1/9, by the name of Garland Greenfield. Get right on it and come back when you know, please."

Within five minutes, Top knocked and came into the office. "General, I've located Greenfield, that's the good news. The bad news is that he is at Kadena Air Base, or he has left Kadena to rotate back home. And, when he gets to the States, he'll be discharged."

The general spoke. "Anybody got any ideas how to locate him either at Kadena, or if he's flown out, to find out the ETA of his flight at Norton Air Base in California so we can be waiting for him. Given the twenty hours or so flight time if he's left, we've got enough time to get NIS to Norton to be waiting for him if his flight has left Kadena. Or, we could maybe get NIS in Hawaii to pick him up when they land to refuel, but first we gotta find him."

Top spoke." General, I believe Major Jacobs has a golf buddy — an Air Force guy — who is stationed at Kadena Air Base. That may be a place to start."

General Dowda picked up the phone on the conference room table and dialed a number. "Major Jacobs, I need you in here, with a legal pad."

Tom Jacobs was a graduate of The University of the South in Sewanee, Tennessee. He enlisted his senior year of college, completed OCS and TBS, and with his intelligence, had steadily risen through the ranks. General Dowda hand-picked Jacobs to be his aide.

Major Jacobs came into the general's office. "Tom, have a seat. I'll introduce these gentlemen later, but first, I've got a job for you. I've got to find out if a Marine named Greenfield — Garland Greenfield — you can get the full name and service number from Top, is at, or going to, or has passed through, transit, at Kadena. As I understand it, he has pulled his tour, and will be discharged from the Corps upon reaching the States. Do you know someone at Transit who can help locate this Marine for us?"

"Yes, sir, I do. Major Mike Foster, Air Force, is actually second in command of transit. He and I have played golf several times at the Kadena base course, last time last Saturday. I have his number. What shall I tell him we need him to do?"

"Tell him that there are orders on the way for this Greenfield — Top, please prepare the orders — changing his transit orders if he hasn't left, and if he has left, we need your buddy to give you the flight number and the travel itinerary of the flight. Also, he needs to do this in a way that doesn't scare off Greenfield. He needs to call Captain McMurry back with his report."

"Yes, sir, I'll get right on it."

"Tom, one more thing. Did you win the match against him last Saturday?"

"Yes, General, the Corps NEVER loses to the Air Force."

Kadena Air Base

When told a Major Jacobs was calling for him, Mike Foster, Major, USAF, wondered if Tom was calling him to set up another golf game, or to razz him about winning the bet at their last match, or both.

Major Foster answered the call. "You were lucky as hell to sink that putt on 18 last week. Are you calling to rub it in?"

"No, Mike, we've got a real problem to deal with, and need your immediate help."

"Sure thing, what can I do?"

After Tom outlined the need to locate and hold Greenfield if he were at Kadena, and to get his flight number and itinerary if his flight had departed, Major Foster said, "There are, maybe, three hundred Marines here waiting to fly back to the States on two different flights. I can check both manifests to see if he's in that group. If he is, how can I find him? Do you have a picture? If I call out his name, he may get jumpy and bolt."

"Mike, I wish I could help you. A description probably wouldn't help becayse he could see the Air Police pulling guys out and asking if their name was Greenfield, and there are no name tags on jungle utilities. He'd know what was going on and bug out. There's got to be another way to get him without his knowing we're looking for him."

"OK, Tom, I'll figure out something and keep you posted. What's your call-back number?"

"Mike, I just thought of something else. I'm loading up on you. We're gonna need a lawyer with you when you get Greenfield, if he's there. He'll need to give Greenfield his Miranda warning, you know, to remain silent, that what he said could or would be used against him — the lawyer will know the drill. If Greenfield says anything, we want to be able to use is. Can you make that happen?"

"Can do. The JAG office is five minutes from here, and one of my poker buddies is a lawyer. I'll call him right now. What is your call-back number?

After writing down Tom's number, Mike started brainstorming. How could he possibly locate Greenfield without Greenfield's knowing he was being looked for?

And then he knew exactly what he would do. He got his barracks hat and put a piece of paper in it, gave instructions to his next-in-command, and left his office.

The terminal at Kadena was large and airy. There were about three hundred Marines, plus their sea bags, ready to board two civilian aircraft for flights back to the States. Mike had checked the manifests of both flights and knew which flight Greenfield was on, but Marines from both flights were all in one place. The terminal had a sound system which worked well, and Mike knew how to use it to get Greenfield.

When Mike got to the center of the terminal, he stood on a bench under the big clock and gave the pre-arranged signal to his next-in-command, who was viewing the terminal from Mike's office.

Mike's next-in-command punched the key to make the announcement to all the Marines. "Marines, the Air Force very much appreciates the service you have given to our great country, and as a show of our appreciation we are going to award a new Seiko watch to the lucky Marine whose name is drawn out of the hat of Major Foster, who is now standing on the bench under the clock. Please listen up."

Major Foster had brought a hand mike with him. He addressed the crowd, all of whom were looking at him. "Jarheads, you've all done a great job, at great peril. We — the Air Force, and all Americans — appreciate your service. We have written the names of each of you, taken from the flight manifests of both aircrafts, and put them in my hat. I'm going to reach into my hat and select the one Marine, from all of you, who will receive a new Seiko watch, courtesy of the Air Force." Mike held his hat above his head, reached with his right hand and made a motion as if he were searching through papers with names on them, and then pulled out of his hat the only piece of paper in it, looked at it, and announced: "The lucky Marine is PFC Garland Greenfield. Come forward, please."

Everyone started looking around to see who the lucky winner was. Greenfield had never won a thing in his life. He smiled bashfully as he moved through the crowd. Everyone was clapping him on the back, calling him a 'lucky dog'.

Greenfield got to the bench where Tom was standing. He didn't notice the two husky Air Police on either side of the bench, or the Air Force captain behind the major making the announcement. Foster extended his hand, as if to offer a handshake, and when Greenfield did the same, the Air Policeman on his right snapped a handcuff on his right wrist, pulled his right arm behind him, and then pulled his left arm behind him and cuffed his left wrist. Major Foster directed the Air Police to take Greenfield to his office, jumped from the bench and followed them. The Air Force lawyer was one step behind Major Foster.

GREENFIELD

"General, there is a call for Captain McMurry from a Major Foster.", Top announced from the doorway. "I'll route it to the conference table phone." McMurry picked up the receiver, introduced himself and listened. Everyone was quiet as they listened to McMurry's end of the call.

When McMurry had finished the call, he placed the phone back in the receiver. "Major Foster got Greenfield. put him in handcuffs and is transporting him to the brig at Camp Hansen. It's a good thing we had an Air Force JAG lawyer with them to warn Greenfield of his rights, 'cause Greenfield started talking as soon as they were on the way to the brig. He said that he was asleep on the night of the fragging when Grant woke him up and told him he was going to play a joke on Lieutenant Speight by tossing a smoke grenade that he — Grant — had swiped from an LZ. Greenfield said Grant said he needed Greenfield to hold open the lieutenant's hooch door since he couldn't because he had a messed-up hand, and that he would toss the smoke grenade with his good hand. Greenfield said he held the door open but didn't see what Grant had in his hand or what he threw into the lieutenant's hooch. Greenfield said as they were running back to the hooch, he heard the explosion and knew Grant had fragged the lieutenant. When they got to their hooch, he asked Grant why he'd thrown a live grenade, instead of a smoke grenade. He said Grant grabbed him and said that he was as guilty as Grant was, and he'd better keep his mouth shut or he'd be charged too. Greenfield may not be guilty of conspiracy or murder, but he sure is guilty of accessory after the fact for helping Grant to keep it quiet."

Colonel Sullivan addressed the general. "Sir, this satisfies me that Jackson didn't do anything, and that Captains McMurry and White, and Lieutenant Ross, were right on the money about Jackson's possibly being innocent. I recommend that you sign the paperwork to overturn the conviction."

General Dowda put his elbows on the table, and leaned forward. "I've got to get my head around this. Grant fooled Greenfield into helping, and instead of throwing a smoke grenade he threw a live M61 — or we think it was a M61 — under the lieutenant's rack. Greenfield was not interviewed by the IO, Lieutenant Breckenridge, but was interviewed when NIS interviewed the company, and I guess denied everything. An attempt to interview Grant was made and he didn't say anything, right?" McMurry nodded. "And Corporal Singletary tells us he saw Jackson go into his hooch right before the grenade exploded, and he then saw Grant and Greenfield — not Jackson — running from the lieutenant's hooch toward their hooch. But because Breckinridge gave him an order to not disclose that info, Singletary told NIS he didn't know anything about it. Greenfield has volunteered he was with Grant and that Grant tossed the grenade, and that would be admissible wouldn't it Colonel Sullivan?" The colonel nodded 'yes'. "And so we've got a rogue Investigation Officer who knew damn well he was not shooting straight when he didn't make Singletary's statement part of the investigation, probably because he was pissed at Jackson. Colonel, would there be a crime in his not making the report of what Singletary said?"

Colonel Sullivan answered. "Yes, sir, it would at least be obstruction of justice."

The general stood up. "Colonel, please prepare the documents necessary to reverse or strike or whatever you do to get rid of the dishonorable discharge and the sentence, and restore Lance Corporal Jackson to his rank, and the return of his pay. But you may think about helping him getting all that money at once. He's been confined all these months, I'd hate to see him blow it all in one night on the town." He went to the door and asked Top and Tom Jacobs to come in and have a seat at the table.

"Top, when we break up, I want you to find out where this Breckinridge is stationed, base and unit, and give that information to Colonel Sullivan. Colonel, in a minute you and I will discuss

Breckinridge. But now, gentlemen, we have done a good day's work for the Corps, and we need to reward ourselves."

The general walked over to a cabinet in the corner of the room, got a tray, put several glasses on it, and brought them to the table and gave a glass to each man. He then went back to the cabinet, opened the cabinet doors, and took a bottle of 101 proof Wild Turkey and a bottle of Old Grouse scotch back to the table. "Gentlemen, pour yourself a strong belt of your preference." After each officer had followed the General's order, the general held out his glass to make a toast, and the other officers and Top stood. "Gentlemen, to the Corps! Semper Fi!" The other officers repeated the toasts, clinked glasses all around and took a well-deserved drink.

"Now, Gentlemen, we're earned that drink. But we're not through. Here's what is going to happen next."

0830 Hours, Wed 12 Nov 69
Camp Hansen, Okinawa
The Brig

The brig for the Third Marine Division on Okinawa was located at Camp Hansen, north of Camp Courtney and south of Camp Schwab.

Lance Corporal Jackson was in the exercise yard of the brig when the guard told him he had visitors. All he could think about was whether he'd survive Leavenworth prison. He had asked one of the brig guards about it, because the guard had served there. After Jackson got the rundown on the prison, he began to summon up the guts to kill himself, because Captain White had told him that it was a long shot, an almost-impossible shot, that the general would overturn the conviction. He knew the visitor would be Captain White, probably with bad news.

Then he realized the guard had said he had visitors, more than one. Jackson couldn't imagine who other than Captain White would be coming to this hell-hole brig to see him.

Family members visited a prisoner in a room where a thick glass partition separated the visitor and the prisoner. Lawyers were permitted to visit with their clients in an open room, at tables. Several guards would remain in the room during these visits, but on this occasion, there were no guards present.

Jackson had been visited by White several times in that room, but this time was different. When Jackson was escorted into the room, Captain White was seated facing him, but two men in uniform were seated across from Captain White, with their backs to Jackson as he cautiously approached the table.

Woody stood up. "Lance Corporal Jackson, you remember these men, don't you?" McMurry and Ross stood up. Jackson recoiled. Then, he saw that they were smiling and extending their hands to shake his hand. Woody continued. "We've got good news — the best news, for you. Have a seat."

Jackson felt as if he were in a dream as Woody recounted the story of the witness file, Lieutenant Breckinridge, the interview with Singletary, Greenfield's confession and the general's asking Colonel Sullivan to return to his office to prepare documents overturning the conviction. There would be no trip to Fort Leavenworth!

Woody continued. "Jackson, here's what's going to happen. You're leaving here with us, as a free man. Here's a power of attorney for you to sign, authorizing me to deposit and control your back pay because you were entitled to pay even though you were convicted and in jail because the conviction was not final. I'll give you money from time to time, until you get used to being on the outside. The last thing you need to do is to blow all of this on beer and women in a weekend. You'll be assigned to first platoon, Delta Company 2/9 which is on Oki, and they know you're on the way. You'll have light duty for some period of time. Your company commander and platoon leader know your story. Any questions?"

Jackson could not speak. He just stared ahead. Then he put his head on the table, and his shoulders shook as he sobbed the cry of a free man. Woody knew that Marines weren't supposed to cry, but this was an exception to that rule.

1245 Hours, Thursday, 20 Nov 69
Office of General Dowda
Camp Courtney
Singletary Is Surprised

Corporal Jason Singletary had no idea that he would again visit the office of General Dowda after meeting with the general about the murder of Lieutenant Speight. But he was told by his platoon leader and company commander that all three of them had been ordered to report to the General's office at 1300 hours on 20 November. He was not told why he was reporting. He just knew that a Marine did what he was ordered to do, without questioning the order.

All three Marines changed from their utilities to their service Charley uniform with the piss cutter garrison hat, and arrived at the General's office at 1245 hours. They were seated in the waiting area. Jason noted there was a lance corporal with a camera also seated in the waiting area.

Promptly at 1300 hours, the general's first sergeant asked them to come into the general's office. The lance corporal with the camera was ordered to follow them. General Dowda was standing in the middle of the room.

The general extended his hand to the company commander and the platoon leader. Then he turned to Jason. "Welcome, Corporal Singletary. I know you have been a corporal in this man's Corps for only eight months, and I know that one is usually a corporal for at least two years before being considered for promotion to sergeant E-5. But your service to the Corps has been so exceptional, particularly in the last few weeks, that it is my privilege and honor to promote you to the rank of sergeant, E-5. Congratulations, Sergeant Singletary." Top handed the general the chevrons of an E-5, three stripes over crossed rifles. The general handed the chevrons to the new sergeant. "Now, Sergeant Singletary, you get that corporal rank off your uniform and replace it as soon as possible with your new rank. "The general smiled and extended his hand, and said, "And that's an order."

Singletary was so overwhelmed couldn't say a word. Those in attendance applauded and the lance corporal took pictures, one with Jason shaking the general's hand.

The general continued speaking. "There is one more thing. In 1943, the Navy Commendation Medal was established, to be awarded to Navy personnel and Marines who have highly distinguished themselves in their service to the Country and the services. The award can be given with the 'Combat V' device when authorized. Sergeant Singletary, the service you gave entitles you to the award of the Navy Commendation Medal with Combat 'V' device. It is my privilege and honor to award this medal to you, Sergeant." Top handed the general a small box which the General opened and held it up, showing the green ribbon with white stripes and the medal, which was six-sided on which the eagle, with its wings spread, held three arrows. This medal would be worn when wearing dress blues or whites. The box also contained a smaller green ribbon with white stripes on which the V was placed, which was appropriate for wearing on the routine uniform shirt. The general nodded to Top, who then read aloud the citation detailing how Singletary had upheld the highest standards of the Corps by following orders. There was applause all around, and then lance corporal took more pictures.

Sergeant Singletary's head was spinning as he thanked the general. His platoon commander and platoon sergeant congratulated him, and the new sergeant, with his new decoration, left the general's office.

As the room was clearing, General Dowda asked Top to hold back. "Top, have we taken care of that thing at Lejeune?" Top grinned, "Yes, sir. The paperwork has arrived and will be carried out in the next four or five days."

0800 Hours, Wed, 26 Nov 69
Rifle Range Bravo Six
Marine Corps Base
Camp Lejeune, North Carolina
Breckinridge

First Lieutenant Donald Breckinridge IV rotated back to the States before the General Court Martial of Lance Corporal Jackson began. He had no idea how the case was resolved, and he didn't give a damn.

For his last posting, Donald requested assignment to the Marine Barracks, at Eighth and I, in Washington DC, which would be an easy drive to his home of record, Philadelphia, and his father's highly successful investment business, of which he would become an associate after release from active duty.

But Eighth and I is a very special place, and the Marines assigned to Eighth and I are the best of the best. Donald did not qualify. He was initially disappointed to be posted to Camp Lejeune, in Jacksonville, North Carolina in late September 1969.

His disappointment abated somewhat when he was told his duty assignment for his remaining three months in the Corps. The Corps tried to assign 'short-timers' to a duty station which involved as little interaction as possible with the command process. Why get used to a unit, and have them get used to you, if you're going to be in the Corps for only a short time? Breckinridge was most definitely a 'short timer'.

Donald was assigned as a firing range OIC — officer in charge. There were multiple firing ranges at Lejeune, used mainly by the graduates of boot camp at Parris Island. Those graduates were assigned to AIT — advanced infantry training — at Lejeune, where, in addition to becoming proficient at firing the rifle, they learned how to take apart and reassemble the M-16 while blindfolded, hand-to-hand combat, squad, platoon and company tactics as well as other exercises to prepare them for combat.

All Lieutenant Donald Breckinridge IV had to do, as OIC of Rifle Range Bravo 6, was to drive out to the range from his rented beach house by 0800 hours weekdays, stay until the range closed, and let the gunnery sergeant run the range. Breckinridge would take the latest edition of *Barron's* or *Forbes* business magazines, or the occasional *Wall Street Journal*, to read after the gunny brought him coffee when he arrived at the OIC's office at the back of the range.

Donald also had a great run of luck lately, although he had not thought of it as luck. Rather, he thought of it as his skill as a man whom women loved and couldn't get enough of. He spent time at some of the many bars in downtown Jacksonville, NC, which existed because Lejeune existed. He drove a sporty red TR-3 convertible, which he thought attracted the ladies. He would hook up with two, three or four different women a week. Sometimes he and the latest 'love of his life' would have dinner at his rented beach house, walk to one of the many beaches of Onslow County, and do their best imitation of Burt Lancaster and Deborah Kerr rolling in the sand.

Since the firing range would not be used on Thanksgiving Day or the Friday and weekend thereafter, Donald had made arrangements to get leave early on the Wednesday before Thanksgiving. His clothes and gear were packed into his convertible, he had gassed up the car, and he was ready to hit the road for Philly late that afternoon.

As Donald drove to work, he was recalling his entanglement with the beautiful, voluptuous redhead he met earlier the week. She was not the kind of woman he'd take home to meet Mom and Dad, but she was a great distraction. Donald was also pissed off, because even though his release date was only three months off, no one had approached him to plan the "getting out of the Corps" party traditionally given to officers receiving their DD 214 and being released from active duty. He didn't realize that no one had approached him because no one wanted to spend time around him, and they were glad he was leaving.

But by and large, Donald Breckinridge IV was just fine with where he was. During his post-Vietnam leave, he went home. His dad had bought him a wonderful garage apartment near his office and gave Donald an unlimited budget to furnish his apartment, a budget which Donald damn near exceeded.

The life of Donald Breckinridge IV was good.

But that life was about to change.

The range was located at the end of a winding two-mile dead-end dirt road, cut through Carolina pines. There was nothing down the road except the range, and no reason for anyone to come down the road unless they had business at the range.

No one had driven to the range since Breckinridge became the OIC of the range.

Until today.

Breckinridge looked up from his morning paper and saw the dust from the two cars coming down the road to the range. After the cars stopped, the gunny ordered the Marines to 'cease firing' and he walked over to the cars. Two men in suits, wearing hats, and two sergeants, wearing side arms, exited their cars. Breckinridge thought that one of the Marines at the range that day must have gotten in trouble.

He was wrong.

The gunny pointed to the office, and all four men walked toward the office. As they entered, Breckinridge stood up and said, "Can I help you?"

One of the men in a suit said, "I am Special Agent Leroy Harmon. You can help if you are the Lieutenant Donald Breckinridge the Fourth who served with First Battalion, Ninth Marine Regiment, at Vandegrift Combat Base, South Vietnam."

"Yes I am, one in the same."

"Well, Lieutenant, I'm with Naval Investigative Service, and I am placing you under arrest for obstruction of justice involving your so-called investigation of the fragging of Lieutenant Speight at VCB, and your failure to report exculpatory evidence given to you by Corporal Singletary about Lance Corporal Jackson." The agent directed one of the sergeants to handcuff the lieutenant. "We are not going to ask you any questions, because we know you are guilty, and because we can prove it. However, I'm still required to advise you that you have a right to remain silent, that anything you say can, and will, be used against you in a court of law, and that you have the right to have an attorney appointed to represent you if you can't afford to hire one. Just so you know, we are taking you back to Base Legal, where the Article and Specification listing your crime will be served on you. You may be interested to know that the charges have been signed by Brigadier General Hugh Dowda of the Third Mar Div. Pretty special to get charged by a general, I'd say. Maybe you can paste the charges on the wall of your cell and look at them the next few years."

The last thing Breckinridge heard as he was pushed into the back seat of the Shore Patrol car was the gunny ordering the Marines at the rifle range, "READY, AIM, FIRE!!"

About the Author

Dallas Clark is a graduate of Wake Forest College and Wake Forest University Law School. After enlisting in the Marine Corps, he earned his Second Lieutenant's Commission at Officer Candidate School. After further training, he was posted in Vietnam. He was licensed to practice law in North Carolina and had an active family law practice until he retired in 2014. His life is blessed by three daughters, two sons-in-law, and five grandchildren. He lives in Greenville, North Carolina.

Note from the Author

Word-of-mouth is crucial for any author to succeed. If you enjoyed *The Investigation Officer's File*, please leave a review online—anywhere you are able. Even if it's just a sentence or two. It would make all the difference and would be very much appreciated.

Thanks!
Dallas Clark

Thank you so much for reading one of our **Military Fiction** novels,
If you enjoyed the experience, please check out our recommended
title for your next great read!

Augie's War by John H. Brown

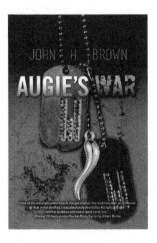

"One of the most powerful novels I've yet read on the
Vietnam War. As a veteran of that awful conflict, I was
absolutely riveted by the tale of Augie and his buddies
and every word rang true."
–Homer Hickam, author *Rocket Boys, Carrying Albert Home*

Made in the USA
Las Vegas, NV
29 May 2021

23712044R00142